ACCLAIM FOR JAMES PATTERSON'S HOTTEST SERIES!

MISSING

"*MISSING* IS, IN A WORD, TERRIFIC. This is a one-sit, fast-paced read that fully satisfies but nonetheless will leave you wanting more." —BookReporter.com

THE GAMES

"FAST PACED...THERE IS NO DOUBT YOU CAN FINISH THIS BOOK IN ONE SITTING."

—Blograma.com

PRIVATE PARIS

"THERE'S NO FLUFF OR DEAD WEIGHT, AND REVELATIONS COME FAST AND HARD...This story is drenched in realism and really strikes a chord, proving to be a worthwhile read."

—matthewrbel.blogspot.com

PRIVATE VEGAS

"NEVER A DULL MOMENT IN THIS ACTION-PACKED PAGE-TURNER." —Writerswrite.co.za

PRIVATE INDIA: CITY ON FIRE

"IT IS UNPUTDOWNABLE AND DEFINITELY A PAGE-TURNER…ONE IS FORCED TO KEEP READING TIL THE END, THOUGH THE END IS OVER 450 PAGES AWAY."

—Winnowed.blogspot.com

PRIVATE DOWN UNDER

"FAST-PACED AND SUSPENSEFUL."

—Upinstitchesblog.wordpress.com

PRIVATE L.A.

"A GREAT READ DEVOURED IN ONE SITTING…[I'M] LOOKING FORWARD TO SEE WHAT HAPPENS NEXT FOR JACK MORGAN AND HIS TEAM(S)."

—RandomActsofReviewing.blogspot.com

PRIVATE BERLIN

"FAST-PACED ACTION AND UNFORGETTABLE CHARACTERS WITH PLOT TWISTS AND DECEPTIONS WORTHY OF ANY JAMES PATTERSON NOVEL." —Examiner.com

PRIVATE LONDON

"THE STORY CONTINUES ALONG QUITE QUICKLY WITH THE TWO-PAGE CHAPTERS FLYING PAST FASTER THAN YOU CAN IMAGINE. I READ THIS BOOK IN ONLY AN EVENING. If you are a Patterson fan then you will probably enjoy this one as well." —TheFringeMagazine.blogspot.com

PRIVATE GAMES

"PATTERSON, HE OF SIX DOZEN NOVELS AND COUNTING, HAS AN UNCANNY KNACK FOR THE TIMELY THRILLER, AND THIS ONE IS NO EXCEPTION...A PLEASANT ROMP."

—*Kirkus Reviews*

PRIVATE: #1 SUSPECT

"[THEY] MAKE ONE HECK OF A GREAT WRITING TEAM AND PROVE IT ONCE AGAIN WITH [THIS] CLASSY THRILLER, THE LATEST IN A PRIVATE INVESTIGATION SERIES THAT'S SURE TO BLOW THE LID OFF A POPULAR GENRE...If you want to be entertained to the max, you can't go wrong when you pick up a thriller by Patterson and Paetro."

—NightsandWeekends.com

PRIVATE

Count to Ten

ALSO BY JAMES PATTERSON

PRIVATE NOVELS

Private (*with Maxine Paetro*)
Private London (*with Mark Pearson*)
Private Games (*with Mark Sullivan*)
Private: No. 1 Suspect (*with Maxine Paetro*)
Private Berlin (*with Mark Sullivan*)
Private Down Under (*with Michael White*)
Private L.A. (*with Mark Sullivan*)
Private India (*with Ashwin Sanghi*)
Private Vegas (*with Maxine Paetro*)
Private Sydney (*with Kathryn Fox*)
Private Paris (*with Mark Sullivan*)
The Games (*with Mark Sullivan*)
Missing (*with Kathryn Fox*)

A list of more titles by James Patterson is printed
at the back of this book.

COUNT
TO TEN

James Patterson
AND
Ashwin Sanghi

GRAND CENTRAL
PUBLISHING

NEW YORK   BOSTON

Copyright © 2016 by James Patterson

Hachette Book Group supports the right to free expression and the value of copyright. The purpose of copyright is to encourage writers and artists to produce the creative works that enrich our culture.

The scanning, uploading, and distribution of this book without permission is a theft of the author's intellectual property. If you would like permission to use material from the book (other than for review purposes), please contact permissions@hbgusa.com. Thank you for your support of the author's rights.

Grand Central Publishing
Hachette Book Group
1290 Avenue of the Americas, New York, NY 10104
grandcentralpublishing.com
twitter.com/grandcentralpub

Originally published by Century in the United Kingdom in 2016 as *Private Delhi*
First U.S. trade paperback edition: November 2017

Grand Central Publishing is a division of Hachette Book Group, Inc. The Grand Central Publishing name and logo is a trademark of Hachette Book Group, Inc.

The publisher is not responsible for websites (or their content) that are not owned by the publisher.

The Hachette Speakers Bureau provides a wide range of authors for speaking events. To find out more, go to hachettespeakersbureau.com or call (866) 376-6591.

Library of Congress Control Number: 2017948579

ISBNs: 978-1-5387-5963-9 (trade paperback), 978-1-5387-6027-7 (large print), 978-1-5387-5965-3 (ebook), 978-1-5387-5962-2 (hardcover library edition)

Printed in the United States of America

LSC-W

10 9 8 7 6 5 4 3 2 1

PART ONE

KILLER

Chapter 1

THE KILLER EMPTIED the final bag of ice into the bath and shut off the cold tap.

With the tub full he stood back to admire his handiwork, watching his breath bloom. Winter in Delhi, it was cold, but the temperature in the small bathroom was even lower than outside and falling fast, just the way he wanted it.

From outside came the sound of footsteps on the stairs and the killer moved quickly. His victim was early but that was fine, he was prepared, and in a heartbeat he left the bathroom and crossed the front room of the apartment, scooping his hypodermic syringe from a table as he passed. A scratching sound announced the key in the lock and the victim opened the door.

The killer attacked from behind, grabbing the victim, pulling him into the room, and smothering a cry of surprise with one gloved hand. He used the syringe and for a second the victim struggled, then went limp. The killer let him drop to the carpet, checked the corridor outside, and then kicked the door shut. He bent to the victim and began to undress him.

Ten minutes later the victim awoke, naked and gasping in the bath. The bathroom light was off and his eyes hadn't yet adjusted to the gloom but he heard the clicking of the ice cubes and knew instantly where he was. His arms had been hoisted overhead, handcuffed to the taps; submerged in the ice, his feet and knees were bound. As he began to struggle he heard someone enter the room and then a gloved hand pushed his head beneath the cubes. He inhaled icy water, feeling his airways fill and his heart constrict with the shock of the sudden cold. When the hand allowed him back to the surface, his coughs and splutters were punctuated by the violent chattering of his teeth.

The figure loomed over him, a shadow in the darkened bathroom. "You'll feel it in your toes and fingertips first," he said. "Tingling. Then numbness. That's your body redirecting resources to protect the vital organs. Clever thing, the body, it can adapt quickly. If you were an Inuit, an Aborigine, even a Tibetan Buddhist monk, then withstanding this kind of cold would be simple for you, but you're not those things, you're..."

The killer moved into view. In his hand was the victim's name badge, taken from his shirt. "Rahul," he read, and then tossed it into the bath. "Oh, I do apologize. I'm sure you know all about the effects of cold on the human body. You know all about the slow shutting down of the various functions, how the brain dies before the heart."

"Who are you?" managed Rahul. He squinted. "Do I know you?" The attacker's voice was familiar somehow.

"I don't know," said the attacker. "Do you?" He perched on the edge of the bath and Rahul could see he wore all black, including a black balaclava. Opaque surgical gloves seemed to shine dully in the gloom, giving him the appearance of an evil mime.

"You're wondering why I'm here," said the man, as though reading his thoughts. He smiled and removed from his pocket a tiny little tool that he showed to Rahul. "Are you familiar with a procedure called enucleation?"

Chapter 2

JACK MORGAN ENJOYED risk. Why else would he be standing outside this door at 4 a.m., barely daring to breathe as he used a tiny lubricating spray on the lock and then went to work with his pick, nudging interior tumblers into place?

But not blind risk.

Again, that was the reason the owner of the world-renowned Private investigation agency had arrived in Delhi two days earlier than his official schedule predicted, and more discreetly than usual. It was because he liked his risk with a little forethought.

He liked *calculated* risk.

He slid into the darkened apartment like a shadow. From his pocket he took a rubber doorstop, closed the front door as far as he could without making a sound, and then wedged it.

Next he listened. For close to five minutes Jack stood in silence by the door, letting his eyes adjust and taking in the scant furniture—a sofa, a television, an upturned packing crate for a coffee table—but more than anything, listening—listening to the noise that emanated from the bedroom.

What he heard was the sound of a man enduring a fitful sleep, a man who mewled with the pain of nightmares.

Jack trod noiselessly through the apartment. In the kitchen he opened the fridge door and peered inside. Nothing. Back in the front room he went to the upturned crate.

On it stood a bottle of whisky. Johnnie Walker.

Oh, Santosh, thought Jack to himself. *Tell me you haven't.*

From the bedroom the sound of Santosh Wagh's nightmares increased, so Jack Morgan finished his work and let himself out of the apartment and into the chill Delhi morning.

Chapter 3

IN THE UPMARKET area of Greater Kailash in South Delhi, in a row of homes, a young couple stood at the gate of an abandoned house.

"This is it," said the boy, his breath fogging in Delhi's winter air.

"Are you sure?" asked the girl at his side.

"Sure I'm sure," he replied. "C'mon, let's go inside."

They climbed over the gate easily and made their way through overgrown grass to the front door. Padlocked. But the boy used a pick to crack the lock in less than two minutes. *Not bad for an amateur*, he thought to himself.

He went to open the door, but it wouldn't budge.

"What's wrong?" asked the girl. She was shivering and cold and desperately wishing they'd decided to go to the cinema instead of opting to make out here.

The boy was puzzled. "I thought it was unlocked..."

"What do we do now, then?" said the girl.

Like all young men governed by their libido, the boy wasn't about to give up easily. Yes, it was cold, but he'd come armed with a blanket and the garden was sufficiently overgrown to screen them from the street.

"We don't need to go inside. Let's just stay out here," the boy suggested.

"But it's so cold," she gasped.

"We'll soon warm each other up," he assured her, leading her to an area close to the front of the house. The grass was damp but he covered it with the blanket from his backpack, and the foliage not only screened them but also protected them from the chill breeze. She tried to imagine that they had found themselves a secret garden, and when he produced a spliff, it sealed the deal.

They sat and spent some minutes in relaxed, agreeable silence as they smoked the spliff, listening to the muted sounds of the city drifting to them through the trees. Then they lay down and began kissing. In a few moments they were making love, cocooned in weed-induced sexual bliss.

"What's that?" she said.

"What's what?" he asked, irritated.

"That noise." Then her senses sharpened. "It's the ground. The ground is—"

She didn't get to finish her sentence. Suddenly it was as though the grass were trying to swallow them. Subsidence. A sinkhole. Something. Either way, the earth gave way beneath them, and the two lovebirds crashed through the lawn and into a nightmare beneath.

Chapter 4

DAZED, THE GIRL pulled herself to her hands and knees, coughing and gagging at a sudden stench, a mix of caustic chemicals and something else. Something truly stomach-turning.

The floor was rough concrete. She was in a low-ceilinged basement. A gray patch of light in the ceiling indicated where they'd fallen through. Plasterboard, turf, and rotted wooden beams hung down as though in the aftermath of a storm.

And pulling himself up back through the hole was her boyfriend.

"Hey," she called. "Where are you . . . ?"

But he was gone.

Naked, wincing in pain, and consumed with a creeping sense of something being terribly, terribly wrong, the girl looked around, her eyesight adjusting to the gloom.

She saw gas masks and coveralls hanging from pegs. A small chainsaw. Dotted around the concrete floor was a series of plastic barrels with some kind of toxic chemical fumes rising from each one. And even in her traumatized state she realized it was those fumes that had eroded the ceiling structure enough for it to collapse.

And then she saw other things too. They seemed to appear out of the darkness. A table, like a butcher's block, with a huge meat cleaver protruding from the bloodstained wood. And from the plastic barrels protruded hands and feet, the skin bubbling and burning as though being subjected to great heat.

Bile rising, she knew what was happening here. She knew exactly what was happening here.

Chapter 5

A CHARNEL HOUSE, thought the Commissioner of Police, Rajesh Sharma, when he returned to the office the next day, with the stink of chemicals and decomposition clinging to him. Rarely had he been quite so grateful to leave a crime scene. Those poor bastards who'd had to stay.

The call had come in at around eleven o'clock the night before. A neighbor had heard screaming, looked out, and seen a terrified young woman, her clothes in disarray, running away from the house.

A short while later it was sealed off. The team had been inside for eight hours and would be there for many more days. They had determined the perp was using hydrofluoric acid to dissolve the bodies in plastic tubs. There was no way of counting how many, but say one for each barrel, that made eleven at least. Quite a death toll. What's more, it didn't take into account any corpses that might already have been disposed of.

But here was the bit that had really taken Sharma by surprise: the house was owned by the Delhi state government.

Mass murder. On government property. He would have to ensure the press did not get hold of this story; in fact, he'd have to make sure the news reached as few ears as possible.

Sharma had washed his hands. He'd rubbed at his face. But he could still smell the corpses as he sat behind his desk at police headquarters and greeted his guest.

The man who took a seat opposite was Nikhil Kumar, the Honorable Minister for Health and Family Welfare. Photoshoot-perfect, not a strand of jet-black hair out of place, Kumar wore simple khaki slacks, an Egyptian cotton shirt, a Canali blazer, and comfortable soft-leather loafers. His very presence made Sharma feel overweight and scruffy by comparison. Well, let's face it, he *was* overweight and scruffy. But Kumar made him feel even more so.

"What can I do for you, sir?" Sharma asked the minister. It paid to be courteous to ministers.

"Thank you for seeing me at such short notice," said Kumar.

"I'm happy to help. What's on your mind?"

"I am given to understand that your men searched a house in Greater Kailash today. I was wondering if you could share some information regarding what you found."

Sharma tried not to let his irritation show as he considered his response. On the one hand he wanted to keep Kumar satisfied; on the other, experience had taught him that it was always better to keep politicians out of police inquiries.

"How about you tell me what your interest in this matter is?" he said. "And how you found out about it?"

"As I'm sure you're about to remind me, I have no jurisdiction with the police. You and I stand on the battlements of two opposing forts in the same city. But I have contacts, and I find out what I can. You want to prevent leaks, run a tighter ship."

Sharma chortled. "This is your way of buttering me up, is it, Minister? Coming into my office and criticizing the way I run my police force?"

"Let me be frank with you," said Kumar. "It may not be wise to delve too deeply into this case."

"Minister, we've got at least eleven potential murders here." He was about to reveal he knew the building was owned by the state but stopped himself, deciding to keep his powder dry. "While I appreciate the need for discretion, we will be delving as deeply as we need to in order to discover the truth."

"Suffice to say that you would be adequately compensated," said Kumar.

Sharma was taken aback. "For what?"

"For your cooperation."

Sharma sat back and made Kumar wait for a response. "I tell you what, Minister—you leave now, and I'll think about your offer."

Sharma watched with satisfaction as Kumar stood and tried to leave the office with as much dignity as he could regain.

Only when the door had closed did Sharma allow himself a smile. This was what they called an opportunity. And when life gives you lemons...

Chapter 6

SANTOSH WAGH OPENED the front door of his home to find Jack Morgan on the doorstep.

"Santosh!" said Jack, and before Santosh could react he had stepped inside.

As ever, Santosh was happy to see his boss. The thing with Jack was that as soon as he appeared, whatever the time, whatever the place, you were simply a guest in his world. It was impossible not to feel reassured by it. It wasn't just the gun Jack carried; it wasn't just the fact that Jack was enormously wealthy and could boast powerful and high-profile friends. It was just Jack, being Jack.

"Welcome to my humble abode," said Santosh. Looking around, he saw his living quarters through Jack's eyes: hardly furnished, dark, and a little musty. "I would give you a tour, but I believe you know your way around already."

"I don't follow," said Jack quizzically.

"Years ago when you hired me you told me you thought I was an exceptional detective. Did you really think you could break into my apartment and I wouldn't notice?"

Jack relaxed, allowing himself a smile. The game was up. "Well, I'm an exceptional cat burglar, so I played the odds. How did you know?"

Santosh's cane clicked on the wooden floor as he made his way to the kitchen and then returned with a bottle of whisky that he placed on his makeshift table. He pointed to the bottle with the tip of his cane. "Perhaps you'd like to check it."

Jack leaned forward, holding Santosh's gaze as he reached for the bottle, inverted it, and studied the almost invisible mark he had made with a small bar of hotel soap two nights before.

"It's just as it was the other night," he said, replacing the bottle. "And I'm pleased to see it."

Santosh blinked slowly. "Not nearly as pleased as I am."

"I had to check, Santosh. I had to know."

"You could have asked me."

"But addicts lie. That's what they do. Besides, why even have it in the house if you don't plan to drink it?"

The answer was that Santosh preferred to face temptation head-on. He would spend hours just staring at the bottle. It was for that reason, not his renowned detective skills, that he had seen the soap mark, and having spotted it he'd studied his front-door lock and detected the odor of lubricant. One phone call to Private HQ later and his suspicions had been confirmed.

Jack had been checking up on him.

But of course he couldn't blame Jack for that. Private was the world's biggest investigation agency, with offices in Los Angeles, London, Berlin, Sydney, Paris, Rio, Mumbai, and, most recently, Delhi. Jack had invested a huge amount of faith in Santosh by making him Private's chief of operations in India.

Santosh had been an agent with the Research and Analysis Wing, India's external intelligence agency, when investigations into the 2006 Mumbai train blasts had brought him into contact with Jack. It had been only a matter of time before he'd recruited Santosh to establish Private in Mumbai. Setting up Private's office in Mumbai had been challenging; his last case had almost killed him and at the very least it had looked as though he might have lost his ongoing battle with the bottle.

Jack had come to his rescue by persuading him to go to rehab, the Cabin in Thailand. Six months later, Jack had persuaded Santosh to move to Delhi to establish Private in the capital.

So Jack had to know that Santosh was still in control of his addiction. And he was. The bottle of whisky had hung around his home untouched for the whole three months he'd been there. Every day Santosh had resisted the temptation to open it and banish his private pain. And every day it got a little easier.

Privately, though, he worried if he could truly operate without it. He worried that his brain might not be able to make the same leaps of logic it once had; he worried that kicking the booze might make him a worse detective, not a better one. These were just a few of the things keeping him awake at night.

"I don't drink it," he told Jack. "That's the important thing."

Chapter 7

JACK LOVED TO drive in Delhi. First of all he always made sure to hire an old car, one that already had its fair share of bumps and scrapes, and then he'd climb in, wind down the window, and plunge headlong into the sheer mayhem of one of his favorite cities.

He liked to drive fast. Or at least as fast as he dared, leaning on the horn like a local and winding his way through lines of busses, scooters, cyclists, and auto rickshaws, past glass-fronted buildings and ancient temples, broken-down housing and luxury hotels with glove-wearing staff at the gates. Delhi was a vibrant, colorful mix of cultures old and new. A genuine melting pot. To Jack it felt as though Delhi's entire history—Hindu Rajputs, Muslim Mughals, and Christian Englishmen—all came to him through the open window of the car, and he breathed it all in—good and bad—breathing its very essence.

At times like that, Jack felt most alive. Blessed. He thought that being Jack Morgan in Delhi was just about the best thing you could be in this world.

Usually, that is.

But not today. Because one thing stronger than his love for driving fast through Delhi was his respect for Santosh Wagh. It was in a car accident that the investigator had lost his wife and child, Isha and Pravir. So, for that reason, Jack drove slowly, with the window closed.

As they made their way through the streets Jack cast a sideways glance at his passenger, a man he was proud to call a friend.

In his early fifties, Santosh looked older than his age. Sleep deprivation and alcohol abuse had taken their toll. His salt-and-pepper stubble was more salt than pepper and the brown wool jacket with leather patches at the elbows gave him the look of a university professor. His eyeglasses were unfashionable and his scarf should have been replaced years earlier. Not that he seemed to care. Aloof and cerebral, permanently ruminative, Santosh was far too preoccupied to care about such trivial matters.

"Tell me about Delhi's political makeup," Jack asked him, more to keep his passenger's mind off the journey than genuine ignorance on his part.

Santosh cleared his throat. "Delhi's a strange place. It's not only a state in the Indian federation but also India's capital—like Washington, DC. The city's government is split down the middle: civic administration is managed by the Chief Minister, Mohan Jaswal, while law and order is managed by the Lieutenant Governor, Ram Chopra."

Jack slowed to allow a pair of motorbikes to pass, and then immediately regretted it when a cab and an auto rickshaw nipped in front of him as well. *Any other day . . .* he thought ruefully.

"The Chief Minister and the Lieutenant Governor. Do they see eye to eye?" he asked Santosh.

"Jaswal and Chopra?" mused Santosh. "Do they see eye to eye? Now there's a good question. Before I answer it, how about you tell me which one of them we're due to meet."

Jack laughed. He loved to see Santosh's mind working. "I tell you what, my brainy friend. How about *you* tell *me* what the beef is all about, and then I'll tell you which one we're due to see."

"Very well," said Santosh. "The answer to your question is no, Jaswal and Chopra do not see eye to eye. As Chief Minister and Lieutenant Governor respectively, they're supposed to run Delhi in partnership, but the fact of the matter is they agree on nothing. There is what you might call a difference of opinion when it comes to interpreting the rules of their partnership."

"They hate each other?"

"Pretty much. A jurisdictional war is not the best path to a lasting friendship."

"One of them would dearly like to put one over on the other?"

"As a means of wresting complete control, no doubt." Santosh flinched slightly as a pedestrian passed too close to their car. "Now, how about you tell me which one it is?"

"Chief Minister Mohan Jaswal."

Santosh nodded. "Has he told you why?"

"Nope. Just that he wants to meet. He asked for both of us. What do you know about him?"

"Jaswal started his career with the army and was part of the Indian Peace Keeping Force sent to Sri Lanka in 1987. He opted for early retirement upon his return—traumatized at seeing Tamil Tigers blowing themselves up with explosives strapped to their chests.

"He then became a journalist for the *Indian Times* in Mumbai, working as the newspaper's senior correspondent in New York. A plum posting that most would have coveted. But not Jaswal. He returned to India to enter the political arena, claiming he wanted to 'make a difference.'

"We were acquainted in the days when he was a journalist and I was with the Research and Analysis Wing. He used to try to pump me for information."

"Were you friendly?"

Santosh looked at Jack. "I didn't particularly trust him, if that's what you mean."

Chapter 8

THE CHIEF MINISTER'S Residence at Motilal Nehru Marg occupied over three acres of Delhi's prime real estate, a sprawling white-stuccoed bungalow reminiscent of the colonial era, surrounded by sweeping lawns.

Santosh and Jack stepped out of the battered Fiat and into the cold Delhi air, where Jaswal's secretary waited for them. They were whisked inside without any of the usual security checks, and then ushered into a book-lined study where the Chief Minister, Mohan Jaswal, sat behind his desk.

Now in his early sixties, Jaswal had a youthful vigor that belied his age. He had not an ounce of fat on his body and he sported a neatly trimmed white mustache. His crisp white kurta pajama and sky-blue turban indicated his Sikh faith.

"Good to meet you, Mr. Morgan," he said, and the two men shook hands.

"Just Jack is fine."

And then to Santosh, Jaswal said, "It's been years."

"I know," replied Santosh curtly.

There was an awkward moment between the two acquaintances, broken only when Jaswal invited them to sit. Tea was served and more pleasantries exchanged: yes, it was cold outside; yes, Jack Morgan had been to Delhi many times before; yes, he was delighted to set up a bureau in the city; no, Santosh had not lived here for very long. Just three months.

All the while the two men from Private sipped their Kashmiri tea, answered Jaswal's questions politely, and waited for him to get to the point of the meeting.

"I need you to handle an exceptionally delicate matter," the Chief Minister said at last.

They waited for him to continue as he took a puff from a bronchodilator. "I hear news of a gruesome discovery at a house in Greater Kailash," he said. "Any more than that, however, is being kept a secret from me."

Questions forming, Jack leaned forward before stopping himself and sitting back to watch Santosh take the lead.

"What sort of gruesome discovery?" asked Santosh, thanking Jack with the merest incline of his head. His hands were knotted together on the head of his cane; his heart beat just that tiny bit faster. Ushered in to see the Chief Minister, he'd wondered if this might turn out to be a dry, political request. Evidently not.

"Bodies," sniffed Jaswal. "Up to a dozen of them, in various states of . . . decomposition. It seems they were being melted down in some way."

"Some kind of corrosive involved?"

"It would seem that way. Body parts were found in thick barrels full of the stuff."

Jack shifted forward. He and Santosh exchanged a look. "What sort of barrels?" asked Santosh.

"Plastic, as far as I'm aware," said Jaswal.

"Hydrofluoric acid," Santosh and Jack said in unison. Even Santosh allowed himself a thin smile at that one.

"That's significant, is it?" asked Jaswal, looking from one to the other.

"Very," said Santosh. "It tells us that whoever is responsible is concerned firstly with hiding the identity of the victims and secondly with disposing of the corpses. In that specific order. Which means that the identity of the victims is extremely important."

Jaswal raised an eyebrow. "Isn't that always the case?"

"Not at all. For many serial killers the process of killing is what defines the act; the choice of victim can be random, based only on the ability to fulfill that need. It's what often makes them so hard to catch." He threw a look at Jaswal. "What's your particular interest in this discovery? Over and above curiosity."

"The house in which this . . . grisly operation was discovered is government property."

"And yet you're not being given any information?"

"It wouldn't be the first time."

For a moment or so, Santosh seemed to be lost in

his thoughts before he collected himself and addressed Jaswal once more. "Do you believe Ram Chopra is the one suppressing information?"

Jaswal shot Santosh a wintry smile. "What do *you* think?"

"What I think is irrelevant. It's what you think that is important."

"Point taken. And the answer is yes, I do."

"Why?"

"That's one of the things I'd like you to find out."

"Of course. But let me rephrase the question. Why *might* Ram Chopra want to keep you in the dark regarding the discovery at Greater Kailash?"

"Possibly to wrong-foot me, make me appear ill-informed. Possibly something more."

"How did you find out about the bodies?" Jack asked.

"Police tip-off," said Jaswal. "Nobody directly involved with the case. I'm afraid you'll be on your own with this one."

Santosh looked at Jaswal, knowing that if Private accepted this job then Jack would jet off and it would be he, Santosh, who entered the lion's den.

Santosh was intrigued. Bodies. Hidden motives. It would be messy. Just the way he liked it.

On the other hand, there was something about the case that troubled him. But he couldn't pin down what it was.

Chapter 9

SANTOSH WAS RELIEVED to leave Jack with Jaswal. Finances were not his strong suit. Haggling, negotiating, "doing business" even less so. Besides, as soon as Jack had finished with Jaswal he was flying back to the States. And Santosh had a crime to solve.

A cab dropped him off on the outskirts of Mehrauli, home to Private Delhi, and he went the rest of the way to the office on foot, his cane tapping briskly and a new spring in his step as he passed quaint shops, restaurants, and pubs near the twelfth-century Qutb Minar tower.

He came to an antiques shop tucked away in the old quarter, bell tinkling as he went inside. He nodded to the proprietor and passed through the shop to a door at the back.

Through that he entered a clinical-looking anteroom, bare save for a second door and a retina-scan unit. Santosh bent slightly for the scan and the door slid open, allowing him to access the Private Delhi office.

The office was well hidden for good reason. The Mumbai team had helped Indian law enforcement agencies solve key cases related to attacks by Pakistani terror groups on Indian soil. Both the Mumbai and Delhi offices were on the radar of Pakistan-based jihadi outfits. It was vital to keep the office impregnable. As was the protocol in Mumbai, established clients of Private India communicated with the firm via a dedicated and secure helpline. The screening process for any new clients was rigorous. Investigators from Private visited clients at their homes and offices instead of the other way round. Private's sanctum remained invisible to the world outside.

Inside, polished marble floors were complemented by a bright-yellow staircase connecting the two levels of the office. White acrylic dome lights hung from exposed beams. Santosh greeted the receptionist and crossed the floor where junior investigators handled routine cases, and then took the stairs to his office.

The first member of the team he saw was Nisha Gandhe, his indefatigable assistant. In her mid-forties, Nisha was still capable of making heads turn. The gym and yoga kept her in good shape. But her beauty could not hide a permanent sadness in her eyes.

It had been a tumultuous six months since her abduction by a serial killer in Mumbai. She had still been struggling with the trauma when her husband, Sanjeev, a successful Mumbai stockbroker, had been diagnosed with pancreatic cancer.

Two months later, Sanjeev had lost his battle with the disease. So when Private had opened in Delhi, Nisha and her daughter, Maya, had taken up Jack's offer of a fresh start and had joined Santosh.

Santosh beckoned her into his office, calling Neel Mehra in too. Neel was a brilliant criminologist. In his thirties and dashingly handsome, he attracted the attention of women around him. However, not much escaped the sharp eyes of the Private Delhi investigative team and both Santosh and Nisha had worked out on their own that Neel was gay. With homosexuality still technically illegal in India, his two superiors respected Neel's privacy.

Five minutes later, Nisha and Neel had been briefed. Half an hour after that they had scattered to the winds, flushed with the thrill of a new case, and Santosh's phone was ringing—Jack was on his way over.

Chapter 10

"HOW DID IT go with Jaswal after I left?" asked Santosh.

Jack sat opposite, lounging in an office chair, one knee pulled up and resting on the edge of Santosh's desk. Admin staff from the floor below found excuses to pass the office window, hardly bothering to disguise their curiosity as they craned to see inside. Everybody wanted a look at the great Jack Morgan. It was like having Salman Khan or Tom Cruise in the office.

"It went well," said Jack. "Terms were agreed. Don't tell me you're interested to know the finer points?"

"Not really," said Santosh.

"What, then? You look even more pensive than usual, which, I have to be honest, is normally pretty pensive."

"What were your impressions of him?" asked Santosh.

"I thought he was a well-dressed little weasel. But he could potentially be an important weasel. If we're to establish the agency in the city then we're going to need friends in high places, and he would be a friend in a very high place."

"But his friendship comes with a price. If the friend of my friend is my enemy then the friend of my enemy is also my enemy."

Bemused, Jack shook his head. "In English please, Santosh."

"I'm thinking from Ram Chopra's perspective. He and Jaswal are enemies. If Chopra discovers we're working for Jaswal then he won't see Private as a friend, but rather an enemy, and as he's Lieutenant Governor that effectively cancels out the advantage of being in with Jaswal."

Jack beamed. "Then be discreet, Santosh." He leaned forward, hoisted a cup of coffee from the desk, and took a long gulp. "That's why I employed you, after all."

Santosh gave a tight smile. "Well, yes and no. As we've often discussed, you employed me for my investigative skills." He inclined his head modestly. "Such as they are. What you didn't employ me for was my political diplomacy. I can tell you now, I do not possess such skills. What concerns me about this case, Jack, is that I'm not being asked to solve a crime so much as collect political leverage for Jaswal—a man I trust as much as I would a hungry tiger."

Jack shrugged, failing to see a problem. Santosh tried again. "Am I investigating murders or gathering information to help political rivals?" he asked simply.

"In this case, it's one and the same," answered Jack.

Santosh stared at him. "I thought you might say something like that."

Chapter 11

NISHA STOOD IN the street in Greater Kailash, gazing through the chain-link fence at the crime scene.

A call to the police had proved fruitless. Just as expected, the shutters had come down. As Santosh had warned her, no one in Sharma's police department would help them now. Sharma reported to Chopra. With Chopra and Jaswal at loggerheads, working for Jaswal meant they would have no help from the police.

So she'd decided to pay Greater Kailash a visit.

The house and its grounds were just as they had looked online: neglected, unkempt, but otherwise an unremarkable home in a street full of unremarkable homes. There was one important distinction—the police presence. Uniformed officers guarded the door, while others stood near the polythene tape that marked out where the ground had given way into the grim scene below.

Careful not to attract the attention of those on the other side of the fence, Nisha began to take pictures, methodically working her way across the front of the house. At the same time she watched where she put her feet, knowing only too well that—

Ah.

Something the cops inside had missed. Nisha had quit the Mumbai Police's Criminal Investigation Department to work alongside Santosh, and what she knew from her time on the force was that cops had a tendency to see only what was in front of them. It was one of the reasons she'd been so keen to work with an investigator like Santosh. A detective with the ability to think outside the box.

Or, in this case, look on the other side of the wire fence.

She bent to pick up a cigarette butt that seemed out of place among the usual detritus on the ground. The filter wasn't the usual brown, but silver, plus it bore a beautiful crest in black.

"Can I help you?" came a voice from above. She looked up to see an older woman standing over her.

Nisha stood, held out her hand to shake, and switched on her most dazzling smile. "I suppose you could say I'm a bit of a ghoul," she said. "My name's Nisha. I run a Delhi crime blog. I wonder: would you be willing to speak to me? For my blog, I mean. Do you live around here?"

Something in Nisha's manner seemed to have a positive effect on the woman. Her scowl subsiding, she said, "I do. Opposite. In fact, it was me who called the police."

"Oh? What was it that made you raise the alarm?"

"A half-naked girl, would you believe? Screaming and running away from the house. By all accounts half the lawn had caved in and underneath it was this awful...graveyard or whatever it is they've found."

"What was she doing there?"

"Most likely there with her boyfriend," confided the woman. "Doing *you know what*."

"I see."

"And you know what?" said the woman. "There's been absolutely no mention of this on the news or in the papers."

"Well, exactly," said Nisha. "I only found out via a contact in the police force."

"It's almost like they're trying to hide something," said the woman, drawing her arms across her chest and tilting her chin. She looked left and right. "I used to see a black van in the driveway."

"Really?"

"Oh yes. It was often there."

"Make?"

The woman gave a slight smile. "The make was a Tempo Traveler, and I know that because we used to have one, many moons ago..." She drifted off a little, evidently revisiting a past with a man in her life, possibly a family too, and Nisha felt her nostalgia keenly, think-ing of her own loss.

Regretfully Nisha pulled her new friend back into the present. "I don't suppose you got a license plate number?"

The neighbor frowned. "Well, no, I didn't. Do you go around noting down license plate numbers?"

Nisha conceded the point then added, "Ah, but what if they're up to no good?"

"Well, I never saw anything *especially* unusual. It had a red zigzag pattern running across the side, which was quite distinctive. Other than that..."

"Would you draw it for me?" asked Nisha. She passed the woman her pad and pen, and for some moments the pair stood in silence as the woman concentrated on sketching the van's paint job.

"My drawing isn't very good," she said with an apolo-getic shrug as she handed back the pad. "But it looked something like that."

"Thank you. Did you tell the police about the van?"

"Of course I did. Not that they were interested."

Which figures, thought Nisha.

They spoke for some minutes more, mainly with the neighbor complaining that the house wasn't suf-ficiently well maintained, and how the police hadn't taken her concerns seriously enough. "My late husband would have taken it further. He would have done some-thing about it, but..." She fixed Nisha with such a pained, searching look that Nisha felt as though the other woman could see inside her—as if the neighbor knew exactly what it was they had in common—and for a second she thought it might be too much to bear.

"Thank you," Nisha stammered, only just managing to control her emotions as the two said their good-byes and went their separate ways.

Chapter 12

THE OFFICE–RESIDENCE OF the Lieutenant Governor of Delhi, Ram Chopra, was located at Raj Niwas Marg. There in the living room, two men in oversized leather armchairs drank whisky and paid no mind to the fact that it was the middle of the day. The crisp Delhi winter made everything possible.

Ram Chopra poured more water into his whisky, added ice, and took a puff of his Cohiba cigar. Opposite, the Commissioner of Police, Rajesh Sharma, drank his whisky neat.

Both were big men who tended to dominate a room. Both had been born and brought up in the holy town of Varanasi. Otherwise the two couldn't have been more different: while Chopra was suave and sophisticated, Sharma was unrefined and coarse, from his constantly ruffled uniform to the toothpick firmly lodged between his teeth.

Sharma had been orphaned young and fended for himself. Growing up in Varanasi had been hard, and from early on he'd known the only two options were flight or fight. He'd chosen the latter and gone from being a victim to the most feared kid at school. The many nights of sleeping hungry had given rise to his voracious appetite and obesity in recent times.

Chopra, on the other hand, had been educated at the prestigious Mayo College and then had joined the Indian Air Force, rising to the position of wing commander. Deputized to the Central Bureau of Investigation to assist in a Defense Department investigation, he'd chosen to stay on, investigating high-profile cases involving terrorism and corruption. He'd eventually succeeded in working his way up to the top job, that of director.

His get-it-done approach had made the Prime Minister a fan. Upon his retirement, the position of Lieutenant Governor had been made available to him as a postretirement sop.

And now he ran Delhi. Or would, if not for the constant interference of Mohan Jaswal, Nikhil Kumar, and Co. Still, it kept life interesting. Chopra would be lying if he said he didn't enjoy a bit of conflict every now and then. It was something else he had in common with his overweight, whisky-swilling friend opposite.

He regarded Sharma through a cloud of blue cigar smoke, feeling pleasantly sleepy and guessing the Police Commissioner felt the same way. "These body parts found in the basement at Greater Kailash," he said. "Any new developments?"

"Investigations continue," replied Sharma.

"One would hope so," said Chopra. With some effort he leaned forward to place his cigar on the edge of the solid silver ashtray. The ash needed to fall gently on its own. Aficionados would never tap a cigar.

"But there's something else," said Sharma.

"Yes?" asked Chopra.

"Kumar wants the matter hushed up. The prick visited me, offering me a bribe."

"I see. Well, if Kumar wants this kept quiet then perhaps it might be fun to see that the case receives maximum publicity."

But Sharma wasn't smiling. "You might not want that, Lieutenant Governor."

Chopra squinted at Sharma through the smoke. "Oh yes? Why so?"

"I'll show you."

Intrigued, Chopra watched Sharma ease himself from the armchair—no easy task—and cross to a briefcase he'd brought with him. The big cop extracted a folder, returned to Chopra, and passed him a photograph.

"This is the house where the bodies were found?" asked Chopra.

"It is."

Chopra studied the photograph a second time then handed it back. "In that case, I concur with our friend Kumar. It might not be prudent to raise public awareness at this stage."

Sharma's chin settled into his chest. "I thought you'd

say that. I've already taken steps to ensure the investigation is as low-key as possible."

"Nevertheless, I'd be interested to know why Kumar wants this kept quiet. You can look into that for me, can you?"

"I can."

"Thank you. You can be certain I shall be most grateful for your efforts."

"There's something else," said Sharma, opening the folder once more.

"Yes?"

"I hear Jaswal wants you to approve the appointment of Amit Roy as Principal Secretary in Kumar's ministry."

"He does."

"Are you going to do it?"

"I haven't decided yet." Chopra grinned. "Jaswal hates to be kept waiting, so..."

"You thought you'd keep him waiting."

"Quite."

"I have something here that might help make up your mind. Have a look at this," said Sharma, handing over the folder.

"What is it?"

"It's as many reasons as you want why it's a bad idea to promote Amit Roy."

In the folder were photographs of Amit Roy with young girls. Children. Chopra didn't bother leafing through the lot. He got the idea. He dropped the folder back on the table between them.

"This changes nothing," he said.

"But it's incontrovertible evidence that Amit Roy is a pedophile. The very worst kind."

"Exactly. And it's for that reason that I plan to let the appointment go through."

"Why?" asked Sharma.

"The bodies at the Greater Kailash house could put Jaswal in a fix. Having an animal like Roy as Health Secretary could put him in an even bigger fix. My thanks for bringing these things to my attention, Sharma. I shall approve Roy's promotion at once."

Chapter 13

NISHA'S HUNT FOR a black Tempo Traveler van sporting a zigzag pattern had taken her to the Regional Transport Office. The visit had cost Private India the price of a bribe, but for that Nisha had been given the name of a workshop, Truckomatic, that might customize vans.

Fifteen minutes later she entered Truckomatic, a large industrial paint shop that rang to the sound of pneumatic lifts and sprays. According to the owner—a gym rat who gave Nisha a long look up and down before deigning to speak to her—Truckomatic customized over a hundred vehicles each month.

Nisha showed him her pad. "Something like that," she said. "I was wondering whether you've anything similar."

"Sure," grinned the owner. "For around two hundred customers at last count. We have a catalog of around a thousand concepts. This is one of the more popular ones."

"This one was on a Tempo Traveler," probed Nisha.

"That certainly narrows it down."

"Does it narrow it down enough that you could give me a list of customers?" asked Nisha.

The owner grinned again. "Give me a few days and I *could*, I suppose. But what's in it for me?"

Nisha sighed and reached for her pocketbook, thanking God for Private's no-questions-asked expenses policy.

Chapter 14

"I'VE NEVER SEEN this cigarette before," said Nisha, placing the butt she'd found on Neel's spotless white table. "Can you find out which brand it is?"

"Easily done," said Neel, crossing to his bookshelf. He scanned the various medical and scientific journals and catalogs until he laid his hands on the book he was looking for. He brought it back to the table.

"What is it?" asked Nisha.

"You see, Sherlock Holmes had his power of deduction, Superman had his X-ray vision, Dick Tracy used his two-way wrist radio, but Bob Bourhill depended on cigarette butts."

"Bob Bourhill?" asked Nisha.

"A sleuth tasked with figuring out the cause of fires

in the forests of Oregon. He spent years cataloging cigarettes, cigars, and cigarette butts. He's the acknowledged
expert in this narrow but important field."

Neel used a magnifying glass to examine the butt and
then consulted his book.

"Bourhill codified the characteristics of cigarette
butts across the world and his book on the subject is
updated each year. If it isn't in the book, then it doesn't
exist. Ah, here we go... This one is a very exclusive
brand. It's by a company called the Chancellor Tobacco
Company in England. The cigarette is called Treasurer
Luxury White. Very expensive. Only sold in England
and only at exclusive locations. Not available through
ordinary retail channels, and certainly not in India."

Nisha grinned. "Remind me to thank Bob Bourhill
when I see him."

Chapter 15

THE SMALL GROUND-FLOOR apartment in Vasant Vihar was ideal for Nisha, her eleven-year-old daughter, Maya, and their maid, Heena. It had been pricey—Vasant Vihar was an expensive area and property prices in Delhi had gone through the roof—but Sanjeev had left her with money and, having bought the apartment, Nisha had saved the rest. Financially she was well off.

But for all that, nothing could fill the emotional hole Sanjeev had left. It was as though his absence were a malignant presence. Like a shadow in their lives. And it was with them now as they sat at the dining table, finishing a dinner prepared by Heena. It was an unspoken thing. *We wish Papa were here. Telling stupid jokes or singing to himself or even just being grumpy. Whatever. We wish Papa were here.*

Not for the first time, Nisha thanked her lucky stars

for Heena. Without Heena she couldn't work. And there were times that Nisha thought work was the only thing that allowed her to cope with losing Sanjeev.

Heena was also blessed with the ability to know when Nisha and Maya needed a little mother–daughter time. Like now, as she cleared the table and left them to settle down into the living-room sofa.

"Why couldn't we just get pizza from that new place down the street?" asked Maya, snuggling into her mother. A cartoon was on TV but neither was really watching it.

"Junk food. Not good for either of us," replied Nisha. "Better to eat healthy home-cooked meals prepared by Heena."

Nisha felt her daughter's shoulders shake, the all-too-familiar signal that tears were imminent, and all Nisha could do was hold her and try to cuddle the pain away.

"I miss Papa," said Maya, the tears now rolling down her cheeks. "I miss the times he took us out for pizza and ice cream. I don't want the pizza or ice cream. I just want Papa back."

"I know, baby, I miss him too," said Nisha, thinking, *God, so much. I miss him so much.*

"I feel so lonely," whimpered Maya. "You're always working." The pain in her little girl's voice, and the bald truth of the statement, made Nisha feel wretched. "But at least when you were late, it was Dad who would tuck me into bed. Now there's only Heena. The apartment feels so cold and empty."

Nisha hugged Maya tighter and thumbed tears from

her face. "Tell you what," she said. "On the weekend, we'll go out. How about a movie followed by pizza?"

Sniffing, Maya nodded and Nisha felt bowled over by her bravery. This frail little thing, forced to cope with so much at such a young age. "You and I make a great team," she said into Maya's hair. "I promise that we'll take a holiday together in the hills soon. What do you think about Shimla? It's not too far from Delhi."

"The last time you said that, we had to cancel the holiday because of work," said Maya, and Nisha cringed at the memory.

"No cancelations this time, I promise," she said.

Maya brightened up more. Nisha passed her a box of tissues to wipe away her tears.

"Now, what about that essay you were supposed to write for your school competition? The one about how to improve the health of Delhi's citizens?" asked Nisha.

Maya rolled her eyes. "It was due earlier today. It's already been submitted."

"I see. And does it have a title, this masterwork?"

"It's called 'Health Care, Fair and Square?' It's about how everybody should have access to health care whether they're rich or poor, young or old, whatever their nationality. How we should treat health care a bit more like we do education, so more people get a fair shot."

Nisha awarded Maya with an impressed look. "Wow, well, that's very, very commendable, Maya. I'm delighted. Can I have a copy to read?"

"I saved one," beamed Maya. She fetched it then

snuggled back into position. "I'm pretty pleased with it, actually. Especially as most people have just talked about, like, how many hospitals there are in the city and stuff."

"Yours has got a bit more substance," said Nisha, leafing through the A4 pages.

"Well, I don't want to be big-headed, but..."

"You're going to be anyway."

"Yeah," laughed Maya. "Fingers crossed I'll win."

"You never know."

"The prize is being handed out by some real bigwig, a guy called Amit Roy from the government."

"Very good. With any luck you'll meet him."

Mother and daughter cuddled on the couch, hugging each other in a home that felt empty. The winter winds of Delhi howled outside and the branches of the Indian lilac tree that touched their living-room window tapped a rat-a-tat-tat rhythm on the pane.

With Maya snoring gently beside her, Nisha lifted the essay to read but had only got through a few sentences before she felt her eyelids grow heavy.

She laid it down, guiltily, promising herself she'd return to it first thing.

Chapter 16

THE KILLER WAS disappointed. Rahul's murder had been relegated to a short piece in the newspaper. Little more than a sidenote.

What disappointed him even more—though of course he was not in the slightest bit surprised—was the fact that no publicity had been given to the find in Greater Kailash. All those corpses. All that evidence. It should have been the lead item on the news. And yet there had been nothing.

The usual suspects were once again covering their asses. But he knew who they were; he had done his research.

Arranged on the surface before him was a series of photographs, a selection of Delhi's great and good.

Men who would whimper when they died. The killer was choosing his next victim. He knew the method, of course.

Now to decide who died next.

Chapter 17

DELHI'S GOVERNMENTAL HUB was the Secretariat, based in the area known as Indraprastha Estate. There, Chief Minister Mohan Jaswal was to preside over a press briefing.

Santosh sat alone, one eye on the lectern at the front of the room from where Jaswal would conduct the press conference, another on the journalists around him. To his left sat Ajoy Guha, a familiar face from DETV. Broadcasting from Delhi's media hub at Noida, and boasting twice the viewership of the other news channels put together, DETV was known for its fierce reporting, outspoken views, and hard-hitting investigations, and the fiercest and most outspoken show of all was Guha's *Carrot and Stick*.

Guha was tall and lanky with slightly thinning hair and a narrow face accentuated by wire-framed glasses.

He sat scribbling into a notebook. Santosh admired his methodical approach. You didn't become the country's highest-paid news anchor for nothing, he reasoned.

Guha stopped writing and put the notebook away. He took out a box of Nature's Way lozenges and popped one in his mouth.

Next Santosh saw Jaswal, standing just outside the door. The Chief Minister took a puff of his bronchodilator then entered, approaching the lectern and adjusting the microphone.

He wore a pale yellow turban, color-coordinated with the kerchief in his pocket. Perfect for TV cameras. There were advantages to being Sikh—the turban and white beard instantly caught the attention.

Like the seasoned campaigner he was, he began to field questions from the press. Innocuous queries at first. Camera flashes went off like little bombs. Santosh watched with interest as the conference rumbled on, wondering if the issue of the corpses in Greater Kailash would come up.

And then India's most fearless reporter weighed in.

"Just one final question, sir," said Guha, waving a sheaf of papers. "I have with me copies of police reports indicating that up to eleven corpses were discovered in the basement of a house in Greater Kailash. The question to you, Chief Minister, is this: why didn't you tell us?"

Who leaked? wondered Santosh. *Let's see how Jaswal gets himself out of this.*

Jaswal didn't miss a beat. "Neither the police nor the

Lieutenant Governor have informed me of this matter," he said.

Good play, thought Santosh. It wasn't a lie but it wasn't quite the whole truth either.

At the lectern, Jaswal went on, raising a statesman-like finger to make a point. "But if what you say is true then heads will roll," he said.

"Ladies and gentlemen, the Chief Minister has another official engagement and hence the press conference must end here," said the press secretary as Jaswal turned to leave. There was a mad scramble as reporters fired off further questions while cameras whirred and flashed.

Santosh followed Jaswal out. He needed a few minutes with him.

Chapter 18

IN HIS OFFICE, Jaswal seethed. "Who is feeding them information, Santosh? Why is it that my own sources of information are being throttled, yet a...*toad* like Guha knows all about it?"

Santosh gave a small shrug.

Jaswal reddened. "But this is what I'm paying you to find out."

"Are you? I thought we were being paid to look into the murders."

"Anything. Just bring me anything."

"In order for you to make political capital out of it? I'm not sure that's Private's style."

"Jack Morgan has no such qualms. If the ethics of the investigation bother you, I suggest you take it up with him. Better still, why not just get on with the case, find the killer, and leave the rest to me. Then we'll all be happy."

Santosh nodded. The man was right. It wasn't up to Santosh to question *why* they were investigating, nor what the long-term ramifications might be. It was up to him to get on with the investigation and try to find the killer or killers. Let the politicians slug it out between themselves afterward.

Outside the building he met Nisha, fresh from procuring information at the Public Works Department.

"How did it go?" he asked.

"They huffed and puffed but I fluttered my eyelashes, opened my purse, and got the information I needed."

Santosh stopped and adjusted his scarf. "Go on," he said.

"Okay, well, the house at Greater Kailash is no ordinary house."

"Apart from the fact that there was a corpse-disposal factory in the basement," said Santosh drily.

"Yeah, apart from that. Get this—it was last occupied by the director of the Central Bureau of Investigation. No one has been allocated the house for the past three years, something to do with a missing structural stability certificate."

"I see," said Santosh, chin raised, eyes gleaming behind his glasses.

"So I need to find out who was heading the Central Bureau of Investigation three years ago," said Nisha.

"There's no need. I can tell you. It was the present Lieutenant Governor, Chopra," replied Santosh, whose memory for such information had not diminished.

Nisha whistled. "Then we have a prime suspect."

Santosh shook his head. "Chopra is a killer who hid the bodies in his own basement? No, Nisha. Somehow I don't think it will be that easy. If only it were. But one thing we do know is why Chopra and Sharma are blocking information from reaching Jaswal. It's not because they hope to hurt Jaswal, it's because the truth is potentially embarrassing for Chopra."

"Are you going to tell Jaswal?" she asked.

"I should, shouldn't I? Given that our original brief was to find that out for him. Except that just now he asked me to continue looking into the murders and for the time being that's exactly what I plan to do."

Chapter 19

HER VISITOR'S PASS bounced against her chest as Nisha strode through the open-plan offices of the *Indian Times* on Parliament Street.

Pratish rose from his cubicle to meet her with a peck on the cheek. In response she gave him a hug and for a moment the two old friends simply enjoyed seeing one another again.

"How have you been, Pratt?" she asked him, taking the seat he indicated.

He pulled a face.

"Oh dear," said Nisha. "Want to share?"

For the next few minutes they talked: he about his messy divorce, bitchy ex, and grueling hours at the paper; she about losing Sanjeev and the difficulty of caring for Maya.

"We make a fine pair," he said at last. "Now, I don't

suppose you came here just to trade hardships. What do you need?"

"Political gossip," said Nisha. "You are, after all, the foremost authority."

He preened. "Subject?" he asked.

"Ram Chopra," replied Nisha.

Pratt whistled. "Smooth operator. Rather hoity-toity...smokes Cohibas like a chimney. Speaks the Queen's English with greater flair than Englishmen. Can't stand Jaswal."

The mention of Chopra's Cohibas made Nisha frown. "Does he ever smoke cigarettes?"

"Not to my knowledge. The cigar is something of a trademark. Why?"

"Nothing. It doesn't matter. What about Jaswal?"

"Ah! One of our own. You know he used to work for this paper? Our Chief Minister was a hack for the *Indian Times*. Who knows, maybe I'll be Chief Minister one day. Anyway, he hates Chopra's guts. Mutual antagonism."

"Who are Chopra's friends?" asked Nisha.

"Follow me," he said, and led the way to the archive room, where he typed "Ram Chopra" into a terminal that gave reel number references. Next he switched on the reader and fed a reel onto the spindle, carefully threading the film under the small rollers. He began advancing the film using manual knobs.

Moments later he had the image he was looking for: Chopra, Honorable Minister for Health and Family Welfare Nikhil Kumar, and another man in a bush shirt.

"Who's that?" asked Nisha, indicating the third guy.

"Samir Patel, the chairman of Surgiquip, one of the largest Indian health care equipment companies. Most of the new hospitals in India have used Surgiquip's services and technology—and according to my sources, that's because Chopra swung a huge deal in favor of Surgiquip. Kumar's in on it too. Eyebrows were raised. Jaswal was livid, especially with Kumar being part of his cabinet. But the matter remained buried."

As Nisha left Pratt with a kiss and a promise to meet again soon, her mind raced. So—Delhi's Lieutenant Governor, Ram Chopra, was the last to occupy a house in which body parts had been discovered. Chopra was at war with Jaswal. And Chopra was dirty—doing shady deals with medical corporations.

Somehow all this was connected, she knew. But how? What Private needed was a break in this case.

They were about to get one.

Chapter 20

NEEL MEHRA ADJUSTED his jacket and muffler in the mirror of the entrance foyer of the Olive Bar and Kitchen. He wanted to look good for Ash. It had been a long time.

He headed into the open courtyard, where outdoor heaters compensated for the cold weather and diners nibbled on thin-crust pizzas and sipped chilled Sancerre. There waiting for him was Ash—Dr. Ashish Lal, the police medical examiner.

Ash was only a few years senior to Neel, but thanks to his gray sideburns and dark circles beneath his eyes he looked a lot older—one of the perks of working for the police department and bosses like Sharma.

The two had met at the Department of Forensic Medicine at the All India Institute of Medical Sciences. Neel had been working on a difficult case that needed a complicated diagnostic test to be performed. The only one capable of handling it had been Ash. The two had become friends, then lovers. Neel was the younger, more desirable of the two men, but Ash had been something of a mentor to him. A strong, lasting relationship had formed.

"Thanks for seeing me at short notice, Ash," said Neel, taking a seat.

Ash smiled and poured Neel a glass of wine, and for a moment or so the two regarded each other, both stirred by the other's presence. "I'm happy to help," smiled Ash, breaking the spell. "But this particular meeting never happened. You know why." He joined the fingers of his hands together—almost like two spiders performing push-ups against one another.

"My lips are sealed," said Neel, taking a sip of his wine.

"It's about the house at Greater Kailash, isn't it?"

"It is."

"And your interest?"

Neel gave a theatrical look left and right. "Can I let you into a secret?"

"Isn't that the purpose of our meeting?"

"The purpose of our meeting is so that we can trade secrets."

"Ah, well then, you better tell me yours before I divulge any of mine."

The waiter arrived, and the conversation paused as pizzas were ordered, and—Ash looked over the table with inquiring eyes—yes, "another bottle of Sancerre, please."

"So, your secret?" asked Ash.

Neel saw a new light in his friend's eyes and was gratified to think it was he who had put it there. "Private Delhi is looking into the bodies at Greater Kailash."

"I see. On whose dollar?"

"Now we really are into the territory of secrets. If I tell you that, do you have details of the investigation to trade?"

Ash shrugged. "Well, as the medical examiner on the case I do indeed have some details. However, they are very scant. The killer is not only extremely good at covering his own tracks but also those of his victims. There's one cadaver that's slightly better preserved than the others. I'll be examining it over the next couple of days."

"And do you think you'll be at liberty to share your findings?"

Ash smiled. "I certainly won't be at liberty to do that, no." His smile broadened lasciviously. "But I might just do it all the same."

"That would be very much appreciated. Anything else you can tell me?"

Ash nodded. "I have something that might be of interest to you. I'm still curious to know who's employing Private, though."

"It'll go no further?"

"Of course not. But you better hurry. Our pizzas will be here soon. Not to mention that second bottle of wine." Ash's tiredness seemed to have disappeared.

"We're being employed by Mohan Jaswal."

Ash smiled, rolled his eyes. "Figures," he said. "And I suppose Jaswal is keen to catch the killer, is he?"

"As I'm sure you can guess, Jaswal is far more concerned with putting one over on Chopra or making sure Chopra doesn't put one over on him. We're stuck someplace in the middle. Such is life. But what else is it you've discovered?"

Ash pulled a face. "Like I say, it's precious little." He reached into his jacket, retrieved a small plastic bag from his inside pocket, and placed it on the table between them. Inside was a tiny piece of fabric. "How do you fancy analyzing that on some of that fancy gadgetry you have at Private?"

"You scratch my back . . ."

Ash twinkled. "I'll happily scratch yours."

Neel pocketed the evidence bag. "You've had a good look at it, presumably."

"I have."

"And?"

"And I'm fairly sure I know what it is. I'd be interested to see if you concur."

"Give me a clue. We're trying to catch a killer here, not play forensic tic-tac-toe."

"All right, then. You win. I think it's a piece of a hospital gown."

Chapter 21

"I THINK HE'S right," said Neel the following day.

He was hunched over a powerful microscope, scrutinizing the tiny piece of fabric given to him the previous night. The thought of Ash made him stop suddenly and he raised his head from the eyepiece, allowing himself a smile of remembrance, and then went back to the job at hand.

Behind him stood Nisha and Santosh. "You think it's a piece of hospital gown?" said Santosh, leaning forward, hands clasped over the head of his cane.

"I do."

"That is very interesting," said Santosh. "It means we have a connection."

"We do?" said Nisha.

"May I?" said Santosh. He laid his cane on the table, shifted his glasses to the top of his head, and took over from Neel at the microscope. For some moments there was silence, broken only by Santosh murmuring his agreement that yes, it was a fragment of hospital gown. "Here," he said to Neel, bidding him scrutinize the evidence again. "Do you see traces of a black marking?"

Neel looked, then nodded. "You think you know what they are?"

"Dhobi marks," said Santosh. "Some public hospitals don't do their own laundry. They outsource the job to teams of dhobis, a specific community that specializes in washing clothes the traditional Indian way—soaking them in hot water and then flogging them against laundry stones in vast open-air concrete pens. Each dhobi uses indelible ink to mark the garments to stop them going missing. So where there is a dhobi mark, there has to be a dhobi. Finding that dhobi will reveal which hospitals those bodies came from."

"And that's the connection," said Nisha, stepping forward. "It's hospitals, isn't it? Ram Chopra is doing deals with medical companies. Fragments of a hospital gown found at Greater Kailash..."

"Precisely," said Santosh.

"Then surely this brings Chopra even further into the frame?" pressed Nisha. "Or...maybe not Chopra himself, then at least his associates. Whatever his dealings with Surgiquip, perhaps they're being blocked and this is him cleaning house?"

"Maybe," said Santosh. "It would be convenient, wouldn't it?"

Nisha rolled her eyes in exasperation. "Just because it seems obvious doesn't mean it can't be the truth."

"Noted," said Santosh. "But the important thing is we now have a thread, and we have to keep pulling at it and see what unravels."

He waved his hands at Neel and Nisha like a crazed scientist releasing his flying instruments of death. "Go. Go. Keep pulling that thread."

Chapter 22

SANTOSH ASKED THE taxi driver to drop him off near the main gate of the Delhi Memorial Hospital. He heard barking and wondered why a hospital needed guard dogs as well as security officers.

He took the elevator to the tenth floor. It was one of Delhi's largest hospitals and was part of the state government's health service. It had over five hundred beds but the corridors were usually to be found overflowing with patients awaiting a free bed. Santosh tuned out wailing babies as he knocked on the door to the office of the chief administrator—a South Indian man whose full name was an awe-inspiring Mangalampalli Gopalamenon Thekkaparambil, everyone simply called him MGT. He and Santosh had known each other at college although they hadn't really been friends. In those days

MGT had hung out with either the stoned or the drunk. Santosh had been neither.

"Come in," announced the voice from inside and Santosh entered, instantly reminded by the stench that MGT was a chain smoker. Out of deference to his visitor, MGT was moving an ashtray from his desktop and waving ineffectually at smoke that still hung in the air.

"Good to see you, Santosh," he said, reaching to shake Santosh's hand. He was tall and lanky, with a full head of jet-black hair and a stubbled chin.

"You too," said Santosh. "Why in heaven's name do you have guard dogs at the gate?"

"Oh, there's a separate VIP wing in the hospital," answered MGT. "Usually top politicians. We need dogs to protect the dogs." He laughed, revealing stained yellow teeth, and then changed the subject with the expertise of a true bureaucrat. "So what was it that you wanted to meet me about?"

"Private has been recruited by a medical services firm to find out the average turnaround time of hospital beds in India," said Santosh. "I was hoping you could help me with that."

"That's privileged information, Santosh."

MGT's secretary knocked, entered, and handed him a small slip of paper. He looked at it, opened his desk drawer with a key, and placed the slip inside, locking the drawer afterward. Santosh watched impassively, wondering what was so important it needed locking away.

MGT fixed Santosh with a hard stare. "Why don't you stop bullshitting and tell me why you're *really* here?"

Rumbled. "Apologies, MGT—old habits die hard," he said, shifting in his seat. "Can you keep a secret?"

MGT gave a slightly noncommittal shrug. "Try me."

"This is about murder," said Santosh and, careful not to reveal too many salient details, went on to explain his theory concerning the body parts at Greater Kailash.

"A serial killer at large?" asked MGT, his eyes widening theatrically.

"It's one of the ideas I'm working on, yes. Whatever the motive, the fact remains that there's a common theme."

"And what would you like me to do about it?"

Santosh looked sharply at him. "Well, I thought you might appreciate being informed."

MGT gave a tight smile. "You wondered if we might have a killer stalking the corridors of the hospital?"

Santosh felt himself shunted to the back foot, not somewhere he liked to be, especially as he wasn't sure whether MGT was mocking him or not. He pressed on. "As well as thinking you might like to know, I also wondered whether anything I might say would have any relevance to you; whether it might ring any bells?"

"Well, I'm afraid it doesn't."

"I see. And this doesn't worry you, this..."

"*Theory* of yours? No, Santosh, funnily enough it doesn't."

Chapter 23

AMIT ROY, THE new Principal Secretary of the Department of Health and Family Welfare, looked at the material on his desk yet again. He took his time over it, like a man eager to commit its contents to memory, which was exactly what he was. He hated getting rid of the stuff but there was no other option: keeping it was a security risk.

Once more he scanned the various photographs laid out on his desk, arranged side by side and in neat rows, like a fleshy tarot reading. A smile played on his lips as he recalled the moments portrayed. His hands wandered and he closed his eyes to allow his fantasies to play out, revisiting the screams, the pleadings, the sheer transgressive pleasure known only to his kind.

But enough. He tore himself away, thinking again how he hated to dispose of such precious things but knowing it was a necessity, and then gathered the material from his desk and scooped it into a carrier bag. He went into his back garden, where a barbecue unit sat, and he opened the hood. Into that went the photographs. *Save them*, urged an inner voice. *Save one at least.* But no. He doused the lot with lighter fluid, lit a match, and watched his prized possessions burn.

Chapter 24

NIKHIL KUMAR TAPPED at the keys of his laptop. Even in the dead of night he was perfectly turned out in a well-pressed kurta and pajama, his hair neatly brushed, his skin radiant from the exfoliating face wash he used every night.

He was drafting another letter to Jaswal requesting that Roy be transferred. He had no option but to type the letter himself because he simply could not dictate it to the department stenographer. The entire ministry leaked like a sieve and anything he dictated invariably reached everyone else before the intended recipient.

He was in his ground-floor study, which opened into the living room of his official residence at Mayur Vihar, a residential zone of East Delhi located just east of the Yamuna river. Two policemen were on guard at the driveway gate, and his wife and son were asleep in a bedroom on the upper floor. His son, only eight years old, always managed to find reasons why he couldn't sleep in his own bed, and Kumar's wife would fly into one of her famous temper tantrums if ever Kumar suggested he try harder.

He typed on. At the gate the two policemen stamped their feet to warm themselves in the cold.

All were oblivious to what was happening in the garden.

Chapter 25

TOWARD THE REAR of the house was a vegetable and herb garden managed by Mrs. Kumar. In one corner was a manhole topped by a solid cast-iron cover. The manhole cover received a little nudge from below and, once it had popped up, was gently pushed to one side.

An intruder dressed in black protective clothing—gloves, boots, and helmet—emerged. On his back was a rucksack containing the tools of his trade. He headed to the service entrance of the house that opened into the kitchen. He tried the door. Locked.

He removed his helmet, boots, and gloves and deposited them near the door. Pulling out a pair of surgical gloves from his rucksack, he snapped them on and removed a lock-picker's tool containing the twelve most commonly used picks. Choosing two of the twelve, he unlocked the door in less than a minute.

He tiptoed into the kitchen in his socks. Empty. Kumar's servants had retired for the night. He reached into his bag, first for the balaclava and then, when that was fitted, his hypodermic syringe. Then he crossed to nudge open the door, seeing Kumar hunched over his computer, his back to the doorway.

But the hinges were old, and the door squeaked as it opened.

Chapter 26

KUMAR SWIVELED IN his chair, irritated, expecting to see his wife, son, a member of staff or security—an unwelcome presence, interrupting his train of thought.

But it was none of those. The figure in the doorway was dressed in black, complete with balaclava covering all but his eyes, and his nose and lips that protruded obscenely through the mouth hole. And for a second, frozen by shock, Kumar dithered, unable to decide whether to scream for help or make a dash for the panic button, when what he should have done was both at the same time. The intruder lurched forward. At that moment Kumar saw what he held. A hypodermic syringe, whose needle was jabbed into his neck.

And for Kumar, the lights went out.

When he regained consciousness it was to find that

he'd been duct-taped to his office chair and moved to the other side of the desk. The man in black stood before him, still wearing his balaclava. Using a flashlight, the intruder checked Kumar's pupils and then stepped back, satisfied, his eyes gleaming in the eye holes of the balaclava, his bulging lips wet.

"I injected you with etorphine, an opioid possessing three thousand times the analgesic potency of morphine," he said. "I find it very useful indeed. However, I'm not going to give you the pleasure of dying while you're asleep. No, you must be fully awake."

The attacker was disguising his voice, yet there was something familiar about it.

"Who are you?" managed Kumar. He was wondering if there'd been enough noise to rouse his sleeping family. Probably not. He was too weak to scream now. The intruder was clearly no madman. He gave every indication of having a well-thought-out plan. It was this more than anything that terrified Kumar. Here he was in a house surrounded by staff and security and yet he was going to die.

But not yet.

"Who are you?" he repeated. "I know you, don't I? If you're going to kill me then why not reveal yourself to me? Tell me what you want."

"Tell you what I want? Very well. I want you, who has done so much taking, to give."

"What are you talking about, 'give'? Give what?"

"I'll show you." The attacker turned to reach into a small rucksack, retrieving a pair of blood bags, each attached to a length of surgical hose and a needle. He arranged the bags on the floor at Kumar's feet. It was only then that Kumar realized his arms had been duct-taped a certain way, palms upward, like a man offering a peace settlement.

The only light in the room was the glow of the laptop screen. In the gloom of his office Kumar looked down to see his attacker peering up at him, and he gazed into the man's eyes hoping to see some shred of mercy or pity, but found none.

"Please don't do this," he whimpered. "I'm a very powerful man. There is so much I can do for you. Name it. Name your price."

"I have already named my price, Honorable Minister for Health and Family Welfare. I have already named it. You are about to pay it. You ask if there is anything you can do for me—the answer is no, you have already done enough. You are corrupt and venal and you have done enough."

The intruder rose, and in his hand he held one of the needles. Kumar's struggles were futile as the intruder used his index and middle fingers to tap up a vein in Kumar's left forearm. The radial artery. In went the first needle. Blood flowed along the opaque medical tube and began to fill the bag below.

"Please..."

But the man in black was not listening. He was now holding the other needle, repeating the process in the other arm.

"Are you feeling your heart rate increasing?" he said,

and drew over a second chair in order to sit opposite Kumar and watch the show. Kumar could indeed feel his heart beating rapidly, suddenly accompanied by a clammy sensation.

"You will now feel dizzy," said the man in black.

Again, that voice. Kumar recognized the voice.

"Soon you will turn pale. Then shortness of breath will kick in. Once your blood pressure has dropped far enough, you will lose consciousness. Anywhere between twenty and thirty minutes' time."

Kumar watched helplessly as the man in black moved over to dismiss the screensaver of his laptop and read the letter on his screen. "Very interesting," he said after some moments. "Very interesting indeed."

And then he deleted the letter. Next he began opening other documents, reading e-mails, pleased at what he learned.

Ten minutes passed. The only sound in the room was Kumar's whimpering, and even that began to fade as he felt his strength recede. As the blood was taken from him so was the will to live, as though his spirit and soul were being taken too. Suddenly he was gripped by a desire to say sorry for everything he had done, but knew the sudden need for what it was—a hypocritical, self-serving reaction to his imminent death. A need to salve his conscience.

His eyelids began to flutter. His blood flowed into the bags more slowly now. With it went hope. With it went everything he had ever been or ever would be. With it came the end.

And then, just as he was about to die, the man in black leaned forward in his chair, took hold of the balaclava from the bottom, and peeled it up over his face.

The last word Kumar ever said was "You."

Chapter 27

THE BELL KEPT ringing. It was a big brass bell splashed in blood. And it was clanging because a swaying corpse was suspended from it.

Shut up, thought Santosh, but the bell kept clanging. Louder than ever.

It took a few more minutes for him to realize he'd been having another nightmare. With a gasp, he pulled himself from its claws, reaching for his glasses on the nightstand. He put them on and then saw the time on his bedside clock. Six in the morning, and the bell in his nightmare was really the ringing of his cell phone. He took the call. Neel.

"Nikhil Kumar is dead," said Neel. "Just got the news."

"Murdered?" asked Santosh.

"Let's put it this way: the circumstances are highly suspicious," replied Neel.

Santosh felt a headache lurking behind his eyes. There was throbbing in his head. While working in Mumbai, he had used to drink himself into a stupor before crashing out on the couch. Rehab had advised him to take sedatives instead, and in place of the whisky hangover he had one from the sedatives. At least the whisky had been enjoyable.

"I'll meet you there in half an hour," he said, rubbing his eyes. "Have you informed Nisha?"

Chapter 28

THE CRIME-SCENE UNIT was at the house, but temporarily too preoccupied to register Private entering. In keeping with the Sherlock Holmes maxim of hiding in plain sight, the three investigators simply walked in as though they had a perfect right to be there, and at their head, Santosh crossed the entrance hall and entered the downstairs office quickly, knowing that despite what Holmes said, it wouldn't be long before they were challenged.

The sight in the office brought him up short. In the midst of the scene-of-crime officers in protective suits and masks was the victim, Nikhil Kumar. Wearing elegant pajamas, he'd been taped to a chair but his head lolled on his chest and by the look of him—his skin a grotesque chalky color—he had been drained of blood.

According to Neel—in other words, according to

Neel's contact, Ash—Kumar's wife had discovered her husband's body early in the morning. Not finding him in the bedroom, she had assumed he would be asleep on the couch in his study. She had brewed him a mug of tea and carried it into the study, only to be greeted by his exsanguinated corpse.

Neel and Nisha entered the room behind Santosh. The investigators were paying them more attention now, exchanging puzzled glances. A challenge was imminent, Santosh knew, and he moved forward to inspect the corpse, noting the way in which the arms had been bound, not to mention the pinpricks that indicated where the blood had been taken. At the same time he ever-so-casually brushed the laptop on the desk to get rid of the screensaver, but the screen was blank. *That's odd*, he thought. *Laptop on, but no document, no web page showing.*

"Excuse me..." said a SOCO.

But then from the doorway came the raised voice of Sharma: "Who the fuck allowed you inside?"

Santosh turned to see the corpulent, red-faced figure of the police chief.

"Why?" asked Santosh. "Is this your house?" He had no plans to reveal that it was Ash who'd tipped off Neel about Kumar's death. Ash stood beside Sharma and Santosh could see the nervousness on the medical examiner's face.

"It's a goddamn crime scene!" shouted Sharma, indignant. "I need all of you to get the fuck out of here, right now!"

At the same time, Neel snapped on his gloves and strode into the study confidently. Ash shouted after him, "Hey, you can't go inside there. I'll have you booked for interfering with a crime scene!"

To the uninitiated the altercation between Ash and Neel was a mere shouting match, but to those in the know—Santosh and Nisha—it was a choreographed argument that served two purposes: first, it would ensure that Sharma didn't suspect Ash of leaking information; second, it would give Santosh time to observe the crime scene.

Santosh seized the opportunity to do a walkabout, leaving the house while Neel and Ash kept up their bickering. He looked at the main gate. A small guardhouse was located to the right of it. It would have been impossible for someone to enter with guards on duty at night. Unless it was an inside job.

He looked at the walls that surrounded the house. They were around six feet high, and solid iron spikes, each about a foot long, were grouted at the top. Glass shards had been embedded into the top surface of the wall. Thin cables ran between the iron spikes. Santosh noticed little yellow signs indicating electrified cables. Difficult for someone to clamber over the wall without doing serious damage to themselves.

He walked to the rear garden and looked at the neat little rows of herbs and vegetables that Mrs. Kumar had planted. Something was out of place. He examined the soil. In one corner it had been disturbed. Santosh gazed at it a little longer. It seemed to be a cylindrical pattern with a rounded end. The manhole cover. If it were shifted sideways, wouldn't it create a similar pattern?

He bent down and grasped the manhole cover. He pulled and it came off easily. He removed his worn scarf and tied it to the underside handle of the cover. He then gently nudged the cover back into place.

Santosh made his way around the house, carefully observing the doors and windows. Nothing had been broken or tampered with. The intruder would have picked a lock to get inside. Which one? Front or rear? The manhole was toward the rear and the main door at the front was visible from the gatehouse. More likely that the killer had used the kitchen door.

"You have exactly five seconds to get the hell out of here before I ask my men to arrest you," came Sharma's voice from behind. He had noticed Santosh's absence from the study and had stormed outside to find him.

Santosh turned. His breath bloomed in the garden. "Whoever executed this murder planned it perfectly. Lots of preparation went into it."

"Murder? Who says it's murder?" bawled Sharma. "Looks like suicide to me. Yes, let's go with that."

"He duct-taped himself to the chair?" asked Santosh.

"I don't need your fucking help, Wagh. Now get out before I take you into custody."

Chapter 29

"WHO HAD MOTIVE to kill Kumar?" asked Santosh as he, Nisha, and Neel made their way to Neel's Toyota. "Who were his enemies?"

"Every politician has hundreds," replied Nisha. "But no one hated Kumar more than Jaswal."

"And who were his friends? Often, real enemies may appear like friends and vice versa," said Santosh.

Nisha took a folded piece of paper from her shirt pocket and handed it to Santosh. It was a printout of a photograph that showed Kumar with Patel and Chopra.

Chapter 30

NISHA LOOKED AT the six names on her smartphone yet again. They were the six remaining Truckomatic customers who needed to be traced. She ran a Google search on each and then she made the first call.

"Hello, could you put me through to your administration department?" she asked brightly.

"Anyone specifically?" asked the switchboard operator.

"No," replied Nisha. "I need to discuss an insurance policy that is due for renewal on one of your company's vehicles."

After a few minutes of elevator music, another voice came on the line. "How can I help you?" asked the man.

"Hello, my name is Sherry," lied Nisha. "The insurance policy on a black van owned by your company is about to expire and I was wondering if you would be interested in renewing it at a lower rate with us."

"Black van? You mean our vanity van?"

"Yes, that's the one," replied Nisha. "My company can beat your current premium."

"Do you charge extra for operating the vehicle outside city limits?"

"We usually do," said Nisha. "But we could look at other ways to compensate for that. Is your vehicle used extensively outside Delhi?"

"Almost entirely," replied the man. "The van is used whenever we have distant shoots, which is most of the time. It's hardly ever in Delhi."

Nisha repeated the process. It turned out that an airline used their van as a shuttle for their staff and it remained in service 24/7; a hotel had their van stationed in the entrance portico; and a pharmaceutical company stored theirs in Chandigarh, 250 kilometers away from Delhi.

Nisha crossed off the four companies and then turned her attention to the two names of individuals left on her list. One was a Bollywood actress. Nisha spoke to her secretary and confirmed that the customized van remained in Mumbai.

"Why did you register it in Delhi?" asked Nisha.

"Because Mumbai has lifetime tax while Delhi has annual road tax," said the secretary. "Substantial cost saving."

That left only one name—a "Mr. Arora." She picked up the phone and dialed the number.

A receptionist answered saying, "Dr. Pankaj Arora's office. May I help you?"

Chapter 31

"WHO IS THIS Dr. Pankaj Arora?" asked Santosh.

Nisha read aloud from the online biography. "Dr. Pankaj Arora, chief surgeon, Delhi Memorial Hospital. After completing his Bachelor of Medicine and Bachelor of Surgery...blah, blah, blah...He worked for several years as general surgeon at Sir Ganga Ram Hospital, New Delhi...blah, blah, blah...currently chief surgeon of Delhi Memorial Hospital."

She showed him a printed page, complete with shot of Arora. His dark hair was slicked back, and an ill-fitting grin revealed a large gap in his front teeth.

"Good work," said Santosh. "This heightens my suspicions about Delhi Memorial Hospital. It's closest to the Greater Kailash house where the bodies were discovered. Now we find that Arora's van could have been spotted at the house. Any information on my college classmate MGT?"

"Leave it with me," said Nisha.

Chapter 32

THE ROLE OF the Irrigation and Flood Control Department was to protect Delhi from floods and provide drainage but, as with every other government department, it had the body of a Hummer and the engine of a lawnmower. Getting anything moving was next to impossible.

"What can I do for you, Mr. Wagh?" asked the superintendent engineer, after Santosh had made his way through a maze of corridors and bureaucrats to his office.

"I believe the drainage system of Delhi was used to access a house and commit a crime," said Santosh, scratching his salt-and-pepper stubble. "I was wondering if you could tell me how someone might go about getting a detailed drainage map?"

The superintendent engineer opened a cabinet

drawer, took out a rolled-up paper, and handed it to Santosh. "No special effort required. Anyone can get a copy of Delhi's drainage map, for a fee."

"And does the department maintain a record of those who paid the fee?" asked Santosh.

"Sure," said the engineer. "But all we have is a name in a register. If someone supplied a false name, we'd have no way of knowing."

Chapter 33

SHORTLY AFTERWARD, SANTOSH found himself at the Indian Medical Association for a meeting set up through the doctor in charge of his rehab at the Cabin in Thailand. Dr. Singh was Indian and his nephew was the president of the association.

Santosh asked directions to the president's office and was soon making his acquaintance.

"Thank you for agreeing to meet with me. I know you're busy," said Santosh when the small talk had all but dried up. "So I'll get to the point. Could you tell me more about Mangalampalli Gopalamenon Thekkaparambil?"

"The chief administrator of Delhi Memorial Hospital?" asked the president. "Sad story. Capable man. Tragic, though. Lost his only child when the boy was just nine."

"How?"

"Wilson's disease."

"What is that?" asked Santosh.

"A genetic disorder," replied the president. "Copper accumulates in the body's tissues. It manifests as liver problems."

"Rare?"

"Very. One in a hundred people is a carrier. The disease strikes only when both parents are carriers."

"Is there no cure?"

"Sometimes a possible solution is a liver transplant. Unfortunately this was not an option in this case."

"Why?" asked Santosh. "Either of the parents could have donated part of their livers, no?"

"The mother died a couple of years after childbirth," replied the president. "The only possible course was for MGT to donate. Unfortunately he was a serious drinker on the verge of cirrhosis at that time."

"No cadaver donations possible?"

"They waited, but sadly the boy died before an organ could be procured."

Santosh nodded, his vision clouding a little as he thought of Isha and Pravir.

Chapter 34

BACK ON THE street, Santosh considered hailing a cab but took a look at the traffic—the constant noise and movement, each blare on a horn signaling a near miss, a driver on the edge—and he found himself cringing away from the idea, his mind still on the accident that had killed his family.

He was back there. In the car with Isha and Pravir. He was driving and from the back, Pravir called, "Papa, look at my score!"

Pravir was playing a handheld video game. Just a silly game. And because Santosh had pledged to be a better father, to pay more attention to his loved ones, he took his eyes off the road. Not really to look at the screen, more to simply acknowledge his son, congratulate him.

Either way, he took his eyes off the darkened, winding road for just a second, maybe not even that. But it was long enough to miss the bend.

Santosh had never been a particularly good driver. His mind was rarely "in the moment," which, ironically enough, was part of the reason he needed to consciously pay more attention to his family. And it was the reason his reaction time was slower than it might have been.

In short, he was not the sort of driver who could afford to take his eyes off the road.

And for that he had paid: Isha and Pravir both dead, him in the hospital. For a long time after that he had walked with a limp until he'd been told that the injury was psychosomatic. He'd lost the limp; he'd kept the cane. There were psychological scars that would never heal.

So he walked, and as he did so, he thought how they had that in common, he and MGT: they had both lost their families. Both for avoidable reasons. If Santosh had not taken his eyes off the road then Isha and Pravir would be alive. If MGT had not been such a heavy drinker then . . .

He stopped. Pedestrians flowed around him; one or two insults were tossed his way but he didn't care because it was as though light had suddenly flooded his mind.

Could it be?

He fumbled for his phone, called Neel, dispensed with the pleasantries: "The bodies at Greater Kailash. Did you say there was one that was better preserved than the others?"

"Yes. Ash was due to examine it any day now."

"Can you call him? Ask him how he's got on?"

"He's working. That might prove difficult for him."

"If you wouldn't mind," insisted Santosh. "There's one thing I'm desperate to learn."

"What is it?"

"I want to know if the body still has all its internal organs."

"I see," said Neel, commendably unflappable. "Something tells me you already know the answer."

"I *suspect* I know the answer. See if you can confirm it for me by the time I reach the office."

Chapter 35

"HELLO," SAID ASH, cautiously.

"Can you talk?"

"Um, not really. I'm busy..."

Neel sensed Ash was on the move, probably finding somewhere private to talk. Sure enough, when he next spoke he sounded out of breath, hissing, "What are you doing ringing me at work?"

"Well, firstly I wanted to say how much I enjoyed the other night."

Ash softened. "Good. I had a great time too."

"And secondly..."

"Of course, there's a *secondly*."

"Secondly, I wanted to ask if you'd conducted the postmortem on the intact cadaver."

"I can't talk about that," hissed Ash. "The walls have ears."

"Can you confirm something for me either way, yes or no?"

"Go on."

"Were the organs intact?"

Ash gave a small, impressed chuckle. "No."

"What was gone?"

There was a pause, as though Ash had waited for someone to pass in a corridor, and Neel held his breath. "Ash? Are you there?" he prompted. "Which organs were missing?"

Ash cleared his throat. "All," he said.

Chapter 36

"WELL?"

Santosh had burst onto the top floor of Private, cane tucked beneath his arm as he threaded his way between desks to where Nisha and Neel stood waiting.

"Ash had conducted the examination," said Neel, relishing the moment.

The end of the cane swung his way. "And?" said Santosh. His eyes glittered. His blood was up.

"All the vital organs were missing. All of them."

"I knew it."

Santosh was as close to happy or excited as Neel or Nisha had ever seen him, and they couldn't resist trading a quick eyebrows-raised look. In a second, though, their boss had switched back to stern-mentor mode, targeting Nisha this time.

"What do you think? Tell me what conclusions you draw."

Her head dropped to think. "Some sort of donation thing?" she said, uncertainly. "Kumar drained of blood. This body missing organs. Like they're being…harvested."

"It could be, couldn't it?" said Santosh. "It could be that our friend Dr. Arora is doing the harvesting. Now, what I want to do is find out whether there have been any similar murders. Something with a similar MO. Neel, while I'm a big believer in using the power of contacts and shoe leather, how would you feel about hacking into the National Crime Records Bureau?"

Neel felt fine about it, and as Santosh waited for the hack to begin he reflected that his belief in nurturing contacts had been inextricably linked with his drinking. Was it a coincidence that giving up booze had left him willing to explore more modern, expedient methods of information gathering?

He'd have liked to think it was a coincidence. But he knew deep down it wasn't.

Santosh and Nisha stood at Neel's back as he worked a laptop and desktop unit at the same time, using the laptop to launch a formal, untargeted attack on the system, the other for a more specific search.

Nisha had her arms folded across the front of her leather jacket, one foot behind the other. "Look at him go," she teased. "Who knew we had such a nerd at Private, eh, Santosh?"

Her smile faded as Santosh looked admonishingly at her over the top of his glasses and then returned to staring into space. Neel threw her a quick look over his shoulder, eyebrows raised, and the two shared a smile. Their boss's epic sense-of-humor fails were a shared confidence, the kind of thing they talked about in hushed tones whenever he was absent.

"Right," said Neel after a few more moments. "Exactly what is it you'd like me to look for?"

Santosh clicked back to the present. "Let's start with murders committed within the past six months."

"This is Delhi. That will be a lot."

"I haven't finished. Murders committed within the past six months in which . . . parts have been removed."

"Parts?"

"Body parts. Bits of the body. Trophies. Some piece of the victim that the killer removed and took away with him."

Neel consulted his laptop. "We have approximately two minutes before they kick us out altogether," he said.

"You'd better work quickly then," said Nisha, nudging him with her elbow.

Neel scooted slightly to the right, chair wheels drumming the boards. His fingers danced on the keyboard of the desktop. Lines of information appeared. As one, Nisha and Santosh leaned forward to look more closely.

"There's nothing," said Neel. "Correction, there *is* something. Here."

He pointed at the screen, indicating a brief murder report. The victim's name was Rahul. He had been found in the bath.

Both eyeballs missing.

Chapter 37

THE JOURNALIST AJOY Guha leaned back in his swivel chair in the DETV editorial office, sucking contentedly on a lozenge. On shelves behind him were neatly organized files, each containing in-depth investigations into various stories. It was well known that Guha required his team to devote hundreds of hours of research before broadcasting a show on any given topic. The sole personal item on the shelves was a photograph of a woman.

He addressed his team, who had assembled in the office, some standing, some perched on the edges of desks. "The suicide of Kumar is a major story," he said. "But we need an angle. Something unique to *Carrot and Stick*."

"How can we be sure that it was suicide?" asked one of the team members.

"Very good," said Guha. "Let's look into that."

The subordinate glowed with pride.

"There's something I think you should see," said a research assistant, passing Guha a bunch of papers.

"What are these?" he asked.

"Financial statements of Surgiquip India Limited," she replied.

"Patel's company?"

She nodded. "One of the largest investors in Surgiquip is an anonymous fund based in the Bahamas. Some of the directors of the fund are known friends of Kumar. There's every reason to believe that the money invested in Surgiquip also included Kumar's money. Effectively, Kumar was Patel's partner and, given his official position, was in a position to favor Surgiquip."

Guha rolled the lozenge inside his mouth as he contemplated the implications of that information. "Let's find an excuse to get Patel into the studio," he said. "We can rip apart those connections once he's in our hands."

"Do you think that's wise?" asked the show's producer. "Some of these companies are our lifeblood. Without advertising bucks, we're nothing."

"These people need to be exposed," said Guha. "You can be either a news channel or a profitable business. You can't be both."

Chapter 38

LOOKING MORE CLOSELY into Rahul's death, the first thing Santosh had discovered was that there were very few details available. Contacts in the force had supplied him with a time of death—sometime between 9 p.m. and midnight—and Rahul's occupation—shift worker—and that was it.

Now he stood in front of the late Rahul's front door, an apartment locked and sealed with a length of police tape, and was about to let himself in when a door to the left opened and the face of an elderly neighbor appeared.

"Can I help you?" she asked, with such an admirable lack of suspicion that he opted to come clean.

"I'm a private investigator," he said. He indicated the sealed door. "I'm looking into the death of your neighbor."

She held herself as though to stop herself from shuddering. "Awful business."

"Would you be willing to speak to me about it?" He shifted his weight onto his walking stick. Totem or not, it had its uses: weapon, pointer, putting elderly ladies at ease.

"You'd better come in," she said.

In a few moments they were sitting together, drinking tea, the neighbor telling him what scant details she knew. No, she had never noticed anything unusual. No strange guests or visitors. Nothing like that. No, she hadn't heard any odd noises. He was a good neighbor. Quiet. Kept himself to himself. Hardly ever there.

"He was a shift worker of some kind, wasn't he?" asked Santosh.

"He worked the hospitals. A porter, I think. Orderly. Nothing medical. Nothing proper, you know. But even so, all these jobs need doing, don't they?"

"Yes, they do," agreed Santosh, thinking that those jobs weren't usually well paid enough for ordinary hospital porters to be able to afford apartments. Not unless they were making something on the side. "Which hospitals did he work at, do you know?"

"No. In actual fact, I think he worked at them all at one time or another. Certainly I saw him in a number of different uniforms."

From the inside pocket of his jacket, Santosh took Arora's bio and showed it to the neighbor. "Did you ever see this man?"

She took a good look then shook her head. "Do you think he did it?"

"It's just a theory at this stage."

"What a horrible thing to do to someone," she said, hugging herself once again.

"The eyeballs?"

"Well, not just that. The ice too."

Santosh's teacup rattled as he replaced it on the table. "I beg your pardon. Did you say 'ice'?"

"Yes. When he was found—it was a colleague who found him—there were empty bags of ice in the bathroom. It had melted by that time, of course, but they think the bath was full of ice."

Ice, thought Santosh. *Like you might use to preserve an organ for transplant.*

Back in the hallway—thanks made and the neighbor installed in front of the TV—Santosh broke the tape, picked the lock, and let himself into Rahul's apartment.

It was not dissimilar to his own in terms of layout and lack of furniture. Whoever Rahul had been in life, he was not a homebody; the single armchair, TV, and coffee table in the front room suggested a person unaccustomed to spending much time in his own abode.

Along one wall was a low bookshelf; the few books on it were beach reads and bestsellers, the usual suspects. Meanwhile in the kitchen were exactly the kind of single-man ingredients and utensils that Santosh had in his own home.

Santosh thought back to Jack breaking into his apartment. Both locks had been easily picked. Had Rahul been at home when the killer had entered? Had he been asleep when the killer had filled the bath with ice? Surely not.

What did he do? Did he let himself in, fill the bath, then wait? Or did he catch Rahul unawares, knock him out, then fill the bath with ice?

Rahul was a shift worker, so it was entirely likely that he could have been asleep early, but even so.

"He would have had to bring his own ice," Santosh said aloud. "He brought his own ice, filled the bath, and waited for Rahul to arrive. Which meant he knew Rahul's movements. He knew what time Rahul was arriving home."

Which meant he was targeting Rahul specifically.

Chapter 39

NIGAMBODH GHAT WAS located along the banks of the Yamuna river toward the rear of the historic Red Fort. On any given day, more than sixty corpses would be burned on Hindu cremation pyres at Nigambodh Ghat.

There was high security that day. The cremation of Nikhil Kumar was a state funeral. An honor guard in dark green turbans and red plumage led Kumar's grief-stricken wife and son to the brick platform. His body, wrapped in homespun cloth, was placed in the sandalwood pyre, his head pointing south, as hymns from Hindu scriptures were recited. His son sprinkled water from the Ganges on the pyre before lighting it.

Among the mourners at the funeral were Jaswal, Chopra, Roy, senior bureaucrats, businessmen including Patel, and politicians from across the spectrum. Jaswal stood respectfully with his head bowed down as the flames consumed Kumar's body. He had worn a white turban because white is the color of mourning.

Santosh had also managed to reach the venue but he chose to remain slightly away from the VIP crowd, clutching his walking stick.

As the ceremony drew to a close, Jaswal walked to his car that was part of a larger security convoy of five vehicles. He nodded to Santosh as he approached the car and Santosh got inside the vehicle along with him. Jaswal pressed a button to activate the glass screen between them and the driver.

"I think we may be dealing with something big," said Santosh once they had privacy.

"Like what?"

"I'd rather not say at the moment."

"Does it involve Chopra?"

"In exactly what capacity I'm unsure."

"Give me a straight answer to a straight question, Santosh. Does it involve Chopra?"

"Yes," admitted Santosh, stopping short of telling Jaswal that the Lieutenant Governor's name was associated with the house at Greater Kailash. He felt a surge of irritation at the gratified look on Jaswal's face. "This isn't a game of political chess, Chief Minister. People are dying."

Beneath his immaculate turban, Jaswal reddened. "Spare me the self-righteous act, Santosh. You were employed for a reason."

"Give me leave to investigate fully. Perhaps we'll both get the result we want," said Santosh, hiding his distaste.

Jaswal shrugged. "Very well. Consider yourself given free rein; I'll discuss the financial arrangements with Jack."

Satisfied, Santosh left—and, not for the first time, he asked himself if Jaswal knew way more than he was admitting.

Chapter 40

THE KILLER STIRRED a cube of sugar into his tea. Scalding hot was the way his mother had used to make it. He never could understand how people could enjoy lukewarm tea. He sipped it and allowed his thoughts to wander back to that eventful day that had changed his life forever.

His old man had been a drunk but that hadn't been the end of it. The bastard had been a vicious wife-beater too. Whenever he'd return home at night he would use the boy's mother as a punching bag. Though the poor woman had found creative excuses to explain her bruises to neighbors, she'd fooled no one.

It was a dark and scary world that the boy had been born into. In fact, it had been a miracle he was born at all. His mother had been beaten so badly when she was pregnant that the boy had been born a month early.

One night his mother had been telling him stories from the Mahabharata when the asshole had staggered in, loaded out of his mind. As soon as he'd seen his wife he'd swung her around and twisted her arm behind her back. She'd screamed in agony. The boy had charged at him but he'd swung his arm crazily, catching the young boy on his lower lip, which had begun to bleed profusely. The boy had slunk away as he'd watched the Neanderthal torment his mother. Her wails had been pitiful, like those of a tortured animal.

The boy had run into the kitchen to grab something with which to attack his father. A gunnysack had been lying on the floor, tied up with jute rope. He'd untied the rope and rushed over to where his drunk father had fallen on top of his wife, about to pass out. The fall had cracked open his mother's skull and a pool of blood had formed around her head.

The boy had been able to see she wasn't breathing. Her open eyes had been unseeing. And although the boy would later cry an ocean of tears as he mourned his mother, what he'd felt in that moment had been fury. As though on autopilot, with no mind or will of his own, he'd slipped the rope around his father's neck and pulled. The hulk had thrashed about wildly but the boy had been strong.

When his old man had stopped flailing and gone still, the boy had removed the rope and replaced it on the gunnysack. He'd climbed on the countertop to fetch a small tin box his mother kept on a high shelf in the kitchen cabinet. It had contained a little money she'd saved doing odd jobs like sewing and cooking for others. It hadn't been much. About two hundred rupees. The boy had pocketed it.

He had then run all the way to the railway station and boarded the first train that was leaving. He'd hidden in corners and toilets and beneath bunk beds in order to avoid the ticket collector, and hadn't gotten off the train until it reached its destination—the holy city of Varanasi.

He had no longer been a boy. He had become a killer.

Chapter 41

SANTOSH SAT AT home, watching the news but not really watching it. His bottle of whisky—as talismanic to him as his cane—rested on the upside-down box in front of him, still bearing Jack's soap mark; his cane leaned against the threadbare sofa on which he rested, not so much sitting as slumped, and, as ever, he was lost in thought.

This case. It was most...perplexing. Everything seemed to add up and yet there were so many unanswered questions.

The news was almost over, and though there had been much coverage of Kumar's apparent suicide and the day's funeral there was still no word of the bodies found at Greater Kailash.

"People are dying, but nobody seems to care," Santosh said to the room. A chill wind that rattled the window and the sound of distant Delhi traffic were the only replies.

Sighing, his eyes went back to the screen, where the news had ended and Ajoy Guha's *Carrot and Stick* was just starting. There sat Ajoy Guha, looking exactly as he had at the press briefing the other day, while the topic scrolling at the bottom of the screen was "INDIA'S HEALTH CARE SECTOR: BOOM OR DOOM?" The camera panned across Guha's guests—and suddenly Santosh was sitting up straight.

One of them was Dr. Pankaj Arora, the chief surgeon of the Delhi Memorial Hospital. He was joined by Samir Patel, the chairman of Surgiquip, and Jai Thakkar, the CEO of a large insurance company called ResQ.

"Well, how about that?" Santosh said to himself, reaching for his phone and scrolling to Nisha's number. "Nisha?"

"Yes, boss." He could hear Maya playing in the background.

"Are you watching *Carrot and Stick*?"

"I could be."

"Put it on if you don't mind."

Moments later she came back. "You do realize I've had to turn off cartoons for this?"

"I'm sorry. I wouldn't disturb you if it wasn't important. Please pass my apologies to Maya. I'll make it up to her."

"She says she wants to see that fancy sword you keep in your cane."

"Tell her it's a deal."

"Okay, well, back to the matter at hand. Who am I looking at?"

"The one on the left with the slicked-back hair."

"Oh my God, that's Arora."

"The very same. Next to him is Samir Patel, chairman of Surgiquip."

"Dodgy dealer, friend of Chopra."

"Allegedly."

"And the third guy?"

"That's Jai Thakkar, the CEO of a large insurance company called ResQ."

They stayed on the line and watched as Guha fired questions at his guests. Santosh wondered whether this was an Ajoy Guha program at all. No one seemed to be shouting or fighting.

Arora was speaking. "We make the erroneous assumption that health care is an industry," he said pompously. "Ultimately, health care is a humanitarian service. Our objective must necessarily be to provide the healing touch to millions of Indians."

Thakkar interjected in a high-pitched nasal voice: "But how will that ever happen if we do not have world-class hospitals and infrastructure? Spending on health care is just about five percent of India's GDP. That's abysmally low. We have a system that is patchy, with underfunded and overcrowded hospitals and clinics, and woefully inadequate rural coverage. It is only private participation that can overcome these limitations."

And thus allow your private corporations to make millions, thought Santosh.

"Would you agree with that view, Mr. Patel?" asked Guha.

"We at Surgiquip have been working hand in hand with the government to upgrade Indian health care infrastructure," said Patel. A ruby-encrusted Marte Omas pen sparkled in his shirt pocket.

Guha rolled the lozenge in his mouth, getting ready for the kill. "When you say you have been working 'hand in hand' with the government, are you referring to the fact that the late Health Minister, Kumar, was an investor in Surgiquip?" he asked.

Santosh was suddenly all ears. He hadn't seen that coming. Guha was famous for throwing curveballs.

Patel's startled expression was captured on camera as he absorbed the revelation. The vermillion mark on his forehead seemed to levitate as his eyebrows traveled north. He had no option but to answer. "That is a preposterous insinuation," he replied.

"So are you denying his involvement in your company?" asked Guha.

"Nikhil Kumar and I were on the same page regarding the need to upgrade and improve our creaking medical infrastructure. Our relationship was entirely based on that common objective."

"You've still not answered my question," said Guha, staring into Patel's eyes like a criminal lawyer. "Were you business partners?"

"This program was meant to discuss the overall condition of the Indian health care sector, not one specific company," said Patel, his face reddening with anger at the persistent line of questioning by Guha.

"The nation wants to know whether the Health Minister could have been killed as part of a deeper conspiracy in the health care sector," said Guha. "That's why I must ask you yet again whether you were partners."

"It is evident to me that this is about you scoring a few cheap debating points in your quest for ratings," said Patel. "I shall not dignify the question by answering it."

"Did you have a falling-out with the Health Minister that eventually resulted in his death?" asked Guha, his fist bobbing up and down as he slammed the desk.

"You will hear from my lawyers when I sue you for libel!" shouted Patel, as Arora and Thakkar looked on. Thakkar seemed relieved that he was not in the firing line. Arora watched the scene with a steely hardness in his eyes. Patel stood up. Thakkar shifted uncomfortably in his chair.

"Where are you going, Mr. Patel?" asked Guha. "The show is not yet concluded."

Patel ripped off his collar microphone. "You're right, Mr. Guha. The show isn't over yet," he said as he stormed out of the studio.

"Nisha," said Santosh, switching off the TV at the same time, "could you pick me up tomorrow? I'd like to pay Greater Kailash a visit."

"Had a brainwave, boss?"

"We'll see. Nice and early, please."

He ended the call, about to return to his thoughts when something occurred to him: for the first time in as long as he could remember, he had not felt tempted by the bottle.

Chapter 42

SHE WAS NOT a particularly fast driver—like most newcomers to the city, she found the Delhi traffic a little intimidating—but even so, Nisha drove slowly out of respect for her passenger. From the corner of her eye she could see him staring straight ahead, impassive, his cane held tightly. The whites of his knuckles the only sign of any inner turmoil.

"So, what's prompted this visit, then?" she asked, hoping to break the ice.

"I have a theory," he said enigmatically. "Bear with me on it, would you, Nisha? All will—or will not—become clear when we have a look at the house. Did you notice anything unusual about it the other day?"

"Well, apart from the police presence, I can't say I did. At least we'll have the advantage of their absence this time around."

"You didn't get a good look, then?"

She wondered if he was questioning her profession-alism. Feeling herself tighten a little, she replied de-fensively: "The terms of the investigation were a little different then."

"Quite, quite," agreed Santosh hurriedly, putting her at ease. "Much has changed in the meantime. Much of it thanks to your investigation, Nisha. Private is fortunate to have you."

Equilibrium restored, the two of them lapsed into si-lence once more, and Nisha watched the road as Santosh stared straight ahead, occasionally gazing out of the pas-senger window at red stone buildings flashing by, the vibrancy of Delhi just a fingertip away.

The silence—such as it was, assaulted by a constant deluge of activity from outside—was companionable, but even so, Santosh broke it, clearing his throat. "How are things at home, Nisha?"

She turned left, using the opportunity to control a sudden heartache. "Maya misses her father, of course. It's difficult for us to come to terms with his death. I don't suppose we ever will."

Santosh nodded.

There was a pause.

"Tell me it gets easier, Santosh. Reassure me of that at least."

"It does. It really does. When you learn to leave behind all the guilt and regrets, the what-ifs and what-might-have-beens. It gets easier. It's just that getting rid of those things is the hard part. Choosing how to do it is the trick." He gave a dry, humorless chuckle. "I can certainly help you when it comes to choosing the wrong methods."

Nisha remembered her boss stinking of whisky first thing in the mornings. Yes, Santosh knew all about self-medication. "I have Maya," she said. "She's what keeps me going. Her and work, of course."

"As long as the balance is right," said Santosh, and Nisha felt a little stab of guilt in return. They both knew full well that the balance was rarely right.

By now they had arrived at Greater Kailash. The house was just as Nisha remembered it, except of course the police were no longer there, just plastic incident tape that fluttered across the front door and bordered a hole in the front garden.

"Here's where I spoke to the neighbor," said Nisha when they had pulled to the curb and stepped out, and were standing on the sidewalk.

"Strange comings and goings," mused Santosh, looking up and down what was a thoroughly unremarkable street. "A black van registered to Dr. Arora. The coincidences are piling up. And yet they refuse to form a cohesive, logical conclusion. Come on."

He led the way to the house, where they made their way through the front gate and into the garden.

"I didn't get this far before," Nisha said with a trace of apology.

"It doesn't matter, it doesn't matter," insisted Santosh with a raised finger. "Our remit was different then. Besides—" But then he stopped. "Oh, that's interesting."

He was heading off the path that led to the front door and onto the grass. Then stopped and knelt down.

Once again, Nisha was half surprised, half amused at how sprightly Santosh was, despite the cane he always carried.

"Look," he said. And Nisha found her attention directed to a bald patch in the grass.

"Yes?"

"Something's been taken from here."

Santosh stood. His head twitched this way and that as though he was looking for something in the overgrown garden, and then he was setting off with great strides toward the far corner. There they found another bald patch, similar to the first.

"Something has been taken from here," he repeated. He pointed with the cane from one empty patch to another. "My hunch is we'll find two, maybe more of these, and that they are—or *were*—some kind of surveillance, security device."

"A laser mesh trap."

"Possibly."

"But one that's been removed."

"*Exactly*." Santosh's eyes sparkled. "And do you know what? I'd bet my life that it was disguised to look like something different, a sprinkler or something. That girl the neighbor saw running away, who fell through the subsidence and into the cellar below—she and her boyfriend presumably triggered the warning system. Some kind of cleanup team came and removed the equipment."

"Why not remove the bodies?"

"No time. The neighbor had already called the police—the regular police."

Then Nisha said, "Something's occurred to me."

Santosh looked at her. "Let's hear it."

It was her turn to lead him across the grass to where the incident tape marked out the courting couple's unfortunate entrance into the basement. They peered into the basement below but there was nothing to see. Forensics had taken everything; crime-scene cleanup teams had done the rest. Not a single shred of evidence would be left.

But then, that wasn't where Nisha and Santosh's interest lay.

"They went through here, yes?" Nisha said. "And given that the neighbor saw the girl's clothes in disarray, we can be reasonably sure what they were up to at the time."

"Yes."

"Well, why *here*? Why outside on a cold night?"

Santosh nodded almost happily. "Of course, Nisha, of course. A neglected, near-derelict, and very obviously empty house—they would have tried to get in first."

"Break a window, pick a lock."

Together they strode to the front door of the house and within seconds they spotted that almost out of sight, close to the door, was a clean space. Something removed.

"A mailbox, perhaps?" said Santosh. "Or some kind of entry panel disguised to look like a mailbox. Our libidinous friends tried to get in, failed, so found a spot over there. It was just dumb luck and no doubt the fact that the acid had weakened the structure that they fell through. Otherwise, this was a virtually impregnable facility."

"Was this what you were expecting?" asked Nisha.

"Something like this, yes. Something to confirm my suspicion that we're dealing with a large conspiracy here, an outfit that is evidently well funded and blessed with top-level access."

"And their business?"

"Organ harvesting."

They looked at one another, both knowing what the other was thinking: this was big and Private was getting close to being out of its depth. They hurried back to the car, both glowing with the thrill of their discoveries.

"There are still so many imponderables," said Santosh. "Why was Kumar killed?"

"Because he was getting in the way. Whatever this outfit is doing, the Health Minister was either blocking it, threatening it, or wanting a slice—and so he paid with his life."

"He certainly did. Drained of blood like that. But why like that, do you think? Why in such an attention-grabbing manner? Why not just a bullet in the back of the head?"

"As a grisly warning to those in the know."

"It could be," said Santosh. "It could be."

Nisha started the engine. "So we have a name: Dr. Pankaj Arora. Isn't that enough to take to Jaswal? Or the police?"

"Not until we can be sure who's involved and who's not," sighed Santosh. "It could be that Jaswal is involved at some level."

"We need to put a stop to it, Santosh," warned Nisha. "People are dying."

But Santosh shook his head, resolute. "I understand, and we must work quickly. But even more people will die if we reveal our findings prematurely. There's no point in standing on the tail of the snake, Nisha. We need to cut off its head."

PART TWO

DELIVERER

Chapter 43

FROM THAT NIGHT when he had killed his drunk father to his escape on a train to the holy city of Varanasi, every detail was firmly etched in the killer's mind. His subsequent experiences had taught him to be prepared and extra vigilant.

Upon arriving in the holy city, the boy had made the railway station his home. What little money he'd had was used to purchase a single meal each day. It hadn't been too long before his money had run out.

One day a priest wearing a white dhoti and saffron shawl with beads around his neck had seen the boy. Realizing he was hungry and lost, the priest had bought him a sumptuous meal. The boy had eaten ravenously as the priest sipped from a cup of masala tea. His hunger satiated, the boy had confided that he had no place to live and that his parents were dead.

The priest had taken the boy to his home, a basic hut by the banks of the Ganges. "You can stay here with me till such time as you find something better," the priest had said. "You will need to help me with all the household chores though." The boy had gratefully accepted the proposal.

The next day they had headed to the woods that bordered the railway tracks to collect firewood for the traditional stove in the priest's house. The boy had gathered all the branches that had fallen from trees, tying them into bundles that could eventually be carried back. The priest had sat under a tree, looking at the boy's sweating torso.

"Let me wipe the sweat off your body," the priest had said, getting up and using his cotton shawl to dry the boy's back. He'd asked the boy to turn around and face him but instead of drying him, he had attempted to kiss the boy on his lips. The boy had backed off in shock, but the priest had been persistent. "Love is a natural thing," he had said. "God tells us to love our fellow human beings. I am merely expressing my affection for you," and he had grasped the boy and pulled him toward his body.

The boy had now been fully alert. It had been as though that terrible night when his father had killed his mother was being played out with him as victim. He'd played along with the priest, allowing the pervert to kiss him and shove his tongue inside his mouth.

And then he had made his move.

The boy had been holding a heavy branch in his other hand when the priest had grabbed for him. He'd now swung it up toward the priest's head with as much force as he could muster. An involuntary scream had emerged from the boy as he'd brought the wood into contact with the man's chin.

The priest had sunk to the ground, dazed by the blow. The boy had continued to smash the priest's skull with the branch until his head was a bloody pulp. "Die! Die! Die!" he'd shouted. He had pulled the priest's lifeless body to the nearby railway tracks and lain him across the line. He'd waited by the side, at a safe distance, until a passing train ran over the corpse.

That day he had realized that as well as no longer just being a boy, he was no mere killer either. He was capable of taking care of himself and cleansing the world of vermin. Delivering purity in a world of filth. Delivering light in a world of darkness.

He was now the Deliverer.

Chapter 44

THE WINDOWLESS OPERATING room of the Delhi Memorial Hospital was freezing cold. Under the surgical lights a patient lay on the operating table, his eyes closed, an anesthesia mask over his face.

Doesn't the patient wonder why a routine gallbladder operation is taking place so late at night? thought the senior nurse. She threw a look at Dr. Pankaj Arora: the slicked-back hair, the gap in his teeth. *If only the world knew what a butcher he is.* She should never have allowed herself to get sucked into his scheme, but the money was good—enough to pay off the staggering debts her husband had accumulated.

The anesthesia machine stood at the head of the table, and a tube ran from it to the mask that had been placed over the patient's mouth and nose.

Wearing protective caps, surgical masks, vinyl gloves,

and long green surgical gowns, the team was led by Dr. Pankaj Arora. It wasn't an urgent surgery; it could have waited until morning. But Arora had insisted and no one ever argued with him. His temper was notorious.

Arora applied antiseptic solution to the areas he'd marked on the body. He then made a small incision above the belly button and inserted a hollow needle through the abdominal wall. This would pump carbon dioxide into the abdomen, inflating the cavity.

"Do we need intraoperative cholangiography?" asked the senior nurse. It was standard procedure to check if there were any stones outside the gallbladder.

Arora gave the woman a terrifying look. No one asked unnecessary questions while he was operating. "If you had bothered to check," said Arora, "you would know that he has no stones outside the gallbladder."

In fact, he has none inside the gallbladder either.

The senior nurse cursed herself for asking a stupid question. It was never a good idea to get on the wrong side of Arora.

He efficiently attached the umbilical port and then made three more incisions, no more than an inch each, in the patient's belly. Next he inserted a wand-like laparoscope that was equipped with cameras and surgical tools into the umbilical port. Immediately, the monitor in front of him came to life with a view from inside the patient.

"How's the blood pressure?" he asked the anesthesiologist.

"Steady—one hundred and ten over seventy," replied

the anesthesiologist, looking at the iridescent numbers and squiggles that mapped the patient's vital signs.

Arora used the laparoscope to pull back both the liver and gallbladder and removed the connecting tissue to expose the cystic duct and artery. The senior nurse quickly used clips to clamp off the duct and artery. Arora cut the duct, the artery, and the connecting tissue between the gallbladder and liver, and used the laparoscope to suck out the pear-shaped gallbladder.

At this stage all the instruments should have been withdrawn, the carbon dioxide allowed to escape, and the patient stitched up. Instead, Arora increased the size of one of the incisions—to almost four inches.

"More suction," he said to the senior nurse. She immediately grabbed a long plastic tube, and began using it to vacuum the puddles of blood. Arora was like a drill sergeant inside the operating room.

He used his instruments to separate the colon from the right kidney. He cut the splenorenal ligament to free the kidney entirely. He then cut the ureter, placed an endoscopic specimen retrieval bag around the patient's kidney, and pulled it out through the larger cut.

From the corner of his eye he saw the senior nurse place the kidney in the Surgiquip LifePort unit, a transport device that would continuously pump the kidney with a cold liquid solution. It would double the organ storage time until it could be transplanted.

Arora began to stitch up the patient.

Surgery completed, he walked over to the scrubbing area, removed his gloves, mask, and cap, and washed his hands. He then walked through the doctors' lounge and into the corridor. The patient's wife was seated in one of the visitors' chairs. She had been looking at the clock anxiously for the past four hours.

She got up instantly. "Is everything all right, Dr. Arora?" she asked.

He smiled at her, his expression softening only momentarily. "Don't worry," he said, placing his hand on her shoulder. "He's perfectly fine. He'll be discharged in two days."

A look of relief was evident on the wife's face. "I was worried when it took so long. I was under the impression that the gallbladder could be removed in two hours."

"Laparoscopy takes a little longer but most patients seem to recover faster and feel less pain after the surgery," he explained, taking off his glasses and using his kerchief to clean them. "We also needed to carry out intraoperative cholangiography to check for stones outside the gallbladder. That's why it took some more time."

Oh, and we also removed a healthy kidney along the way.

Chapter 45

IN HIS OFFICE, Santosh pressed a button on the multipoint controller and watched the oversized LCD screen spring to life. There was a time difference of twelve and a half hours between Delhi and Los Angeles. It would be ten thirty in the morning for Jack, a good time to reach him.

"What's bugging you?" asked Jack, picking up on Santosh's worried expression.

"The case," said Santosh. "I'm wondering whether it leads Private Delhi into a political quagmire."

"Well, it was always a bit boggy," drawled Jack. "But how come I'm getting the funny feeling that it turns out to involve the suicide of your Health Minister."

"Kumar," offered Santosh. "That's what they're saying in the States, is it? That it was suicide?"

"I'll be honest, Santosh, it's not that big a story here. But yeah, that's what they're saying."

"Well, it wasn't. I saw the body. It was murder. We've established a link between the city's hospitals and the body parts found at Greater Kailash. We think there's a link between that find and an earlier murder in which the victim's eyeballs were removed. And now Kumar, who was drained of all blood and the blood taken. The theory I'm currently working on is that we've stumbled across some kind of organ-harvesting or illegal-transplants operation. And my instinct is that this goes right to the top."

"Okay, hang in there. I'm on my way back to Delhi to address the Global Security and Intelligence Conference. We can talk more when I arrive."

"The one being held at Vigyan Bhawan?" asked Santosh.

"Precisely," said Jack. "Grab a cab, pick me up from the airport, and we'll chat in the car on the drive into town."

"Will do. Just one small request in the meantime."

"Shoot."

"I need you to find out whether any American insurance companies encourage their customers to come to India," said Santosh.

"For what?" asked Jack.

"For organ transplants or medical procedures," replied Santosh. "It's called medical tourism."

"Anything else?" asked Jack.

"If any of them do encourage clients to have their procedures performed in India, then which ones? I'm particularly interested in one company: ResQ."

Chapter 46

JACK MORGAN SAT at the round ink-black lacquered table in the octagonal "war room" of Private Los Angeles. Padded swivel chairs were clustered around the table, jumbo flat-screens mounted wall to wall.

Opposite sat the CEO of the National Association of Insurance Commissioners, headquartered in Kansas City—a man called Denny. Jack had helped him with several delicate investigations involving insurance frauds worth millions. Requesting Denny's help that morning, he had not expected him to be in LA for a meeting, but as fortune would have it ...

"So here's the deal, Jack," said the insurance man, adjusting his horn-rimmed glasses to read from a folder on the table. "There is indeed an increasing trend to send American patients to India on account of the new super-specialty hospitals that have been established there.

Doctors' services are a fraction of the cost. In addition, postoperative care is also cheap. Insurance providers can cut costs tremendously by doing this."

"And clients are willing to travel halfway around the world for medical procedures?" asked Jack.

"Around a hundred and fifty thousand patients travel to India each year for medical procedures. The size of the industry is already around two billion dollars per year."

"Any specific insurance companies that specialize in the India game?" asked Jack.

"Leading the pack in this effort is a company called ResQ," said his friend. "It's listed on the NASDAQ but their main operations are now in India. The name of their CEO is Jai Thakkar."

Chapter 47

RAM CHOPRA SIPPED his morning coffee as he scanned the newspapers. In New Delhi, the commonly accepted joke was that the *Times of India* and the *Indian Times* were read by people who ran the government; the *Hindustan Times* and the *Daily Express* were read by people who thought they ought to run the government; the *Indian Express* was read by the people who used to run the government. The *Mail Today* was read by the wives of the people who ran the government. And *The Hindu* was read by people who thought the government ought to be run by another government. The readers of the *Delhi Times* weren't bothered about who ran the government as long as the women on page three had big tits.

Chopra was almost unique because he read them all. His routine started with the mainstream dailies published in Delhi, followed by the morning dailies from outside Delhi. The tabloids came last. They were usually vulgar but utterly delicious.

His wife and daughter were asleep, both being late risers. Usually, Chopra enjoyed the solitude of his mornings with a cup of coffee and the first cigar of the day.

But not today. The butler had just poured him a second cup of arabica plucked from the plantations of Coorg when Chopra clumsily dropped the cup. It fell to the floor, the delicate china shattering to little pieces along with the rich brew. "Bastard!" shouted Chopra, crushing the offending tabloid page in his hand and flinging it across the table.

The butler hurriedly brought a mop to clear up the mess on the floor and wondered what had set Chopra off. He noticed the tabloid that Chopra had been reading now lay in a ball on the floor. He vowed to read it later to find out what had caused his boss to detonate.

Chopra got up from the dining table and headed to his study. The butler hurriedly cleared up the coffee spill and the broken cup fragments along with the crumpled newspaper and headed back to the kitchen. He made himself a cup of tea and retrieved the balled-up tabloid pages. The news item instantly caught his eye. It was on the gossip page.

So, darlings, it's me, back again this week with another installment of juicy chatter. News is that one of the high-and-mighty politicos of our great capital city is miffed with a powerful business-man. It seems that the politico has a sweet daughter of marriageable age and the business-man had swept her off her feet. But (gasp!) he's had a change of heart! The princess was left standing at the altar with her father waiting to give her away. The whisper in town is that the old man is fuming at the humiliation and has vowed to avenge his family's "honor."

Chapter 48

THE DELHI GOLF Club dated back to the early 1930s and was home to the championship eighteen-hole Lodhi Course that was part of the Asian PGA Tour. Samir Patel played there twice a week. On Thursdays he would play with just one colleague while on Saturdays it was usually a four-ball.

He was dressed in his customary bush shirt. The only concessions he had made for the golf course were checkered pants, a sleeveless sweater, and a cap that covered the vermillion mark on his forehead. And today, as he returned to the clubhouse following his game, he was feeling very pleased with himself indeed. It was time to enjoy what he liked to call "a couple of swift libations."

In the parking lot outside sat his chauffeur-driven Mercedes. The driver, a good man known to Patel as Babu, was well enough acquainted with his boss's habits to know that there would be precisely three "swift libations" taking around an hour and a half, at which point his boss would stride slightly unsteadily from the clubhouse and onto the gravel of the parking lot, aglow with the morning's golf and the afternoon's alcohol, making more conversation than usual as he was transported back home to his luxurious, well-appointed home.

Not for the first time, Babu thought how sweet it must be to be one of the big bosses. *What a life*, he mused as he set his phone alarm for an hour's time—an hour in which he planned to continue his nap.

But first, a piss.

And off he went to the course-side restrooms, unaware that he was being followed.

Indeed, he remained unaware, even as he stood at the urinal, barely hearing the restroom door open as a man in black slid in behind him. His first—and, as it turned out, his last—thought was, *Why is someone standing behind me?* But he never saw the man in black. He didn't see the skewer the man held. His only sensation at the point of death was a sudden fierce pain in his left ear as the skewer was rammed hard and fast into his brain.

The man in black let the chauffeur's body slump into his arms. He was already using a rag to staunch the flow of blood from Babu's ear. Moments later he had maneuvered the corpse into a stall and was helping it out of its clothes.

An hour later, just as the recently deceased Babu had predicted, Samir Patel was exiting the clubhouse. An extremely happy Surgiquip chairman, he had won his game and been the recipient of exactly three celebratory drinks, and intended to spend the rest of the afternoon at home. His domestics had the afternoon off, and he planned to fill the remainder of his day slumped in a leather armchair, reading the papers, and catching up on an occasional e-mail, knowing he had complete privacy.

Or so he hoped.

Babu stood holding the door open for him. "Thank you, Babu," he said, hearing a slight slur in his own voice as he settled into the lush leather interior. He really shouldn't drink on an empty stomach. The door closed. Babu took his seat in front. The central locking clicked.

In the next instant Patel knew—even in his relaxed state—that something was amiss. Babu had been his driver a long time. He knew the man's mannerisms. He knew how his presence felt.

And he knew this wasn't Babu.

"Hey," he managed, but then the man in the front was swiveling in his seat and God, no, it wasn't Babu, of course it wasn't Babu, because this man was holding a hypodermic syringe.

He recognized the man.

"No. You" was all he managed before the hypodermic needle was jabbed just under his jaw. It was too late to throw himself toward the door in order to escape, because the sedative had already started to work.

Chapter 49

WHEN PATEL SURFACED it was to the relief of knowing that the man with the hypodermic syringe had been an illusion of the mind, for he had awoken in his own bedroom, lying on his back in bed.

"Thank God," he whispered to himself, feeling like Dorothy in *The Wizard of Oz*. "It was just a dream," and he went to turn over in bed and find a more comfortable position—only to realize that he couldn't. His outflung arms were held in place, tied with rope, and when he tried to turn his head the movement was prevented by a wide band of something around his forehead. His eyeballs skittered madly in their sockets as he tried to see his legs, knowing that they, too, were strapped to the bed.

Another thing: he was naked.

He became aware of someone else in the room, moving around.

"Are you awake?" said a voice. Bright light beams made his pupils contract.

"Please. Please. Please, don't do this," he said in a whine that was disgraceful to his own ears.

"Do what, Mr. Patel?" came the voice.

The familiar voice. Yes. That was right. He knew the man. He knew his attacker and if he knew his attacker then surely he could reason with—

"What are you doing?" he said, seeing something in his peripheral vision. The man was moving closer to the bed, a shadow that refused to fully form in his drug-fogged mind. All Patel knew was that once again a syringe was coming toward him.

"Just some pain relief, Mr. Patel. I want you to remain conscious, so you can see everything I am about to do to you. So you can appreciate its enormity."

The needle sunk deep. The plunger depressed. Next it was as though a wave of bliss and well-being rolled through Patel, so that even though his eyes were wide and straining in their sockets, there was something almost comforting about the roll of surgical instruments that was unfurled on the bed beside him.

The figure retired and then moments later reappeared, only this time the man wore hospital scrubs and a mask. He had moved a mirror from the bathroom and angled it so that Patel could see his own abdomen.

"The doctor is in," said the intruder.

He lifted a scalpel from the roll of instruments and held it up for Patel to see. Even with the etorphine working its magic Patel felt the first tremors of terror, knowing this was no dream; that there was no escape.

He was going to die.

"Anything," he slurred, "I'll do anything."

"*Anything?* You have done nothing—nothing but take, take, take. And now it is your turn to give."

He made his incision. Patel did not feel it, but he heard it, and he saw the blade pierce his flesh between the ribs, the scalpel held between index finger and thumb, angled and then drawn down, opening a red ribbon to just above his belly button. Patel saw his own flesh part, the glistening meat visible beneath, bits of himself he would have hoped never to see.

Damage! screamed his mind, like some kind of automated response. *Damage, damage!* But in the next second he was thinking, *But if my attacker stopped there I might be all right. I might heal.*

I could still live.

The intruder placed the scalpel back onto the bed and then brought something else into view. A clamp. Then another. The man inserted them onto each side of the incision and still Patel felt no pain—one part of his brain screaming while yet another competing part insisted that he might be okay, he might be okay.

And then the man was opening the incision in his chest, opening it wide, so wide, and Patel was seeing his own exposed insides and he was no longer thinking that everything was going to be all right, he knew now that his death was imminent and was thankful that at least it would be painless. The attacker reached inside with two hands and his forehead furrowed in concentration as he rummaged within Patel's chest cavity.

Patel felt pulling. A sucking sensation below.

And then his eyes bulged as he saw what his attacker held up before him.

It was his own heart.

Chapter 50

THE BLACK VAN stood at the corner of Jama Masjid Road and Chawri Bazar Road in the congested Chandni Chowk area of Delhi.

Windows had been replaced by mild steel panels that had been spray-painted to match the black exterior.

A frightened old man entered. The interior was nice and warm but the smell of disinfectant was overpowering. The inside of the vehicle was fitted out in a style similar to an ambulance.

Iqbal Ibrahim motioned the visitor to be seated. Ibrahim was a burly fellow dressed in blue jeans and a green T-shirt that bore the first line of the Quran in white calligraphy. On his head was an embroidered white skullcap. His hooked nose was big—almost like the beak of a bird.

Ibrahim had been brought up in the slums of Delhi,

one among nine children of a rag picker. When he was just six, their shanty had collapsed while he was inside. His parents and the neighbors had pulled him out of the rubble to find him unhurt. It had been a miracle. Four years later a car had missed him by inches while he was playing cricket on a public road. At age twelve, he had been swimming in the Yamuna with his friends when the authorities had released water from the upstream dam without warning. Two of his friends had perished but Iqbal had survived. Ever since that day Ibrahim had believed in his own superhuman nature. He could never fail.

The superhuman had struggled through school and had managed to get into med school via a special quota but had flunked. In spite of failing, he had turned out to be much more successful than the average doctor. On his desk were two cell phones, identical except for their covers. One was red while the other was green. He had nicknames for both: the red one was called "Supply" and the green one was called "Demand." The choice of colors was significant. Supply implied bloody surgeries, hence the choice of red. Demand implied money, often dollars, hence the choice of green.

"Have you brought the money?" asked Ibrahim as the old man sat down. The old man nodded wearily as he passed a brown-paper-covered parcel across the desk.

Ibrahim opened the parcel and took out the individual bundles of cash. He placed each one into a currency-counting machine on his desk and totted up the result. Six lakh rupees. Around nine thousand dollars.

"You realize this is only half? The other half is payable immediately before the transplant?" asked Ibrahim.

"Yes," said the old man, who had sold off his wife's jewelry in order to pay for his only son's operation. The previous year, the boy had been diagnosed with alpha-1 antitrypsin deficiency, an absence of a vital enzyme in the liver. They had tried every possible treatment until the doctors had eventually advised a liver transplant.

"Where should I admit my son?"

"Check him into Delhi Memorial Hospital and sign him up with Dr. Pankaj Arora as the doctor on record. We have identified a donor. Inshallah, your son will get a new liver tomorrow. You are lucky there is no foreigner in the queue for this one. I make them pay twice what you are paying!"

Chapter 51

THE SENIOR NURSE felt inside the pocket of her starched white uniform. The syringe containing epinephrine was right there. Every fiber in her body wanted to run away. But then an image of Arora would appear before her. It was the fear of Arora that kept her there.

Epinephrine, also known as adrenalin, was a hormone that could be used as medication for a number of conditions. The common side effects included anxiety, sweating, increased heart rate, and high blood pressure. The amazing thing about epinephrine was that it could make the vitals of a patient appear as though a heart attack was being experienced.

She walked past the nurses' station and the janitors who were mopping the floors of the long corridor. She stopped only when she reached the door of room 303. She opened it gently and entered the dimly lit room. The sole occupant appeared to be asleep on a bed that was slightly elevated toward the head. An IV line ran into the patient's hand while a bedside monitor mapped the patient's vital signs. He had been in a persistent vegetative state for the past four years.

The nurse took a deep breath, knowing she was crossing a line, for it was one thing when paired organs were taken from a living donor; people could live on a single lung or a single kidney. Similarly, blood, bone marrow, and parts of livers could be taken, knowing that they would regenerate eventually.

But it was quite another when it came to organs such as the heart.

The problem was that harvesting organs without getting the patient into the operating room was impossible. Epinephrine would do the trick by simulating a heart attack.

She held the IV port and inserted the needle into the lumen of the IV line. She prayed to her god as she slowly pressed the plunger, knowing that she was no longer a mere accomplice but a killer in Arora's perverse plans.

He had convinced her that the vegetative-state patient was dead by acceptable medical criteria and that harvesting his useful organs would be a service to humanity.

Nonsense! the alternate voice in her head said. What they were doing was wrong. Beyond wrong. It was monstrous.

Chapter 52

SANTOSH HAD LEFT his cane behind for this particular expedition. He was walking through the underground tunnel, sloshing through a foot of water, wearing a black plastic coat and pants. On his feet were rubber boots and on his head was a miner's helmet with a battery-powered light. He wore a rubber filter mask around his mouth and nose to avoid methane poisoning.

He trudged through the water, oblivious to the stench of sewage. In his hand was a laminated map. It showed the major arteries that ran under the streets of Delhi as well as access points. He had marked his destination in red and the route in blue.

It was mostly quiet inside the tunnel, but every drop of dripping water seemed to be amplified and echoed, and was punctuated by the squealing of rats. He kept walking but he had a nasty feeling he was being followed. He stopped for a minute and strained his ears to check for the sound of footsteps. There were none.

He looked at his watch. He had been down there for over thirty minutes. He sped up and took a final turn. And above him he saw the manhole. A rusted iron ladder snaked up from the drain to the manhole and he carefully climbed it, ensuring that he tested each rung before actually using it.

At the top of the ladder, he examined the manhole cover. He could see his scarf—now soiled and stained—hanging from the underside handle. Just to make sure his theory was right, he held on with one hand and used the other to nudge the cover. It did not require too much effort. A single arm was sufficient to nudge open the cover and slide it away with minimal noise. Switching off the light beam of his helmet, he popped his head above ground in the darkness and pulled himself out. He looked around to ensure that it was the house that he had estimated on the drainage map.

Satisfied that it was, Santosh headed back into the drain, closing the manhole behind him. He had proved his hypothesis: it was indeed possible to access Kumar's house by following a drainage map obtained from the Irrigation and Flood Control Department.

Now, if only he could find who were the people who had bought similar maps. Unfortunately, the list provided by the superintendent engineer had been useless. Anyone could provide a fake name and the department would accept it at face value.

Chapter 53

HYPERION HOSPITAL IN Delhi looked more like a five-star hotel than a hospital. Each patient enjoyed a luxurious private room with a flat-screen television and a room service menu. The lobby downstairs featured a waterfall and a vertical garden. The hospital was the brainchild of the scion of a pharmaceutical conglomerate. It was specifically targeted at delivering efficient—and luxurious—services in the health care sector at a fraction of the amount they would cost in America. All of the design, planning, and equipment had been supplied by Patel's company, Surgiquip.

The couple from Minneapolis were dropped off in a chauffeur-driven Mercedes-Benz van. Their "relationship manager" waited at the entrance to greet them. Every detail had been taken care of for them. This included procuring Indian visas, arranging business-class travel, blocking rooms at the Imperial Hotel for the first night, arrangements at the Joint Commission International–accredited hospital, doctor consultations, diagnostic tests, postoperative care, and even leisure travel in India after recovery.

The husband sat in a wheelchair pushed by a nurse provided to them from the moment they had landed in Delhi. Their relationship manager greeted them as they entered the lobby of the hospital.

"When will you operate?" asked the wife.

"I have been in touch with the Delhi Memorial Hospital," replied the relationship manager. "The matching kidney will become available tonight."

Chapter 54

NEEL WAS HUNCHED over his computer, palms sweating. He was accessing a grim, dark world of human filth, a deep web of depravity that was hard to define. It was an Internet beyond Google, Amazon, and eBay but the markets were no less robust. In fact the underworld of the web was far larger than what appeared above the surface. It was large and anonymous, making it relatively easy to hide from law enforcement.

He was using Tor, an abbreviation for "The Onion Router," an anonymizing filter that could resolve addresses that could not be identified by a regular browser. These websites ended in .onion instead of .com or .org, and were in a constant state of flux so that they were never in a given place for too long.

It was pretty incredible what was on offer. The Hidden Wiki, a directory to all the illegal stuff, had 3,099 listings under drugs alone. In addition, you could find passport forgeries and fake driver's licenses from around the world, firearms, counterfeit bills, contract hit men accepting fees in Bitcoin, human experimentation, child pornography, sex slaves, snuff films, and human organs. Neel felt sick to his stomach as he continued to explore.

On a thread that helped wannabe murderers, there was someone suggesting that dissolving a body in lye was the quickest way to dispose of it. The message board had other users contributing their own dark expertise to the knowledge forum. An active user seemed to indicate that 70 percent of the bones and teeth would remain if lye were used. He advised using acid to dissolve the remains. Yet another thread was entitled "Producing Kiddie Porn for Dummies." This was the smelly underbelly of the World Wide Web that highlighted the greatest depravities of human nature.

Neel clicked into the organs marketplace and was dumbfounded to see a price list as though they were offering items from the daily specials of a restaurant:

Pair of eyes: $1,525
Scalp: $607
Skull with teeth: $1,200
Shoulder: $500
Coronary artery: $1,525
Heart: $119,000
Liver: $157,000
Hand and forearm: $385
Pint of blood: $337

Spleen: $508
Stomach: $508
Small intestine: $2,519
Kidney: $262,000
Gallbladder: $1,219
Skin: $10 per square inch

He scanned the comments below the price list. Someone had posted: "If you are reading this thread, it means that you are searching for a human organ for yourself or a loved one. Ignore all the crazy prices that are listed here. We can get you reliable donors at a fraction of the cost from India." The seller was using the handle "Dr. O. S. Rangoon." An Indian cell phone number accompanied the message.

Chapter 55

NISHA AND SANTOSH watched the five men working along the banks of the Yamuna river. They hefted heavy, soggy sheets on their heads and dumped them into a milky concoction of bleach, alum, and other compounds before giving them a final rinse in the river. Without this chemical rinse, the men knew they would never be able to get the filth out of the fabric because an extended soak in the effluent-laced river water would always leave a grimy patina on cloth.

The work had used to be much easier some years before. The river's waters had been clean and had done most of the work. The overall increase in Indian prosperity had, ironically, reduced the prosperity of the dhobis. The washing machine had eaten into the business of dhobis but the men at the Yamuna had faced a double whammy owing to the degeneration of the river. Even hospitals were wary of sending their stuff to the Yamuna. Fear of infection from effluents had stopped most of the better ones. In previous years there would have been fifty men at work instead of five.

Santosh walked up to the group along with Nisha. "Terrible work these days," he commented. One of them looked up wearily to see a man who looked as though his clothes had been washed by them in the river.

"It's the only way we know how to keep hunger from our doors, sahib," said the man. "Most households have given up on us. After a wash in the Yamuna, their garments are often returned reeking of sewage."

"So how do you survive?" asked Santosh, leaning on his walking stick.

"The cloth sellers still need their fabric to be shrunk before tailoring," replied the man. "In addition there are government hospitals that still send their bed linen to us."

Santosh took out a five-hundred-rupee note from his wallet and handed it over to the man.

"What is this for, sahib?" asked the man. His colleagues also stopped their work, eyeing the money.

"It's for all of you," said Santosh. "Go have a good meal. It's my good deed for the day. My good deed."

"Thank you, sahib," said the washerman. "May God bless you and the memsahib. If there is anything that I can ever be of help with..."

"Now that you mention it, there *is* something that you could help me with..." began Santosh. At Private, Neel had reconstructed a larger sample of hospital gown from the tiny fragment they'd been given. Santosh pulled it from his pocket...

Chapter 56

SANTOSH PICKED UP his phone. It was Neel. "Patel has been murdered," said Neel. "It's our boy, no doubt about it. His driver was killed and he was kidnapped from Delhi Golf Club then taken home. A housekeeper found what was left of the body this morning."

"What do you mean, 'what was left'?"

"He'd been eviscerated. The housekeeper found most of his internal organs nailed to a wall."

"Most?"

"The heart was missing."

"Certainly sounds like our man," said Santosh.

"So we can assume that Patel was an enemy of the organ-harvesting operation?"

"We never assume, Neel."

"True," replied Neel. "You want to visit the crime scene?"

"Better that I stay away," replied Santosh. "No point getting Sharma all worked up. In any case, I have a meeting at noon."

"You want me to go instead?" asked Neel.

"That would be good," replied Santosh. "Oh, one more thing, Neel."

"Yes?"

"That hospital gown came from Delhi Memorial Hospital. Chances are that most of the bodies were from there. Everything seems to be adding up, given that it's the closest hospital to the Greater Kailash house and the black van seen there was owned by Arora, their chief surgeon."

"Your hunch turned out right," said Neel.

"Any luck with the online search?" asked Santosh.

"The biggest supplier from India seems to be a Dr. O. S. Rangoon. I'm searching various databases to find if someone matches up."

"What did you say the name was?"

"Dr. O. S. Rangoon."

"Don't bother with an online or directory search," said Santosh.

"Why?" asked Neel.

"Dr. O. S. Rangoon is simply an anagram of 'organ donors.' Try tracing the cell phone number instead."

Chapter 57

SANTOSH MADE HIS way to his appointment on foot, partly savoring the heart of Delhi as he moved through the streets, partly thinking about the case.

He passed newspaper vendors and cast his eye over headlines. Patel's murder dominated the front pages, of course—no attempts made at suppression or spin there—and one or two of the newspapers had linked his death with that of Kumar.

Suddenly a free-sheet was thrust into his hand. They were being handed out by a young man who walked on swiftly, moving against the tide of pedestrian traffic and giving out leaflets to whoever would take them. The leaflet showed pictures of Kumar and Patel, doctored with bloodstains, and the headline: "RIP THE 'GREAT' AND THE 'GOOD.'"

Santosh caught sight of a police car in the road and

watched the young agitator shove his pamphlets into a backpack and melt into the crowd. He pocketed his own, moving on, wondering about the mood in the city.

There was no doubting the mood at the building occupied by ResQ Insurance. Fear and paranoia ruled over a reception area that teemed with security guards. Santosh passed through a metal detector where his cane was inspected—not very efficiently: the blade inside remained undiscovered—and then he was approached by a guard wielding a wand of some kind.

Finally he made his way in the elevator up to the seventeenth floor of the steel-and-glass tower. Five floors of the building were entirely occupied by ResQ Insurance, a company that had built its fortune by taking advantage of lower health care costs in India.

Founded by two brothers from Cleveland, ResQ had originally started out as a third-party administrator for the large insurance companies that found it more efficient to allow an outsider to process claims and perform other administrative services. Given that back-office tasks were easily outsourced to India, ResQ had built up a strong team in Gurgaon. At that time the company had been known by a different name.

The company's NYU-educated CEO, Jai Thakkar, had realized India presented an opportunity to offer medical insurance at significantly lower premiums, and he had succeeded in putting together an investor consortium to buy out the founders. He had changed the name of the company and then put into action his plan to offer low American insurance premiums linked to medical services in India. Thakkar's idea had worked wonders and ResQ was now one of the most profitable insurance companies in the U.S., with the bulk of its operations in India even though the majority of its customers lived in America.

Santosh exited the elevator on the seventeenth floor and entered a world of soft carpets, deep leather sofas, and understated elegance. He felt slightly intimidated, partly owing to his disheveled appearance.

He passed another security check. Two more armed guards with wands. This time he was asked if he was able to walk without the cane. He agreed that he was. In that case, could he collect it after his meeting with Mr. Thakkar?

Next came Thakkar's secretary, who surveyed him with a snooty air then led him through corridors to a large corner office with views of the other towers in the business district.

Thakkar was on the phone but hung up when he saw Santosh enter. He rose from behind his desk to shake Santosh's hand. "I had a call from Denny, the CEO of the National Association of Insurance Commissioners, saying that I had to see you," he said, friendly enough.

Santosh nodded. "Thank you for meeting me," he said as he sat. "I was hoping you could help me understand the economics of medical tourism."

He glanced at the credenza that ran along one side of Thakkar's desk. On it was a photograph of Thakkar along with Mohan Jaswal. "Where was that taken?" he asked.

"NYU alumni meet," replied Thakkar, the word "alumni" like the buzzing of a bee due to his nasal twang. "Both of us attended but many years apart. He went first to attend a program on journalism during the period that he was posted there by the *Indian Times*. I earned my MBA from NYU several years later. We became friends because of the alumni association."

Santosh kept his expression neutral, not wanting to register a reaction. Thinking, *Thakkar and Jaswal. Friends.*

Thakkar looked like the typical Indian-American on Wall Street. Well educated, groomed, and urbane. Indian residents deridingly called them ABCDs— "American-Born Confused Desis," the word "desi" implying Indian descent. Thakkar's parents had moved from Delhi to America in the seventies but there were enough family ties in Delhi for him to call it home.

"So, coming back to my question," said Santosh, "I was wondering whether American clients come to India simply on account of lower prices for procedures or because they are able to obtain vital transplant organs that they would be unable to procure back home."

Thakkar's face fell. He recovered quickly, though. He was used to dealing with difficult questions from the press and the regulators. "India has become a preferred destination because of the excellent doctors, modern infrastructure, plentiful and qualified nursing staff, and lower prices. Recent technology upgrades and modernization of facilities have made India's hospitals very attractive to foreign clients."

Thakkar's cell phone began to ring. He looked at the number flashing on the screen. "Excuse me for a minute," he said, getting up from his chair. "This one is urgent." He gestured for Santosh to remain seated while he took the call in the adjoining conference room.

Santosh got up as soon as Thakkar left and walked over to the desk phone. Looked at the last call, memorized the number, and then texted Neel to run a trace on it. Then he went back to his chair, sat down, and waited for Thakkar.

"I have just one more question to ask," he said when Thakkar returned.

"Fire away," smiled Thakkar.

"Why have you beefed up security in the building? Not frightened, by any chance, are you, Mr. Thakkar?"

The smile slid from Thakkar's face for good. Shortly afterward, Santosh was shown from the office.

Chapter 58

GALI PARANTHE WALI was a narrow street in the Chandni Chowk area of Delhi that was famous for the multitude of shops selling parathas—or stuffed bread, a culinary favorite of North India.

Nisha found herself in a shop no bigger than a closet, along with one of her college friends, Abha, now a senior columnist for a tabloid. She wrote the lifestyle column.

Abha, a strikingly beautiful Punjabi woman, ordered parathas for both of them without bothering to consult Nisha. They quickly sat down on two of the empty chairs in the shop and waited for their lunch.

Nisha would have preferred to meet at the newspaper's editorial office but Abha was researching an article on the street food of Delhi and had requested Nisha tag along. Nisha had obliged. Not because she particularly savored the food but because Abha always knew the latest gossip in Delhi. Which businessman was down on his luck, which man or woman was having an extramarital affair, which politician had indulged in an outrageously corrupt deal... there was nothing she wasn't up to date on.

Their food arrived. Stuffed with potato, peas, and cauliflower, the piping-hot breads were served along with sweet tamarind and mint chutney. Abha tucked in. *How does she manage to look so good with all that junk going into her?* wondered Nisha.

"What's the matter?" asked Abha, stuffing another delectable morsel in her mouth with her glossy-pink-nail-polished fingers. "Why aren't you eating?" Nisha reluctantly took a bite.

Nisha continued nibbling as they chatted. First about themselves, then their kids, and then the entire world. The conversation veered to politics. "What's happening in Delhi these days?" asked Nisha.

"The Lieutenant Governor is pissed off."

"Why?" asked Nisha.

"It seems that Chopra's daughter was engaged to Jai Thakkar, the CEO of that insurance company ResQ. The creep broke off the engagement after a few romps in bed with her."

"Big deal," said Nisha, licking tamarind chutney off her fingers. "It's quite common these days to have terminated affairs and broken engagements."

"True," said Abha. "But Chopra is old school. You know, 'family honor' and all that. He's vowed to set

Thakkar right. You watch—that Thakkar will get into trouble one of these days. He's been going around town bad-mouthing Chopra and his daughter. News is that Chopra sent him a chopped-off tongue as warning. I did a little snippet for the paper without mentioning names the other day."

"Thakkar is quite powerful himself, right?" asked Nisha. "I'm told that ResQ is among the most profitable insurance companies in the States. He was on Guha's *Carrot and Stick* the other night."

"True, but you can't live in Delhi and piss off the Lieutenant Governor. For the life of me, I can't understand people these days. And that Ajoy Guha is another thing—he's like a leech. Once he latches on he doesn't let go of the story until he's sucked every drop out."

"Committed, eh?" offered Nisha.

"He lives for it. I don't think he has much else. Tragic marriage," said her friend. "The show is the perfect outlet for him to vent all his frustrations. There are also some pretty unsavory rumors about that new Health Secretary, Amit Roy. So high and mighty, yet the word is that he likes them young . . ."

Chapter 59

AMIT ROY STOOD in the wings of the school assembly hall, tired after what had been one of the best nights of his life. Images of the terrified girl still vividly played on a loop inside his head and he felt, not just euphoric, but exalted somehow, sensing a change within himself, as though his disconnection from a society that despised his kind was at last complete. What happened to him now was an irrelevance. He was at one with himself.

Oh, but first, there was this rather boring duty to attend to. Prizegiving at the Vasant Valley School. Yawn.

On stage, the principal made his announcement. "We have a special guest with us today. Mr. Amit Roy is the Principal Secretary in Delhi's Health Department, and he is here to tell you about how each one of you can contribute toward making Delhi a healthier city. Please welcome him with a round of applause."

Roy walked on, adjusted the microphone to his height, and spoke, his Adam's apple bouncing. "I am delighted to be here today in order to award the prize for the best essay on the topic 'Delhi's Health: Is It Only the Government's Problem?' We received over five thousand submissions from across schools in Delhi but the winning one was from Vasant Valley, so you should be very proud of your school."

He waited for the applause to die down and then spoke briefly about air pollution, availability of clean water, sanitation, and all the other difficulties the country's capital was still grappling with, and what ordinary folks could possibly do to play a positive role.

"And that brings me to the end of my talk," he said, eyes scanning the room. "I shall now announce the winner of the state essay competition."

The children waited with bated breath. After all, the winner was one among them.

"And the winner, for her essay entitled 'Health Care, Fair and Square?', is Maya," said Roy. "Maya Gandhe."

He stood back as the auditorium erupted in applause, and from the crowd stood Maya Gandhe.

And the moment he saw her, Amit Roy decided this event wasn't such a drag after all.

Chapter 60

SANTOSH WALKED THROUGH the congested by-lanes filled with vendors selling kebabs and waited for the man to appear. Neel had double-checked the records and confirmed that the cell phone number dialed from Thakkar's desk phone belonged to someone called Iqbal Ibrahim, whose residential address was near the Jama Masjid.

As it turned out, Ibrahim was praying in India's most famous mosque, the Jama Masjid. Built in 1656 by Mughal emperor Shah Jahan, the mosque was vast. Three great gates, four towers, and two forty-meter-high minarets constructed of red sandstone and white marble overlooked a gargantuan courtyard that could accommodate more than twenty-five thousand faithful for prayer.

Neel had given Santosh a photo of Ibraham he'd

managed to retrieve from a database. He'd also supplied Santosh with the latest gizmo he'd developed. It was a pair of regular-looking eyeglasses that accommodated a camera and mic capable of transmitting to the Private Delhi office.

Reaching the mosque, Santosh put on the glasses. He noticed a crowd of people exiting. Prayers seemed to have ended. Then, after ten minutes, Santosh saw a man who resembled the picture he had. He continued staring in his direction, knowing that the camera would be relaying the image to Neel. Santosh watched as the man walked toward him, removing his prayer cap as he approached.

Santosh took a few tentative steps in the direction of the man and held out his arm for a handshake. "Mr. Iqbal Ibrahim? Could I have a few minutes of your time?" he asked.

The man smiled at him. "Please don't be formal, Mr. Wagh," he said courteously. Santosh had half a second to register the fact that the man knew his name, because Ibrahim's statement was accompanied by an almost imperceptible nod of the head. A baton slammed into the back of Santosh's head and he crumpled to the ground, his cane and phone falling along with him, the handset shattering.

Chapter 61

JACK HAD A stopover in Dubai on his way from LA to Delhi. Unfortunately, his Emirates flight from Dubai to Delhi had been delayed. The result was that he arrived at terminal three of Indira Gandhi International Airport almost two hours after the scheduled time.

He cleared immigration, collected his single suitcase from the luggage carousel, passed through the green channel of customs, and emerged expecting to be greeted by Santosh. Instead he saw another familiar face: Nisha.

He rolled his baggage cart toward her, pecked her on the cheek, and asked, "Where is he?"

"He had to meet someone," said Nisha as she led Jack toward the parking lot where her car awaited. "He asked me to do the honors instead."

"My lucky day," said Jack with a smile.

They stowed the suitcase in the trunk and took their seats inside. "Where to?" asked Nisha. "We've booked you at the Oberoi Hotel."

"No, not yet," replied Jack. "We had better go directly to the conference. My session starts in ninety minutes. In the meantime, fill me in on this case."

They set off, and as Jack relished the sights and sounds of Delhi once more, Nisha explained their theory.

"And it *is* just a theory at this stage," she clarified when she had finished.

"Give it to me as a percentage."

"Santosh is almost certain."

"Shall we say ninety percent?"

"We could."

"So, you're ninety percent certain that some kind of war has broken out over an organ-harvesting operation. That about sums it up?"

"It does."

"Do we know who's involved?"

Nisha blew out her cheeks. "Well, now it gets really interesting. As you know, Ram Chopra and Mohan Jaswal are at war anyway—a political war, I should add. Chopra's name is connected to the house in Greater Kailash where the bodies were found, and we think he's been doing deals with a medical corporation called Surgiquip, run by Samir Patel—the recently deceased Samir Patel. Somewhere in the mix we have an insurance company called ResQ—a company run by Jai Thakkar, a friend of Jaswal's, who's fallen out with Chopra."

Jack cleared his throat. "You realize you're going to have to run this past me again when I haven't just stepped off a plane."

Nisha laughed. "Yeah, I understand. Okay, look, the short version is that all the signs point to Chopra, but Santosh feels it's a bit too convenient."

"Sometimes the obvious answer is the right one."

"Tell that to him."

"Either way, it sounds like there's a mountain of political dog shit we need to avoiding stepping in. How is the police investigation proceeding?"

She shrugged. "At the moment it feels as though the police couldn't care less. As you know, the general feeling is that Sharma is running things in a way that benefits Chopra. And if Chopra is involved in the organ-harvesting scheme..."

"If they're fighting we could just leave them to it. Let them all kill each other and let God sort it out."

Nisha gave him a sideways look. "Do we want to do that?"

Jack chuckled. "Tempting though it is, no, Nisha, I suppose not."

Chapter 62

THE MORGUE OF the Delhi Memorial Hospital was like most other morgues in the city: understaffed and overstuffed.

Located in the bowels of the hospital, two-thirds of its area consisted of a refrigerated section that contained individual drawers kept at a constant temperature of four degrees Celsius, while the remaining third was made up of a stark autopsy room tiled entirely in white, with two stainless steel operating tables in the center. A scale for weighing body parts hung from the ceiling over each table, much like a butcher's shop, in addition to a trolley that held Stryker saws for ripping bone, suturing materials, knives, and scalpels.

A hosepipe fitted with a washing nozzle was at hand to sluice blood and tissue down the drain and into the septic tank. Unfortunately it wasn't used often enough.

There was always a long queue of gurneys waiting with bodies that needed to be autopsied or refrigerated.

Patel's mutilated body was wheeled into the morgue along with another gurney. Patel's body was transferred to a surgical table, waiting to be dissected like a laboratory rat. The autopsy technician placed a block of wood under the corpse's shoulders, making it look as though it was sitting. He then made an incision from the top of one ear to the top of the other and pulled the skin from the top and middle of the head down over the face. Patel's face was now grotesquely inside out. The technician used the Stryker saw to cut the skull and expose the brain for tissue sampling and weighing.

In the meantime, the second body was uncovered and placed on the nearby surgical table. The autopsy technician took a quick look. He knew who it was. He had received a call from Ibrahim about him. Whenever Ibrahim needed to eliminate someone without having the headache of body disposal, he would send the case to him.

"I don't have time for this one right now," he said, putting on a casual face. "Put him in the refrigerator and I'll deal with him later."

The assistants wheeled Santosh Wagh into the refrigeration chamber, opened one of the refrigeration drawers, placed him inside it, and slammed the drawer shut.

Chapter 63

THEY WERE IN the Private Delhi conference room.

"Where is he?" asked Jack.

Nisha tried Santosh's cell phone once again. A message indicated that the phone was either switched off or outside the coverage area.

"What did he go out for?" asked Jack.

"He had several meetings lined up," replied Nisha. "One was with Thakkar, the CEO of ResQ. He also had a meeting with someone called Iqbal Ibrahim near Jama Masjid."

"I have some bad news," said Neel.

"What?" asked Nisha.

"I tried to find the IP address of the person calling himself Dr. O. S. Rangoon," said Neel.

"Wouldn't he have been using a proxy server?" asked Nisha.

"Exactly," replied Neel. "He was using a proxy server to hide his IP address from the administrators of the systems that he was posting on. But all individuals who hide behind proxy servers always leave a trail of digital bread crumbs. I tried following the bread crumbs."

"And?" asked Jack.

"Dr. O. S. Rangoon used a single proxy server to mask himself. I figured that if I could access the proxy server logs, I would be able to find his connection requests to the target server."

"Go on," said Nisha.

"The proxy server is located in Russia. Usually such companies would demand a court order to reveal their logs but the idiots had left their own server exposed and I was able to access their logs."

"Excellent," said Jack. "You have the source IP?"

Neel nodded. "It belongs to Iqbal Ibrahim, the man Santosh went to meet. Dr. O. S. Rangoon and Ibrahim are one and the same."

"But the phone number Santosh asked us to trace— which turned out to be that of Ibrahim—was not the same as the number listed on the website by Dr. O. S. Rangoon," argued Nisha.

"He's obviously using two phone numbers," said Neel.

"Is Santosh's RFID chip working?" asked Jack. "I'm authorizing you to track it."

All employees of the Private organization across the world were required to be fitted with a small locator chip embedded under the skin of the upper back. It enabled the Private team to locate them during emergencies. In order to prevent misuse, only Jack Morgan had the power to authorize tracking.

Neel logged into a laptop that generated an e-mail to Jack. Jack clicked on the authorization link and entered his password.

"Can't locate it," said Neel after a minute. "He could be in a basement or a vault, preventing the signals from being picked up."

"He took his spy glasses with him, Neel," said Nisha. "Don't those glasses have GSM? Can you track the signal?"

"No luck," replied Neel after a minute. "He's definitely in an area without signal."

"Did the camera in his glasses send in any feed?" asked Nisha.

"Let me check," replied Neel, quickly accessing the secure server of Private Delhi from his notebook.

Jack and Nisha hunched behind Neel to look at the video footage that had been sent in by the glasses to the server. The first ten minutes were uneventful. Santosh had simply stood, waiting for Ibrahim, near the Jama Masjid. The footage showed hundreds of worshipers emerging from within the mosque after prayers.

The footage soon focused on one particular man, removing his prayer cap as he walked toward the camera. "Mr. Iqbal Ibrahim? Could I have a few minutes of your time?"—words spoken by Santosh and recorded in the audio.

The words of Ibrahim had also been picked up: "Please don't be formal, Mr. Wagh." Ibrahim was smiling. Suddenly the camera jerked. The view seemed to oscillate all over the place until it settled on the blue sky above.

A few seconds later, Ibrahim's voice could be heard again. "Put him in the van and give him a high dose of midazolam," he said. Two burly men lifted Santosh and placed him inside a black van. "Inshallah, it should be sufficient to keep him asleep for four hours. Also, discard his broken cell phone."

One of the men could be heard asking if he could keep the walking stick for himself.

Then Ibrahim's voice: "He doesn't need it. Dead men can't walk."

Nisha froze. Did that mean . . . ?

"He can't be dead," said Neel.

"Why?" asked Nisha.

"Midazolam is a sedative," said Neel. "Why sedate someone who is already dead?"

Nisha sighed with relief. "Let's review the rest of the tape."

The audio was punctuated by the sound of a van door being slammed shut. The next forty minutes were blank because a white sheet had been placed on top of Santosh, covering the glasses he was wearing. The audio contained traffic noise and honking.

The Private Delhi conference room remained silent as Jack, Nisha, and Neel watched the video intently. Then there was the sound of the van door being opened. The sheet was removed as a couple of orderlies peered over Santosh's face. They only seemed interested in removing valuables from his person—watch, pen, wallet, shoes, and eyeglasses. The video blanked out as one of the orderlies pocketed the camera glasses. The moment he folded the glasses, the transmission had stopped.

"He could be anywhere," said Neel. "That's anywhere within a forty-minute radius of Jama Masjid. And that's a lot!"

"Just play the last bit again," said Nisha. "The orderlies who removed the stuff were wearing white shirts with a logo on the pocket. Can you zoom in on the shirt?"

Neel tried but it was of no use. The image was just a pixelated mess. "Let me try something else." He left the conference room for his lab to have a go with SmartDeblur, a software program that could partially restore and enhance blurred images.

"Thank God you're here, Jack," said Nisha as they waited in the conference room. "I just hope Santosh is safe."

"The man knows how to look after himself," said Jack. "Stop worrying." He was not very convincing.

"He obviously received a blow from behind," said Nisha. "But that doesn't explain why he remained motionless in the van. I'm praying he isn't..." The word "dead" was still on her mind but she was unable to bring it to her lips. Neel's observation about the midazolam had given her hope.

Neel came back a couple of minutes later. "I've successfully zoomed in on the shirt logo," he said, handing Nisha a printout. "The logo says DMH."

"Delhi Memorial Hospital. Let's go," said Nisha, running out.

Chapter 64

SANTOSH OPENED HIS eyes. He blinked a few times, struggling to see, but his world remained dark. *What's happened to me? Have I gone blind? Or am I dead?*

His body was wracked with an involuntary tremor. He realized he was shivering. It was freezing cold. He tried moving his arms but his body seemed to be confined within a tightly restricted place.

He tried to wiggle his feet. He was able to but just for a few inches in either direction. His back felt frozen solid. It seemed to be resting on cold metal. He desperately wanted to curl up into a fetal position but there simply wasn't any space to do that. The realization suddenly hit him: *I'm in a morgue.*

Santosh attempted to calculate how much time he could survive inside the refrigerated coffin. He remembered reading somewhere that body heat is lost twenty-five times faster in cold water than in cold air. Most morgues are kept at around four degrees Celsius. At that temperature in water, a person would survive around an hour. Theoretically, he had several hours left provided he remained conscious and kept some movement going.

He succeeded in lifting an arm but there was simply no way to bend it. There was a metal ceiling above him that was only a few inches above his nose. He touched it with the back of his hand. It was just as cold as the floor on which he lay. He touched his thigh with his hand. He was pretty certain he was naked even though the freezing temperature had reduced the sensation in his body. Then the panic attack set in.

He suddenly felt a hot flash in his toes. Then his fingers. To shut down the loss of heat from the extremities, his body was inducing vasoconstriction—a reflexive contraction of blood vessels. But the muscles required to induce vasoconstriction had failed. It was causing warm blood to rush from the core to his extremities.

Santosh tried screaming but couldn't be sure whether any sound was emerging from within him at all. His body seemed to have slowed down to a point where no physical activity was possible. The sounds that did emerge were slurred, almost as though he were under the influence of drugs or alcohol. He felt dazed. Disoriented. Confused. The effects of hypothermia had begun to set in.

He tried getting his mind to remain focused. He knew that if the hypothermia became severe, it would eventually slow down his respiration and heart rate, making him lose consciousness before the onset of death.

He attempted to recall what had happened before he'd passed out. He had met Ibrahim and had then received a blow behind his head. They had obviously brought him here later. But why was he in a morgue? Had he been assumed dead? Or were they trying to kill him by freezing him? Which morgue was he in? Did Nisha or Neel know he was in trouble?

Santosh felt suffocated. It wasn't claustrophobia—it was his lungs giving up. He felt himself slipping out of consciousness. He imagined he was back in the hospital after the car accident in which he had lost his wife and son. Then he was back inside the Tower of Silence, battling Assistant Commissioner of Police Rupesh Desai, with the vultures circling overhead. The scene quickly changed. Santosh imagined he was at an Alcoholics Anonomous meeting. The members had surrounded him and pinned him down to the floor. They were attempting to forcibly pour whisky down his throat.

Santosh sensed his pulse slowing as he slipped into an abyss of darkness.

Finally, there was no pulse at all.

Chapter 65

"HELLO."

Maya Gandhe stood at the school gates, her school bag slung over her shoulder, a copy of her essay in one hand and her prize, an iPad, in the other. Heena was late but let's face it, Heena was always late and, on this occasion at least, Maya didn't really care. Friends filed past her on their way to school busses or for lifts home, teachers inched past in their cars, and every single one of them gave her a wave and a smile.

This is what it's like to be famous, thought Maya. Being new at school had been hard—she and her mother had only lived in Delhi for three months—but now it was as though everybody knew who she was; as though she were a friend to them all.

And that, decided Maya Gandhe, was a great feeling, especially when it was earned—a result of her essay proposing, or at least arguing in favor of, a fairer health care system for all. People didn't know her name because she was good at sports or pretty or any of the normal, boring reasons. They knew her name because she'd used her brain.

Mom would be proud, she knew. Very proud. And Dad? Well, wasn't that funny. It wasn't as if she'd stopped thinking about Dad. More that the thought of him had temporarily changed. Instead of his absence being like a darkness, it was as though he was looking down on her.

Looking down on her and smiling. Proud.

And now Mr. Roy, the Principal Secretary, the very man who had commended her on her essay and presented her with her iPad, had drawn up in his Audi, the window purring down.

"Hello, Maya."

He didn't have a very nice face. It was as though the smile he wore didn't quite fit, but even so, it was Amit Roy, and he was...well, he was important.

"Are you waiting for a lift?" he said brightly, like someone trying really hard to be friendly.

"My nanny's coming."

He looked around. The crowds had thinned out.. They were now the only people at the school gates. "It doesn't look like she's here."

"Oh, she's always late," shrugged Maya.

"Why don't I give you a lift?"

"Oh..." faltered Maya, "I'm not allowed..."

"Of course. Of course not, Maya." He smiled his awkward smile. "Very sensible indeed. But you see, that puts me in a very difficult position, because I can't in all good conscience leave you standing here. And besides, I was rather hoping you could read me your essay."

"But haven't you read it?"

His smile faltered a little, and later she would remember that moment, and think it was the moment his mask slipped. But for the time being nothing could ruin her sunny mood, and in a blink his smile had returned. "Ah, but I'd like a *personal* reading from the author, especially one whose ideals are so close to my heart."

And so it was flattery that compelled Maya to get into the passenger seat of the Audi. That and the assurance that they would encounter Heena on the way.

He drove, taking directions from Maya and talking at the same time. "Remind me of the title of your essay?" he said.

" 'Health Care, Fair and Square?' " she answered proudly.

"Exactly. I was impressed to read such an egalitarian treatise from such a young mind."

"I'm sorry. I don't know what egalitarian means. Or treatise," she said.

"It means you have a very fair mind," he explained. "It means you believe everybody should have equal rights, regardless of their status in society, young or old, rich or poor."

"I do," she said boldly.

"And you get that from your parents, do you?"

"Yes," she said, and pictured them together, Mama

and Papa, feeling a great rush of love for them that threatened to bring her to tears right then and there.

"They must be very proud. What a shame they couldn't make the prizegiving. Perhaps they will be at home, will they?"

"Later on, my mom will get home. Not my dad."

"I see."

The car slowed. "Do you know," said Roy, "I seem to be more familiar with this area than I thought. I could take a right turn here and get you home more quickly."

Maya was nervous about the idea and was about to say so when she caught sight of Heena on the street and before Roy could stop her was lowering the window and calling out to her.

From the corner of her eye she caught sight of the expression on Roy's face.

That mask slipping again.

Chapter 66

THE LIEUTENANT GOVERNOR, Ram Chopra, was sweating ferociously on his treadmill, feeling every single cigar and glass of whisky. *God, these workouts hurt.*

He was watching TV at the same time. *Carrot and Stick*, and Ajoy Guha was warming up for a sensational disclosure. Referring to notes through wire-framed glasses, Guha wore a determined look, like that of a soldier prepared to die in battle.

The words "Viewer discretion is advised" scrolled across the foot of the screen.

Oh yes, thought Chopra. *What's all this then?*

Guha cleared his throat and said, "We at DETV have always believed in the primacy of the truth, no matter how it may affect anyone. Today we bring you footage that we have accessed through a source that shall remain unnamed for reasons of security. The footage is explosive, and we have had to blur out and mute portions of it in order to play it on national television. The person shown in the video is Mr. Amit Roy, the Health Secretary. Ladies and gentlemen, this is a man responsible not only for our hospitals and hygiene but also for the welfare of families. What you are about to see will shock you, and indeed you should not only be shocked but also outraged. I for one am absolutely sickened by it."

The studio and Guha's blue jacket and red tie disappeared from view and a video of Roy sitting on a bed inside a small room appeared. He seemed to be ripping the clothes from a frightened little girl and forcing her to sit on his lap.

Chopra watched, and then switched off the TV. He stopped the treadmill, reached for his phone.

"Sharma," he said a moment later, "were you watching *Carrot and Stick*?"

The police chief chuckled. "I was indeed."

"I take it that Guha's informant is you?"

"And I take it that the next call you make will be to Jaswal?"

"I'm glad you're on my side, Sharma," said Chopra.

Sharma laughed some more. "In the meantime, I'll see to it that Roy is arrested, shall I?"

Chopra thought. "Yes, but wait an hour or so, would you?"

"And why would I want to do that?"

Chopra draped a towel around his shoulders, using a corner to wipe sweat from his brow. "Well, what would *you* do in Roy's position?"

"Me?" said Sharma. "I'm no pedophile."

Chopra sighed. "No, Sharma, I know you're not, but just for a second try stepping outside your own rather limited mind and using something we like to call deduction, or imagination, if you prefer. What would you do if you were a pedophile who had just been exposed? If you were Amit Roy."

"I'd kill myself."

"Exactly. And it might just be more convenient for all concerned if he were to do exactly that. Let's give him time to fall on his sword, shall we?"

"Consider it delayed," said Sharma. "By the way, while you're on the phone: Kumar."

Chopra grinned. "The dear departed Kumar, may he rest in piss."

Sharma sniggered. "The very same. You asked me to look into his interest in the Greater Kailash house, remember? Why he wanted the whole thing hushed up? Well, I've done as you asked, and it looks as though he may have been on the periphery of something going on at the hospitals."

"He was the Minister for Health and Family Welfare. You'd expect him to be slap bang in the middle of *everything* going on at the hospitals."

"Without spelling it out on an open line, I'm talking about something on the side—something with corpses as the end result. A certain *donation* enterprise, shall we say. You're aware he didn't really commit suicide, I take it?"

"It's the worst-kept secret in the city. I'm told that social media is having a field day with the deaths of Kumar and Patel. All kinds of conspiracy theories. They were lovers, is the latest one."

"Naturally," growled Sharma. "But even a stopped clock tells the right time twice a day, and it seems that Kumar and Patel may have had a financial relationship. Now, of course, I'd be willing to pursue this on the off chance that it leads right to the door of Jaswal, but I have a feeling that you, too, had certain business dealings with Patel of Surgiquip."

Chopra slumped on the bars of his treadmill. *Why the fuck is it these things always come to haunt you?* "I may have had, yes," he hissed, without wanting to say more on the phone. "What of it?"

"Well, your name can be linked to the house at Greater Kailash. You can be connected to Patel. You don't want to find yourself ending up as collateral damage if and when the details of their little side business come out, do you?"

"Of course not."

"So we can't just start making arrests. You see what I mean?"

"I see what you mean. And thank you for your counsel, Commissioner."

"It's my pleasure. And going forward?"

Chopra draped the towel over his head and stepped off the treadmill. "Going forward, I plan to make life hard for Jaswal. And as far as you're concerned, if you could continue with—*discreet*—investigations into what the fuck our friends with scalpels are up to, that would be very much appreciated too."

He ended the call. Collected himself. Thanked God again that Sharma was on his side.

Then dialed Jaswal.

"What do you want?" came the reply, loaded with enough venom to make Chopra's next question redundant.

"I was just wondering if you'd seen *Carrot and Stick* this evening?"

"*What do you want, Chopra?*" came the even more bile-filled reply.

"Well, given that you appointed a pedophile as Health Secretary, what I want is for you to tender your resignation immediately."

Chapter 67

"WHAT A LOVELY apartment," said Roy, stepping inside. Maya skipped ahead happily; the childminder, Heena—a dried-up, middle-aged shrew if ever he'd seen one—was fixing him with the latest in a series of disapproving looks as she moved to switch on the radio and start making tea.

I'm going to have to do something about that bitch.

"Well, thank you very much for seeing us home, Mr. Roy," she was saying, trying to get rid of him, dismiss him as if he was the hired help. "I'm sure we needn't take up any more of your valuable time."

"Oh, there's no rush," he said to her. "I'm very keen to hear our little social healer read me her essay."

"Oh, I'm sure that can be arranged at another time, Mr. Roy," said the middle-aged shrew, adding pointedly, "when her mother, an ex-police officer, is present."

His phone was ringing. A text message arrived. And then another one. He pulled the handset from his trouser pocket and stared at the screen, blanching. "You're on the news," said one text. He dismissed an incoming call, but another one came. Another text message. This one said, "Die, pedo." Another that said, "You better run."

They know, he thought. *The whole world knows.*

And it wasn't despondency or shame he felt, but once again a kind of exaltation. He knew now that he would need the sleeping pills he'd kept for an occasion such as this, because there was no way he could live in a society that despised his kind. But even so, he greeted the thought of his death, not with fear or resignation, but with a serenity. His suicide would not be a passing so much as an ascendancy. He would rise. His tormented soul would finally be at peace.

His being filled with joy at the thought, he failed to notice what was happening in the apartment. The news was on the radio, the lead item was the very public disgrace of Amit Roy, and the first he knew of it was Heena shrieking, "*Maya, get out of here now!*"

Roy came back to himself. He saw Maya come flying from her bedroom into the front room, a worried look on her face. "Heena, what's wrong?"

"We've got to get out of here—he's a monster."

"Wait," he said, rounding on Heena. "There's been a terrible mistake."

"You can tell that to the police. Maya, come over here, sweetheart, stay with me."

"No," said Roy. He advanced on Heena, who pulled Maya to her, placing herself between Maya and Roy as he moved toward them.

"You stay away from me," she warned.

But her voice shook and she was stepping backward, going into the kitchen.

"I can explain," said Roy, "really I can. You don't need to be afraid, either of you."

He snatched a knife from the knife block. Flipped it to hold overhand.

"Get away," screeched Heena, and she too tried to reach for a weapon, grabbing blindly for something, anything, from the counter, protecting Maya to the last, keeping herself between the man and his prey.

Even when Roy buried the knife in her chest.

Her mouth dropped open. Roy pulled the knife free with a wrench and then stabbed again, pitilessly, enjoying the pain and defeat in his victim's eyes, her lungs filling with blood, her eyeballs rolling back.

"Don't worry, Maya," he called over the loud gurgling sound Heena made as he stabbed her a third time— feeling blood drizzle his face, Heena dropping to her knees before him. "Don't worry, my darling."

Chapter 68

THE AUDIO OF Guha's *Carrot and Stick* program was played on radio stations belonging to DETV. Nisha heard it in Neel's Toyota as they rushed toward Delhi Memorial Hospital to find Santosh.

"Is everything all right?" asked Neel.

"No..." said Nisha distantly, thinking. "It's just that Roy was supposed to have been in Maya's school earlier today, awarding a prize for the essay competition."

"I'm sure she'll be okay," said Neel.

"Can't hurt to be sure," said Jack.

She checked her watch. Maya should have reached home by now. But when she called there was no answer. She tried Heena's cell phone, then Maya's. Neither answered.

She told herself it was nothing. A coincidence.

Ten minutes later they screeched to a halt in front

of the Delhi Memorial Hospital. Jack and Neel rushed inside, making a beeline for the morgue while Nisha clambered into the driver's seat to park the car.

She steered one-handed, trying Heena's and Maya's numbers.

She needed to know her little girl was safe.

Chapter 69

JACK AND NEEL bypassed the elevators and took the stairs to the morgue in the hospital basement. The autopsy room and the refrigeration chamber were lined with gurneys, on each of them a covered body.

Jack held his kerchief to his nose as the stench hit him but his experience with corpses made Neel oblivious, and he began drawing down sheets to see the bodies beneath, moving quickly from one to the other until an orderly came running over. "Hey! Who are you?" he demanded. "You're not allowed in here."

Jack turned to him. "Does a thousand rupees change your mind?"

The attendant looked wily. "It might."

"Good." Jack reached for his wallet. "Then how about I give you a thousand now and another thousand when we leave just to make sure we're given the executive treatment. And if you wouldn't mind keeping anything you see to yourself, that would do nicely too."

With a nod the assistant pocketed the cash and stepped aside.

In the meantime, Neel had finished checking the gurneys. "He's not here."

"Must be in the refrigeration chamber," said Jack, motioning Neel to follow him through a door leading to the freezing units. One by one they tried the drawers, until they found what they were looking for.

Chapter 70

WITH NO ANSWER from Heena or Maya, Nisha abandoned plans to park the Toyota and instead pointed it toward Vasant Vihar and home. Her heart was racing wildly, her hands clammy. Would such a situation have occurred if Maya's father were alive? He was the one who had always taken care of Maya whenever Nisha would be late.

Nisha cursed herself for not being around for her poor baby. She narrowly missed a pedestrian who was crossing the street without bothering to look left or right, and slammed her hand on the horn to let him know he was a prick. She pressed her foot on the gas and broke two red signals along the way.

"I feel so lonely. You're always working. But at least when you were late, it was Dad who would tuck me into bed. Now there's only Heena in the house. The apartment feels so cold and empty."

But then again, wasn't she overreacting? Forming worst-case scenarios when she had no reason to be so fearful? Roy might be a predatory pedophile, but he wouldn't be the first and he certainly wouldn't be the last to visit a school. The simple fact of him presenting a prize at Maya's school meant nothing.

And yet Nisha couldn't lose the nagging feeling that something was wrong, something was seriously wrong. Why weren't they answering their phones? And if she *was* overreacting? Well, she'd laugh about it later. Call it motherly concern. What were a few red traffic lights when you were worried for the most important person in your life?

The Toyota tires complained as she pulled into the parking area in front of her block. Dark now, most of the apartment lights were on but not hers. Both units on either side of her ground-floor apartment were lit up. Hers was dark.

Heart hammering, telling herself that maybe Heena had taken Maya out for an ice cream, maybe the two of them were paying a friend a visit—still desperate to be worrying unnecessarily—Nisha crashed out of the car, leaving the driver's door open as she fumbled with her keys and almost collided with her own front door.

It was open. On contact it creaked slowly inward and maybe it was a smell, maybe it was just gut instinct, a mother's instinct, but she knew something was wrong, and never in her life had she wished so much for a gun in her hand.

"Hello? Heena? Maya? You in there?"

The hallway yawned emptily at her. Beyond that, their living room. From there came a noise, a rustling, slithering sound, followed by something like a gasp or a hiccup.

"Hello?" she called, moving faster now, along the hallway and into the front room, where training and instinct made her crouch to present a smaller target.

The lights in the room were off. She noticed a lamp lying on its side on the floor, signs of a struggle that made her want to cry out with anguish. From the kitchen doorway was a faint glow of light within.

And then she saw what lay on the kitchen floor. She saw the blood. She heard the gurgling sound that Heena made.

In a second she was over to her, kneeling down, fumbling for her phone, trying to do so many things at once. Check the pulse. *Oh God, so weak.* Evaluate the injuries. Three, maybe more, stab wounds. On the floor nearby was Nisha's own bread knife, gleaming with Heena's blood. Stem the blood. Call an ambulance. Check that whoever did this—*Roy*—was no longer in the apartment. And most of all, find Maya.

Blood bubbled at Heena's mouth. Her eyes rolled and went in and out of focus as she struggled to stay conscious. One clawed hand reached to Nisha.

"He took her. The beast took her," she managed.

"Roy? Roy took her?"

Heena nodded weakly. "Go get her, Nisha," she breathed. "Go and save your little angel."

"Stay with me, Heena," urged Nisha. "Stay with me."

She had her phone to her ear, calmly giving instructions to the emergency services. But it was too late. Heena's hand that held her jacket relaxed and splashed into a pool of blood on the kitchen floor. Her eyelids fluttered then closed. And when Nisha checked her pulse, there was none.

Chapter 71

NISHA SAT ON the kitchen floor, head swimming, momentarily stunned into inaction. For perhaps twenty seconds she wondered if she was up to this task—if life had finally given her a challenge she could not meet.

And then with a curse she shook the thought out of her head. She stood up. Her head was clear. Her only priority was to kill the bastard who had abducted her daughter and get her baby back. At that moment Nisha was the embodiment of Shakti—female power.

She scrolled to the browser of her phone, Google-searched "Amit Roy, Ministry of Health and Family Welfare," and clicked the link for the ministry. Once it had loaded, she clicked on the "Contact Us" link. On that page were the e-mail IDs and phone numbers of the senior officials of the ministry.

Roy's name was the first one on that page. It was

followed by an e-mail ID, office phone number, and residential phone number. She copy-pasted the residential phone number into a reverse lookup website and waited impatiently for the result to pop up.

And she had it. New Moti Bagh. She looked at the map on her phone. Sixteen minutes to get there at this time. In the distance she could hear the sound of sirens and she knew that by rights she should remain behind for the ambulance but she couldn't. Time was all that mattered now. She dashed to the bedroom, reached to the back of her bedside table, and found her old .38 police special. She clipped it to her belt as she scrambled outside, back into the Toyota, and a moment later she was pulling out into traffic.

"I'm coming, baby," she said. "I'm coming."

Chapter 72

NISHA DROVE THE car recklessly as she crossed Rao Tula Ram Marg on her way to Moti Bagh. She would have preferred to take the shorter route via Hare Krishna Mehto Marg but roadworks blocked the way. She cursed her luck and followed the longer route.

I'll kill him if he's touched her. So help me.

A cab in front of her refused to yield in spite of her repeated attempts. Nisha switched the headlights on full beam, jammed her hand on the horn, and overtook it, avoiding grazing it with just a couple of millimeters to spare. The man in the car shouted obscenities at her. He tried to chase her but was unable to keep up.

She wondered whether she should call Jack or Neel but decided against it. Santosh's death was a body blow to everyone. She was on her own.

Like a tigress protecting her cub.

Chapter 73

JACK LOOKED AT the corpse.

It was Santosh.

He couldn't believe what he was seeing. Santosh's knees were slightly lifted off the ground and his arms were bent at the elbows. He had obviously been attempting to adopt the fetal position in order to fight the bitter cold as he died.

Beside him, Neel was staring at his dead boss, a vacant expression on his face.

"Hey, bud, you okay?" said Jack, and put his hand to the other man's upper arm.

It was as though the contact spurred Neel into action. "Help me," he said.

"Help you what?"

"Get the body out. Please, quick—time is of the essence."

They maneuvered the corpse onto a gurney and in the next instant were wheeling it out of the morgue.

"What are we doing, Neel?" Jack asked as they went at full speed to the elevator.

"Follow my lead," said Neel. "I'll explain when we get there."

They loaded the trolley into the elevator and Neel pressed for the fifth floor—the Intensive Care Unit. When the doors opened they were greeted by a doctor about to step into the elevator.

"What's going on?" he demanded, eyes flitting from the two men to the corpse on the gurney. "Where do you think you're going with this body?"

"He's not dead," said Neel.

"He looks dead to me."

"He's not. His arms are slightly bent at the elbows," urged Neel. "Just try straightening his arms."

The doctor looked from Neel to Santosh, took hold of a hand, and tried to straighten the arm. It bounced back a few inches.

"You see?" said Neel. "Dead muscles cannot contract. He has severe hypothermia but he's not dead."

The doctor was nodding his agreement. "Okay, right, we need to take him to an ordinary room," he said. "Intensive Care is kept freezing cold to prevent infections. We need to crank up the temperature of the room.

"Nurse!" he called. "Let's put him in 1016 and get me an electric blanket. We'll need heat packs for his abdomen and groin." They wheeled Santosh toward the designated room. Neel and Jack followed, disregarding the rules that prevented visitors—no way in hell they were going to leave Santosh now.

"What the fuck's going on, Neel?" whispered Jack. "Santosh has no pulse."

"He's gone into forced hibernation," explained Neel. The doors of the treatment room swished shut behind them. "There was limited oxygen inside the refrigeration unit. The combination of freezing temperatures and low oxygen resulted in suspended animation—a sudden halting of chemical reactions."

They watched, feeling suddenly useless as nurses covered Santosh, cranked up the central heating of the room, and slipped an oxygen mask over his face. Hot-water bottles were placed under his blanket and heart and blood pressure monitoring equipment was hooked up.

"There are plenty of examples of humans who appeared frozen to death," said Neel, to reassure himself as much as Jack. "They had no heartbeat and were clinically dead but they were successfully revived after spending hours without a pulse in extremely cold conditions."

Chapter 74

AMIT ROY PASSED through the gates of his house, glanced in his rearview, and saw them slide shut behind him. The Audi came to a stop haphazardly on the gravel in front of the house, and for a moment he simply sat there, panting, trying to process the sudden turn of events.

And the feeling—*this* feeling: giddy, dizzy, a great rush of profound internal energy. Having barely recovered from the unexpected euphoria of killing the old woman, he now had the little girl to look forward to, all the while basking in the knowledge that she, his last victim, would be his best; that he would ascend in such superlative circumstances.

His one problem was lack of time. It had been an hour or so since the broadcast. Sharma would no doubt be dispatching his men to execute a high-profile arrest, complete with news footage as he was led in cuffs to the squad car. His gates would keep the press at bay for the time being, but they wouldn't deter cops with a warrant.

Meantime he emerged from his reverie with the realization that his phone was still ringing. Had it ever stopped? Looking at the screen: no. There were twenty-five missed calls. God knew how many text messages.

"*Well, fuck you!*" he cried, then stepped into the chill night and slammed his phone to the gravel, stamping on it again and again. "*Fuck you!*" he screamed at the sky, grinding the phone under his shoe, alive with the thrill of his emancipation. "*Fuck you, all of you, every single one of you!*" he bellowed, his voice cracking with the effort.

And then he went to open the trunk.

Inside cowered Maya Gandhe. Having killed the interfering childminder, he had grabbed the girl and carried her kicking and screaming out to his car, thrown her in the trunk, not caring if the Gandhes' neighbors saw what was happening. It hardly mattered now, and though she'd mewled and thumped at the trunk lid all the way home, as with his cell phone he'd simply tuned out the noise.

Now she screamed again, in shock and fear, this time at the deranged apparition looming over her, this terrifying man who responded to her cries not with reassurance or even anger, but by joining her, so that for a moment they both yelled into the night until the sheer strangeness of the situation tipped her over into silence.

Now he reached in and yanked her bodily from the

trunk, a demented strength to him as he manhandled her into the house, leaving the Audi on the gravel drive, its engine still running.

In the kitchen he bundled her to the floor and she screamed with new fear and pain as he reached into a kitchen drawer for a knife and a roll of tape. From his inside jacket pocket he took her essay.

"You're going to read to me now," he said, red-faced and gasping for breath. "You're going to read to me, do you hear?"

And despite everything, some fast-receding chink of light in Maya hoped this was all he wanted: just for her to read.

But now he was backing her into the front room. His eyes were wide and foam flecked his mouth. Indicating a chair with the knife, he made her sit and then began to tape her to it.

"Please, please, don't hurt me," she pleaded. "Please, please let me go back home now."

"No—no, I can't do that," he told her, spraying her with saliva. "You're staying here with me; we're both going up together. We'll ascend together in union, don't you see?"

"Please, please—I'll read my essay."

"*Fuck the essay!*" he roared, and screwed it up and cast it to the floor. The light inside of Maya died.

Now the monster stood. The low light in the room skimmed along the blade he held. He shrugged off his suit jacket and with his other hand reached to his belt buckle.

"Together," he was saying. "Together."

And then from behind him came a movement.

Maya saw it. "Mama," she called, but it wasn't Nisha. And as Roy swiveled to see what was happening, the sight of the new arrival did nothing to reduce Maya's terror. It was a man dressed all in black. Face covered by a balaclava. He carried something that Maya thought at first was another knife but then realized was a syringe. And he stepped forward and plunged it into Roy's neck.

The Principal Secretary's trousers fell to his ankles as he raised a hand to the side of his neck and then dropped to his knees.

The man in the balaclava stepped smartly away to allow Roy's body to fold to the floor, before turning his gaze on Maya.

Maya was paralyzed with fear. "Please don't hurt me," she whimpered.

"No, no," said the man, his tone gentle. He reached down and placed the syringe on the floor, held up his hands to show he was no longer armed. "I won't hurt you, I promise. Is this...?" He reached for her essay, the screwed-up bits of paper belonging to another life now. "Is this yours?"

She nodded furiously.

He looked at the title page. " 'Health Care, Fair and Square?' " he read. She couldn't be sure, but she thought he was putting on some kind of voice, as though he needed to clear his throat. "You wrote this?"

Again she nodded.

"There is hope, then," he said. "A hope that lies with the young. Do you mind if I take it?"

She shook her head.

"Thank you." He pushed the essay into his back pocket. "I look forward to reading it. I have a feeling I will like it. Now, I'm afraid I'm going to have to move you to another room in order that you don't witness any more unpleasantness. I will let you go afterward, I promise. Trust me."

Chapter 75

LYING ON HIS front, Roy regained consciousness. The first thing he saw when he raised his head was that the girl was gone. Her seat was empty. Bits of severed tape were curled on the floor. He registered that his shirt had been taken and his trousers were around his ankles. At the same time he tried to raise himself from the floor then realized his hands were somehow pinned to the boards, outstretched on either side of him.

And then he saw the nails. Driven through both hands, deep into the wood. Blood ran from the backs of his hands and dripped to the floor. And almost as though it had been lying in wait ready to get him, the pain pounced and tore through his body, making him scream through bared teeth.

"Oh God," he whimpered when the pain had died down. "Kumar, Patel, and now me. You've come for me."

"Very astute of you. Yes, I have. I have come for you. You are my next, but by no means my last."

"But why?"

"Really? You have to ask?"

"Kumar and Patel were in it up to their elbows, noses in the trough. But not me."

The pain in his hands was white hot and searing, and yet he had the feeling it was merely an aperitif.

"How? Tell me how Kumar and Patel were corrupt?"

"You know!" screeched Roy. "You already know! Isn't that why you killed them?"

"Tell me anyway."

"Because Kumar helped fund Surgiquip and awarded them contracts in return for a backhander. He and Patel were in it together. Like I say, noses in the trough."

"And ResQ?"

"ResQ and Surgiquip are in bed together. But it's *them*, not me. I had nothing to do with it."

The intruder crouched. He placed something on the floor that when Roy twisted his head to look he saw was a field roll. Nimble fingers untied and spread open the fabric. Scalpels glittered beneath. Roy whimpered.

"You had nothing to do with what?" asked the man in black.

"You know."

"Say it."

"I'm in too much pain. I can't think straight."

"Say it."

"Will you let me go if—"

"*Say it.*" The man in black placed the heel of his palm

to where the nail pierced Roy's right hand and applied pressure. The searing pain intensified.

"All right, all right, I'll say it! Organ harvesting. Illegal transplants. Whatever you want to call it. Patients having their organs removed then sold on. You know that. You know that. But I promise you, I had nothing to do with it."

"You had nothing to do with it, yet you knew it went on. You did nothing to stop it."

"Nothing *yet!*" squealed Roy. "I was biding my time. Change can only come from within."

The man in black chuckled drily. "I can't believe you're honestly telling me you would have tried to change things."

"I could have. I would have. Let me go and I'll prove it. We'll join forces."

"Oh yes? Just as soon as you do something about this pesky child-abuse allegation, eh? I don't think so. If not for that then for two other reasons: one, because they are greater in number and way, way more powerful than you could ever hope to be. And two—and given what I've just walked into, I think this is probably the most important—because you are a deviant more interested in serving the perverted pleasures of your own flesh than helping the city you are appointed to serve. Each man on my list deserves to die, Amit Roy, but none of them deserves to die more than you."

Roy's eyes were wide as a gloved hand reached to select a long-handled scalpel. The hand was out of sight and he heard the cutting before he felt the pain, the scalpel piercing the flesh of his back as the man in black diligently began to peel the skin away, exposing the scarlet, fatty tissue beneath.

The pain exploded in stars in front of his eyes. Pain so fierce and intense it was all-consuming, so white and blinding it was almost perfect. Then, as the man in black went to work on his upper thighs and Roy understood that his death—from blood loss, or bodily trauma, or whatever else his attacker had in store for him—was just moments away, he accepted that this celestial pain was in fact his ascendancy in action.

And so, as the man in black pulled off his balaclava so that Roy might recognize the face of his killer, he embraced his death and went to it willingly, knowing that ultimately, and agonizing though it was, the pain of his death was preferable to the pain of his life.

Chapter 76

BLACK WROUGHT-IRON GATES at the entrance to Roy's home brought Nisha to a skidding halt, and she scrambled out of the Toyota, looking for another way in.

Nothing. Just a keycode panel, intercom. Sensor.

Fuck it. She dived back into the Toyota and reversed twenty yards or so, offering up a silent apology to Neel as she revved the vehicle, making herself low in the driving seat, before jamming her boot on the accelerator.

The Toyota shot forward and hit the gate. The hood crumpled; the airbags deployed. She looked up from her low position in the driving seat, pawing the airbag out of her way to see that the gates were a twisted mess— not exactly open but wide enough apart for her to get through.

She squeezed through and ran along the approach road toward his driveway. Tasteful lights glowing from within the borders lit the way. On his drive she saw Roy's car, engine running, doors open. Now the gun was in her hand as she hit the front door, found it open, dropped to one knee, and held the .38 two-handed.

"Roy, you in there?" she called. "Maya?"

To her left was the kitchen. Through that Nisha had sight of what looked like a front room and in there was a body.

A body and an awful lot of blood.

But an adult body.

Slowly she rose, keeping her center of gravity low and staying balanced as she took two quick but careful steps into the entrance hall. The gun barrel moved with the quick darting of her head as she covered her angles and checked blindspots.

"Maya!" she called, hearing the desperation in her own voice.

There came a noise. From her right.

"Mama, it's me"—and Maya appeared from a side room, a tiny, shaking, frightened thing, but alive and unharmed.

"Oh my God, baby, are you all right?" Nisha rushed for her and gathered her up, tears of relief streaming down her cheeks.

"Yes, Mama, I'm all right. The good man came and saved me from the bad man."

Instantly Nisha was alert again, gun up. "What good man? Where?"

"He's in there." Pointing back toward the room she'd just left.

"Stay there, honey, stay there," said Nisha then hit the door, rolling into a study and coming up once again with the .38 in two hands. The window was open and in the distance she could see a man in black running back down along the drive toward the gates.

In a second she was out of the door, down the entrance hall, and out of the front door, scrunching on the gravel, finding the fleeing man in her sights as she took a wide-legged, two-handed stance and shouted, *"Freeze! You in the black! Freeze or I'm putting you down!"*

From behind, Maya screeched, "No, Mama, don't hurt him!" and Nisha found herself with a split-second decision to make as the running man veered off the approach road and into the undergrowth: should she fire on the man who'd saved her daughter? Hurt him? Risk killing him, even?

Or let him go?

"Freeze!" she shouted again, uselessly. The moment was gone.

She had let the killer go.

Nisha lowered her gun, trying to tell herself the only thing that mattered was Maya, trying to convince herself that she hadn't just allowed a serial killer to escape.

Chapter 77

THE NURSES ASSURED Jack and Neel that it would take up to twenty-four hours before they would know whether Santosh would pull through.

Together, the two Private men left the treatment room, trudged out into a waiting area, and took a seat, reluctant to leave just yet: the quintessential American, complete with stubble and polo shirt open at the neck; the sharp-dressed young Indian man—side by side, each lost in his own thoughts.

Not for the first time Jack asked after Nisha. Where had she got to?

Neel shrugged. "Perhaps she's still looking for us in the morgue."

At the same time his eyes traveled to a TV mounted on the opposite wall. The news was showing. Live coverage of the sensational Roy revelations. In the foreground a journalist with a microphone delivered her report, evidently live from Roy's home. As they watched, the reporter turned to indicate what looked like a scene of devastation behind.

"Oh my God," said Neel. "That's my car."

Chapter 78

YAMUNA PUSHTA WAS the embankment on both sides of the Yamuna river, stretching from the ITO Bridge up to the Salimgarh Fort. It was home to a string of slum colonies and clusters of shanties.

Iqbal Ibrahim, aka Dr. O. S. Rangoon, did not bother to get out of the van. All his meetings happened inside. It was his office. Instead, one of Ibrahim's henchmen walked into the largest hut and informed the slumlord that his boss had arrived.

The slumlord was a shifty-eyed man with a permanent trickle of betel-nut juice at the corner of his mouth. He was master of all the expanse of tin roofs and blue tarpaulins that dotted the Yamuna banks and he ruled his kingdom with an iron fist. Rent had to be paid on the first of each month, failing which a dweller's meager possessions would be confiscated. If rent remained unpaid after a week, the occupant would be thrown out along with his family. Desperate families would cry piteously as they were thrown out, ready to do almost anything in order to be allowed to stay.

The slumlord quickly gathered his papers and entered Ibrahim's van. "Al-salaam alaykum," he said, sitting down on one of the visitors' chairs offered by Ibrahim, who was wearing a new green skullcap.

"Wa-alaykum al-salaam," replied Ibrahim. "So, who are your tenants who haven't paid their rent on time?"

"There are always a few," replied the slumlord.

"Inshallah, we can clear up your dues efficiently," said Ibrahim, winking.

At a safe distance, the man who had kept Ibrahim under surveillance for several weeks continued to make notes. It was becoming evident to him that Ibrahim was a resource worth recruiting.

The slumlord laughed, his betel-nut spittle splattering Ibrahim's desk. "What is the exchange rate for a kidney these days?" he asked.

"Two livers," replied Ibrahim matter-of-factly. "Or three hearts, or four hundred liters of blood. What do you have to offer?"

"I'll show you, shall I?" grinned the slumlord.

He made a call. Five minutes later two of his men appeared, carrying a younger man slumped between them.

Chapter 79

THE YOUNG MAN recovered consciousness from the blow that had knocked him out and realized he was lying on the bed that was part of Ibrahim's mobile hospital. He had been arguing with the slumlord when one of the thugs surrounding him had delivered a knock to the back of his head. He had lost consciousness and crumpled to the floor. Now in front of him stood a stranger dressed in scrubs, surgical mask, and gloves.

"What have you done to me?" he whimpered.

"Nothing yet," replied the masked doctor. "We just took some blood and ran a test to check your blood type. I have good news. You're a match."

"What does that mean?" asked the man.

"It means that we can now operate on you," said Ibrahim, emerging from behind his desk, "remove one of your healthy kidneys, settle what you owe to your landlord, and, inshallah, still leave you with a tidy pile of cash—fifty thousand rupees—for the future."

Fifty thousand rupees. This to a poor man who toiled at a construction site. Work had dried up owing to bad weather and he could no longer pay rent for the mud-and-tin shack he occupied along with his wife and three children.

Fifty thousand rupees.

"Will I live?" he asked.

"Sure," replied the doctor. "I'll give you a shot to knock you out. When you wake up it'll all be over. Just remember that if you tell anyone what happened to you, we'll find you and we'll kill you. Is that clear?"

The patient swallowed, eyes swiveling in fear.

"Stop worrying," insisted the surgeon. "I've done this many times. If anyone does an MRI later, they will find that the surgery has been done professionally and that the kidney has been removed with precision."

The surgeon didn't bother to reveal that all his surgeries had been carried out without a medical license. He had flunked his final year at med school and was only qualified to perform autopsies. He worked part-time for Ibrahim and spent the rest of his time disposing of corpses at Delhi Memorial Hospital.

The patient nodded. He looked at the bodyguard who was standing at the door of the van. If he tried to get up and run, he knew he would be shot. He had never seen fifty thousand rupees in his entire life. One kidney was a small price to pay for a large sum.

Ibrahim could see the cogs turning inside the man's

head. He knew that the seven hundred and fifty dollars he paid the man would be recovered twenty times over by the time he sold it off. This chap's kidney was of a rare blood type, and there was a specific patient on the United Network for Organ Sharing database who had been told he would have to wait eight years for a matching kidney owing to his rare blood type. He would pay a handsome price to get it from Ibrahim.

"Will it hurt, sir?" asked the patient.

"Not during surgery," replied the surgeon. "You'll be knocked out. But when you regain consciousness, you will have pain in your lower abdomen. That will take some time to go but we will give you painkillers to manage it. We will also transfer you to a guesthouse on the outskirts of Delhi so that you can stay there for a few days in order to recover."

Chapter 80

"I WANT TO see my daughter now, please," said Nisha, steel in her voice. "You've had more than enough time to interview her."

Two hours, to be precise. Sharma's assistant, Nanda, had spent the time reviewing events with Nisha, increasingly frustrated at what he claimed was her lack of cooperation. The truth was, she was hiding nothing. But that didn't stop the insinuations, the suspicions.

"*Now*," she said, slamming a fist to the interview-room table. "I want to see her now."

Nanda stared at her awhile, just to show her who was boss, that he wouldn't be ordered around by her. Then with a nod to the duty officer he let himself out of the interview suite and Nisha settled down to wait.

After twenty minutes or so—a decent enough show-her-who's-boss interval—the door opened once more, this time to admit Maya, followed by Sharma.

The interview-suite chair scraped as Nisha stood and rushed around the table, kneeling to take Maya in her arms. "Sweetie, I'm sorry. There was nothing I could do about that. Were they nice? Were they nice to you?"

"The lady looking after me was nice," said Maya, then shot a baleful look at Sharma.

"I was doing my job, Mrs. Gandhe," said Sharma. "Take a seat, would you? My colleague Nanda told me you've been about as much use as she has: 'He wore a mask. He was disguising his voice.' "

"Then what else do you expect? What else can we tell you?"

They were all sitting now, Sharma huge on the opposite side of the table, filling the room with the stink of smoke, sweating with agitation and last night's whisky. "What I want to know is why when Mommy was pointing her gun at the bad man she didn't pull the trigger."

"He wasn't a bad man," blurted Maya suddenly. "He was a good man."

Sharma's eyebrows shot up. "A good man, eh? Do you want to know what he did to Mr. Kumar, or Mr. Patel, or Mr. Roy? Shall I tell you?"

"Commissioner!" warned Nisha, beginning to rise from her seat.

"Sit down," warned Sharma.

"He was about to hurt me," said Maya. Her eyes shone with tears and her voice shook. "He was about to do really, really horrible things to me. I know the kind of things. Things you hear about on the news when children go missing and their bodies are found. Things like that. And the man in black stopped him, and I don't care if he killed him because it serves the bad man right. It serves him right for what he was going to do to me and what he's done to other children."

Sharma sat back. His eyes were hooded. To Nisha he said, "Quite a chip off the old block, isn't she?"

"She's been through a lot."

"Is that why you didn't take him down? You think he's a good man, do you?"

Nisha leaned forward. "Listen. I used to be a cop, just the same as you. And like you I don't discriminate. A killer is a killer."

"Even if he's a hit man with a heart of gold?"

"That's what you think this guy is, do you?"

"What about you? What do you think?"

She sighed and threw up her hands. "Oh, come on! This is getting us nowhere, Commissioner. We've told you everything we know. If you don't plan to charge us with anything, then I'll thank you to let us go. My daughter has been through a terrible ordeal."

"Charge you? What did you think I might charge you with?"

"I don't know. You can think of something. Criminal damage on Roy's gates..."

Sharma nodded. "Yes. Maybe that. Or maybe aiding and abetting."

She rolled her eyes. "Oh, for God's sake, Commissioner. You're reaching. This is ridiculous."

Now it was his turn to sit forward. "Who's employing Private, Mrs. Gandhe? It wouldn't be Mohan Jaswal, by any chance, would it? You know full well that I report to Ram Chopra and that Ram Chopra and Mohan Jaswal aren't exactly the best of pals."

"Where are you going with this?"

"I'd watch yourselves if I were you. That's all it is. You tell that to your friends at Private. You tell them that I think you, Mrs. Gandhe, deliberately allowed a serial killer to escape. You tell them that the next victim's blood is on your hands."

Moments later, Nisha and Maya emerged into reception, where Jack and Neel were waiting.

"Santosh?" she said.

Jack grimaced, looking tired. "Well, first we hoped he was alive, and then we thought he was dead, and then we hoped he might come alive again, and now we're not sure. I think that's about the size of it."

Nisha put her hands over Maya's ears. "For fuck's sake, is he alive or is he dead?"

"What Jack's saying is right," Neel assured her. "The prognosis is good. We're hopeful he'll make it."

"Thank God," she said, then shot an apologetic look at them both, particularly Neel. "I'm sorry about your car," she said.

"Don't worry about the car, we'll cover the car," said Jack. "Also, Nisha, I'll put you and Maya up in the

Oberoi until you feel comfortable moving back into your own home and..." he held out his hands, "there's no rush, no rush at all. You take your time."

Privately, Nisha wondered if she and Maya would ever be able to move back into the apartment.

"In the meantime, I think we have another theory to work on," she said.

"Let's hear it," said Jack.

Nisha glanced back to where the desk sergeant sat behind glass, engrossed on the phone. "I don't think this is some kind of organized-crime war we're talking about. I don't think our guy is a hit man; I think he's a vigilante."

PART THREE

MARTYR

Chapter 81

DEATH IS THE great equalizer. The Deliverer had seen hundreds of corpses being cremated at the burning ghats as he grew up in Varanasi. From ashes to ashes, from dust to dust. It didn't matter if you were rich or poor, king or beggar, saint or sinner. The River Ganges could wash away your sins, and if you were cremated by its banks, you could also be guaranteed salvation if your ashes were immersed in the river. Instant *moksha*.

After he had killed the priest, the Deliverer had run to the Ganges to bathe and wash off his sins. He had taken up the worst job—that of a "Dom." Cremations occurred at the burning ghats throughout the day and night. After the cremation, the leftovers would be immersed into the river by the chief mourner, usually the son of the deceased. The bones did not burn completely, so the Doms were responsible for collecting the remaining bone fragments and immersing them in the river. It was a sickening and filthy job. The smell of death had seemed to permanently attach itself to his skin, no matter how many times he took a dip.

One day a young army captain had arrived at the burning ghats in order to cremate his father. He'd noticed the boy scavenging for bones when the cremation was over. The captain's heart had gone out to the boy doing that despicable job. He'd pulled him aside and asked him his name.

"Deliverer," the boy had replied.

"Well, Deliverer, do you go to school or do you simply deliver?" the army man had asked. "What do your parents do?"

"My parents are dead," the boy had replied without any expression. "I work here to earn enough to feed myself."

The army captain had taken the boy to the cantonment school and convinced the reluctant headmaster to accept him. It would be a tough slog with this one. It had taken several days just to get him clean. When food had been placed on his plate in the canteen, he had eaten ravenously like a dog, almost immersing his face in the plate. Not surprisingly, he had been picked on by one of the seniors, a cruel bully.

One day he'd found that his plate had been replaced with a dog bowl. The bully and his friends had been shouting "Woof! Woof!" as the boy looked at the bowl. He had been desperately hungry, so he'd eaten from the bowl, ignoring the howls of laughter from the bully and his friends.

At night, when he'd retired in the dormitory, he had made sure all the boys were asleep before pulling out a small fork—much smaller than an ordinary dining fork—from under his mattress. It had been presented to him by a wandering sadhu who'd been happy with the respect the boy had shown toward him.

The sadhu had explained to him all the intricacies of different types of poisons and the different ways by which human life could be expended—stabbing, decapitating, shooting, strangling, drowning, poisoning, and burning. The knowledge had been delivered with a disclaimer, though: that human life was a gift and should never be taken unjustly.

The fork that the sadhu had given him was no ordinary fork. A vegetable extract known as *Abrus precatorius* was mixed with powdered glass, opium, datura, onion, and alcohol to create a thick paste. Sharp spikes were then fashioned out of this paste by drying them in the sun. Once hardened, two spikes measuring less than two centimeters each would be mounted on a wooden handle to create the fork. The distance between the two mounted needles was carefully calibrated to resemble the fangs of a viper.

The Deliverer had crept up to the bully's bed and plunged the fork into his thigh. The bully had screamed in agony but the lights of the dormitory had been off. The Deliverer had retrieved the fork and crawled back to his bed, pretending to be asleep. By the time the lights had been switched on a few minutes later, the bully had been writhing in agony.

He had been quickly transferred to the Army Hospital and was declared dead from snake bite—a common occurrence in Varanasi—six hours later.

The Indian Machiavelli, Chanakya, had said in 300 B.C.E., "Even if a snake is not venomous, it should pretend to be so."

The Deliverer had stopped pretending. He knew he was venomous.

Chapter 82

SANTOSH LAY PROPPED up on his hospital bed, with Jack, Nisha, and Neel at his bedside. A nurse popped in to check his blood pressure and temperature then left. It had taken almost an entire day for him to emerge from his near-dead state.

"You really need to stop landing up in hospital," joked Jack, going on to tell Santosh of the timely intervention that had stopped him from dying.

"How did you know your approach would work?" Santosh asked Neel.

"There is significant research on this subject," replied Neel. "A case in point is the ordinary garden worm. Research shows that ninety-nine percent of garden worms die within twenty-four hours of exposure to temperatures just above freezing point. But if they are first deprived of oxygen, their survival rate is almost ninety-seven percent. Upon rewarming and reintroduction of oxygen, the worms reanimate and show normal life spans."

Santosh thanked him with a nod. "And now we find ourselves in the lion's den," he said.

He looked at Nisha. After just two days off looking after Maya she'd insisted on returning to work—ignoring Jack and Neel, who'd urged her to spend more time with Maya—and she looked exhausted.

"How is Maya?" asked Santosh.

"She's being looked after at the Oberoi," said Nisha, flashing a tired but grateful smile at Jack.

"Little Miss Gandhe could charm the birds out of the trees," laughed Jack. "She already has the entire staff wrapped around her little finger."

"I can't imagine what she's been through," said Santosh.

Nisha dropped her eyes. A sympathetic, respectful silence fell across the room. "She needs me at night but otherwise she doesn't want to talk about it. She's repressing it. Outwardly she seems fine. Like Jack says, she gives the appearance of having the time of her life, and yet she witnessed Heena's murder. She was tied up—on the point of being assaulted by Roy. I can't even begin to comprehend what that might do to a little girl."

"Children are very resilient," said Santosh. "More so than adults."

"I hope so," said Nisha quietly.

"And now you're in the position of having had contact with the killer," said Santosh.

"I saw him briefly on the drive. He was running away."

"But you've formed the opinion that he's a vigilante?"

"Yes. We've been assuming that it's some kind of organized crime war going on. But what if we were talking about a personal vendetta? What if this were the family of one of the victims? What he said to Maya suggests someone driven by a desire to do . . ."

"Good?" said Santosh.

"In his mind at least, yes."

"Saving Maya was a humane act, but even hit men have a moral code," said Jack.

"It's not just that. It's his interest in the essay, not to mention his MO."

"You said yourself, the gruesome murders could be a warning," Santosh reminded her.

Jack cut in. "I gotta say, I'm warming to Nisha's theory. The *Godfather* movies get it right: when organized crime cleans house they do it in one fell swoop. *Boom, boom, boom.* Not one at a time like this, giving the enemy time to regroup and prepare. You said yourself, Santosh, that Thakkar's increased his security."

"So have Jaswal and Chopra," said Neel. "Whatever our killer's motives, he has the great and the good of Delhi in a spin."

"It couldn't happen to a nicer bunch," said Nisha tartly, earning a penetrating look from Santosh.

"There are armed guards in this very hospital, too," noted Jack. "No doubt here to look after Dr. Arora. They've all got them. Nisha's right, Santosh, this is a rogue agent we're dealing with here."

"Then the motive is revenge, and we must work out who is the killer's next victim," said Santosh.

"In the meantime, I'm not comfortable leaving you here," said Jack. "It seems we're investigating on two fronts now: a vengeful serial killer and an organ-harvesting operation—and they're as defensive as each other. Someone tipped off Ibrahim about you. What's to stop them having another go?"

"I'll be on my guard, Jack," said Santosh. "But for the time being here is where I want to be. What are your plans?"

Jack pushed his hands into his jeans pockets and stood thinking for a moment, chewing his lip. "I think it's about time I had a word with our friend Mohan Jaswal."

The Private team went to leave but Santosh called Nisha back. She hung by the door, unwilling to meet his eye.

"It's not just Maya who went through an ordeal the other day, is it?" said Santosh, pulling himself up in bed a little.

"You almost lost your life."

"That's not what I mean, and I think you know it."

"She's alive and unharmed, that's the important thing. If only I could say the same for Heena."

"For Maya things could have been much worse."

Anger flashed across her face. "You don't say."

But Santosh plowed on. "Things could have been worse if not for the intervention of the killer. I can't be the only one who feels that if this killer is targeting the men behind an organ-harvesting scheme, and if he's killing the likes of Amit Roy, then maybe he's doing the world a favor."

And now she was rolling her eyes. "Oh God, not you as well. I got this from Sharma. He went as far as to insinuate that the killer and I were in league together."

"You're an excellent shot, Nisha."

"It was dark. What if I'd killed him? What if I'd killed him and he turned out not to be the killer but a burglar who was in the wrong place at the wrong time?"

"We have to stop him, Nisha. The fact that he saved Maya cannot have a bearing on that."

"I know," she said tightly. "Can I go now, please, and get on with the business of trying to catch him?"

"Just as long as you are," he said.

And now she rounded on him. "You're sounding fairly sanctimonious for someone who sat on evidence! We knew Arora had links to the bodies at Greater Kailash and we haven't done a thing about it. For all your talk about cutting off the head of the snake, we've done precious little cutting of any description, and in the meantime more people have died, and my little girl..."

For Nisha that was as much as she could take. Choking on her words, she wheeled, snatched open the treatment-room door and stormed out, leaving Santosh alone.

"I'm sorry," he told the empty room, judged by the silence.

Chapter 83

JASWAL SAT IN his usual place in the Delhi Legislative Assembly, attempting to stay calm. The doors were covered by armed guards, strong and impassive, silent sentinels amid the ruckus. The opposition seemed to have ganged up to accuse the government of every conceivable crime. Jaswal consoled himself by stroking his beard.

The leader of the opposition, a balding, chubby man in his sixties, was attempting to have his voice heard over the din. "This government has lost the moral authority to rule. Multiple corpses of patients were discovered inside a house at Greater Kailash. We have been kept in the dark regarding who these victims were. Three key people associated with the health sector— the Health Minister, a health care tycoon, and the Health Secretary—have died in mysterious circumstances.

We're being told that Kumar committed suicide when, as anybody knows, he was murdered, just as Patel and Roy have been murdered. It is evident that there is a deeper conspiracy that the government is attempting to hush up." He brandished a poster satirizing the recent murders, adding, "You see this? Even rabble-rousers on the streets know our system is corrupt. We demand that the Chief Minister must resign."

Almost all seventy members of the house were on their feet, shouting at each other. The helpless speaker of the house kept urging the honorable members to sit down in order to restore order but nobody was interested in listening. Jaswal was probably the only person who remained seated and utterly quiet. He looked positively haggard.

Chapter 84

THE LOTUS TEMPLE was a Baha'i House of Worship and an architectural symbol as striking as the Sydney Opera House. Inspired by the lotus flower, the temple was composed of twenty-seven free-standing marble-clad "petals" arranged in clusters of three to form nine sides. The nine doors to the temple led into a vast central hall more than forty meters tall and capable of holding up to two and a half thousand people.

In a corner of the massive hall sat an odd couple: TV reporter Ajoy Guha and the police chief, Sharma. A fine pair they made: the overweight, perspiring Sharma; the tall, bespectacled Guha. The meeting had been initiated by Sharma but Guha had been happy to oblige.

"So, what did you want to see me about?" he asked Sharma, regarding the cop through his wire-framed glasses.

"For a start I thought you might want to thank me for giving you the lowdown on Roy. That little scoop sparked off the most dramatic thing to happen in Delhi for years. You must be very pleased."

Guha preened a little. "Well, if the cat wasn't already among the pigeons it certainly is now. It's a good time to be a newsman in the city, watching its high rollers run around like headless chickens. I suspect the security companies are pleased too."

Sharma chuckled. "The whole city is awash with conspiracy theories, bloodlust, tales of corruption, lies, and more damned lies, and it's only getting more and more fervent. The other day I saw a bit of graffiti that said, 'Are they telling us the truth?' Today I saw graffiti that said, 'You are being lied to.' " He smirked, evidently enjoying himself.

"In such circumstances revolutions are born," said Guha.

"It won't go that far. You know why? Because the likes of you and me won't let it. The current system favors you just as much as it does me. I think we'll give the city a shake-up and see who comes tumbling out of the bag afterward. No doubt there will be changes, but all for the better, I'm sure of it."

"In other words, changes that favor your boss, Ram Chopra."

"You're wrinkling your nose at the smell of dirty tricks, are you? Let me tell you, Jaswal is not above employing them himself. Rumor has it that he's hired himself a detective agency, the Private agency, no less, to do his dirty work for him. Anyway, what does it matter to you? A scoop is a scoop."

Guha frowned. "You might be right."

"And now I've got another one for you," said Sharma. He handed over a small package.

"What's inside?" asked Guha.

"Details of preliminary investigations into how illegal organ removals are being carried out at the behest of a company called ResQ," replied Sharma.

"Aha, now I see," said Guha. "Head of ResQ is Jai Thakkar, who just happens to be good buddies with Jaswal, your boss's mortal enemy?"

Sharma shrugged. "I say again, does it matter? Any man involved in organ harvesting is a man who needs to be stopped."

Guha stood. "I'll see what I can do."

"Oh, and Guha?" Sharma stared up at the journalist. "I'm continuing my investigations, so watch this space."

Chapter 85

THE TWO MEN sat at a table of the upmarket Cafe E, in the opulent surroundings of the DLF Emporio Mall, Delhi's best luxury mall.

The well-dressed Thakkar sipped mineral water with a calm, meditative air that belied how he really felt, which, if he was honest, was a touch on the nervy side. Added to the recent spate of murders—among them his business associate Samir Patel—was the distinct sense that things were coming apart at the seams. It was an impression not helped by the somewhat harassed and bedraggled appearance of Arora, who sat opposite, an untouched coffee in front of him.

On tables at either side were their security details, four men in total, two for each man. They wore sharp suits tailored to disguise a bulge at the armpit, and dark Ray-Bans to hide eyes that constantly scanned the area around them, ever alert for danger. Cafe E occupied the entire ground floor of the mall, giving them unrestricted sight, which was just how they liked it.

Thakkar set down his glass. "We have over a hundred patients from the United States lined up to visit Delhi next month," he said. "As of now you have arranged organs for less than fifty percent of them."

Arora swallowed. "Why does everything become a crisis with you? You have now started bypassing me and have been directly in touch with Ibrahim. I'm the one who set him up. I even provided him with the van. And now you bypass me and go to him?"

"I wouldn't need to directly contact Ibrahim if you delivered on your commitments," replied Thakkar.

"But this is getting dangerous," argued Arora. "You know what happened at Greater Kailash."

"Was that Ibrahim's fault?"

"Of course it was. And now he's going after poor residents of the slums at Yamuna Pushta. Such an aggressive strategy is a recipe for disaster."

"What's the harm in that?" asked Thakkar.

"He and that hack he calls a surgeon do not have the required medical capabilities," hissed Arora. "Surgeries are being performed in his fucking van! We will all get into trouble...He's using guys who don't even have a medical license. If this were ever to get out—"

Before Arora could finish the sentence, Thakkar's cell phone rang. He took the call. "Hello," he said, "who's this?"—already regretting instinctively answering his phone when he didn't recognize the number.

"Mr. Thakkar? Is that Mr. Thakkar?"

And now Thakkar regretted answering the phone even more bitterly, because though he didn't outright recognize the voice, there was something about it that pointed to the drawer marked "irritant," "troublemaker," "enemy."

"Who is this?" he repeated cautiously.

"Why, this would be Ajoy Guha of DETV. You were recently a guest on my program, *Carrot and Stick*."

"Yes, I remember. I remember it being a most unpleasant experience."

"Well, I must apologize for that. It is not our aim to make our guests feel uncomfortable. Perhaps you would like to make another appearance, a return visit, so to speak? There is a most important issue I would be very keen to discuss."

Thakkar felt his insides clench. First Arora's doom-mongering. Now this. He had a sudden flash of insight: he should have got out while the going was good. He had taken things too far. He hardly dared ask his next question. "What *issue* are you keen to discuss?"

Now Guha's voice took on a different tone, as if—yes, of course—the bastard would be recording it. "Mr. Thakkar, I have information that you are illegally trading organs. Would you like to confirm or deny the allegation?"

Oh God, oh God, oh God. This was what it felt like when your world came crashing down.

"Of course I deny it," hissed Thakkar, "of course I fucking deny it."

But as if Guha's call wasn't bad enough, Thakkar now

saw another situation develop. Opposite him Dr. Arora's
eyes had risen from the tabletop and gone to something
happening at the far end of the mall. Thakkar turned to
see a squad of four armed police enter, and his mouth
dropped open. Guha forgotten about, he ended the call,
watching as the squad led by the chief, Sharma, made
their way across the mall toward the cafe.

As one, the security guards rose to their feet, their
seats skidding back on the marble flooring as they
reached inside their jackets. At the same time two of the
armed policemen brought assault rifles to their shoulders and the other two moved smartly to one side as
though to outflank the security detail. Sharma's voice
boomed: "Draw your weapons and we will open fire,
gentlemen. It's that simple."

To a background of audible gasps from shoppers
as they realized what was happening and took shelter
behind columns lining either side of the atrium, the security men froze mid-draw, looking to their respective
employers for guidance.

Arora gave a nod. *Do as you're told.* Thakkar the same.

"Good lads." By now Sharma was on top of them.
"Thakkar," he boomed, and the ResQ CEO shrank in
his seat, "I have a warrant for your arrest under the
provisions of the Transplantation of Human Organs Act
1994." He turned his attention to Arora. "And who
might you be?"

Thakkar could see the temptation to lie flick across
Arora's face, but evidently he chose to come clean. "Dr.
Arora," he whimpered. "I'm just a doctor."

"*Just* a doctor, are you?" sneered Sharma. "Just a doctor in league with this one, perhaps?"

"No, no, no," protested Arora, giving himself away in the process.

"I see. What's so bad about being in business with Thakkar that you'd deny it so vigorously? Not telling me he's up to no good, are you?"

Locks of greasy hair fell across Arora's forehead as he grew even more agitated, realizing he was digging himself into a hole. "No, no. I don't know anything."

"We'll soon see about that, won't we?" said Sharma. For a moment or so it looked as though he was seriously considering arresting Arora, but then for whatever reason thought better of it. With a wave of his hand he indicated to two of his men, who yanked Thakkar from his chair. A moment after that they were gone, leaving Dr. Arora perspiring, despite the arctic chill of the mall's air conditioning.

Chapter 86

SHARMA LET THAKKAR stew. Of course he did. Despite his fear of the situation, not to mention the temptation to kick himself very hard and repeatedly at pushing his luck over this whole transplant network, Thakkar still felt a wave of contempt for the fat policeman and his ancient, desperately banal methods of intimidation.

The cell was small, hot, and stuffy. He dreaded to think how it felt in summer. He took off his jacket and let the act of neatly folding it shoulder to shoulder calm him, before sitting, smoothing his trousers, then crossing his legs.

Okay, he was in trouble. But he had money. And what was money good for if not for buying yourself out of trouble? What's more, and perhaps even more importantly, he had friends—or at least one very powerful friend—in high places. They weren't going to kill him in prison. They couldn't just keep him here indefinitely. So while there was no doubt he was about to embark on a period of discomfort, it would surely be a relatively short period of discomfort. No, keeping things in perspective, he had nothing overly serious to worry about. At least he was safe from the killer.

Unless the killer turned out to be Sharma. And . . .

No. No, that was just ridiculous.

Now the cell door opened to admit Sharma and his assistant Nanda. The pair of them looked at Thakkar, perched on the edge of the cot, then Sharma indicated for him to rise. A short time later they were installed in chairs in some kind of interrogation room. An interview suite, they called it, but Thakkar wasn't fooled.

"We have a lot of questions to ask you, Thakkar," said Sharma, his customary toothpick wedged between his teeth, "things about your relationship with Jaswal, what you know about the Private detective agency and what they're doing in Delhi, the role played by this Dr. Arora that I met at Cafe E. But first this racket that you and your friends are running. Let's start with that."

"Racket?" said Thakkar disingenuously.

"You've been running a racket that buys or steals organs and makes them available to your American insurance patients," he said. "You may as well come clean. We know your entire modus operandi."

Thakkar remained quiet. He had asked to see his lawyer but Sharma denied him the privilege.

Then, "You have nothing against me," he said defiantly.

"We have accessed your company's bank statements and balance sheet," said Sharma. "You have made hundreds of payments to an unregistered firm. We've done our investigations. That unregistered firm belongs to Iqbal Ibrahim, someone who is notorious for the thriving black market he runs in human organs."

"Then go get him," replied Thakkar. "As CEO of a multinational company, you can't seriously expect me to know every small payment that is made by my managers and staff!"

Sharma ignored the interjection and continued, "At first we were confused. The Indian arm of ResQ buys human organs. American patients are charged insurance premiums that cover this service. The question in my mind was this: how would the Indian operation ever make a profit?"

"So now you're a chartered accountant?" asked Thakkar sarcastically.

"And then we realized that you don't care," continued Sharma, refusing to rise to the jibe. "You have a web of companies and subsidiaries and so long as they make money in the aggregate, individual losses are irrelevant. I think we have an excellent case to prosecute you as well as your company under the Transplantation of Human Organs Act 1994."

Thakkar was quiet.

"In effect, you transfer profits to the American parent while bearing all the organ procurement expenses in India," continued Sharma. "And since the money is a consequence of an illegal act, this is a perfect case for prosecution under the Prevention of Money Laundering Act too."

"You do know that the Chief Minister is my friend?" said Thakkar, his cockiness having disappeared.

"I don't report to fucking Jaswal," snapped Sharma, the toothpick falling out of his mouth. "My boss is Chopra and he hates Jaswal. You also fall into the enemy camp by association. Hell, I'll even get promoted if I make your life miserable. It's only fair given that you fucked and then abandoned the boss's daughter!"

"Bastard!" shouted Thakkar as he stood up.

He received a resounding slap from Sharma. "Sit down unless you are told that you can get up!" commanded Sharma.

Thakkar was stunned. His cheek had turned red from the slap but his other cheek went pink from the embarrassment and shame. He had never been treated this way.

"Now, here's how this can play out," said Sharma. "Either you cooperate with me or I will have to take you out of Tihar Jail."

"I get out of jail for not cooperating?" asked Thakkar, confused.

"You are then taken to a place that is much worse," explained Sharma. "There are a few interrogation rooms at the Red Fort. Usually they are only used by the intelligence agencies when they wish to break terror suspects. The big advantage of using these rooms is that anything goes. I can do whatever I want to make you squeal."

Sweat dripped down Thakkar's face. His throat was parched.

"My men will strip you naked and string you up spreadeagled," whispered Sharma into Thakkar's ear. "Then we will go to work on you with our interrogation tools. You will wish that you were dead by the time we are finished with you."

"Could I get some water please?" whined Thakkar.

"Sure," replied Sharma. "After we're done. So, are you ready to cooperate or not?"

Chapter 87

ARORA HOPPED ABOARD the Blue Line train of the Delhi Metro at Indraprastha station and sat down. He waited for the next stop—Yamuna Bank. Apart from an elderly gentleman who sat reading a newspaper bearing the headline 'WHEN WILL WE HAVE ANSWERS?', he had the carriage to himself.

The doors opened at Yamuna Bank and a familiar face appeared. Ibrahim. A mere nod was exchanged between them before the train took off.

"I had told you to stop. Now Thakkar has been picked up by the cops!" said Arora, the urgency in his voice all too apparent.

Ibrahim looked at him and smiled. "It bothers you that, inshallah, I'm able to get the same stuff at a fraction of the price, right? You're worried that your tidy little business model is getting disrupted by me. You were happy to use me as a conduit to Thakkar in the early days, only to cut me off when it suited you. You were happy to use me to dispose of the bodies..." Ibrahim grinned, revealing brown, crooked teeth. "Tell me, what *did* happen at Greater Kailash?"

With a curse, Arora looked left and right. "You know full well. You—that's *you*, my friend—were supposed to destroy the...*evidence* in a safe, controlled space provided to you by myself, MGT, and Thakkar. We gave you the venue. All you had to do was concentrate on melting down the bodies."

Ibrahim spread his hands. "Well then, I fulfilled my part of the deal because the bodies were indeed melted."

"The operation was discovered."

"A technicality. Answer me this: were any of the victims named? Were any of the bodies identified as patients of Dr. Pankaj Arora—the famous Dr. Pankaj Arora? TV's Dr. Pankaj Arora? Did the discovery of those bodies result in policemen knocking on your door in the middle of the night? No, none of that happened, did it?"

Arora's crimson face conceded the point.

"Let me tell you something else," continued Ibrahim, warming to his theme. "That particular—what was the word you used?—*venue* was provided for a reason, was it not? So that if the operation was discovered then suspicion would fall on Mr. Chopra."

"Well, that didn't happen, did it?"

"Presumably because you failed to take into account the strength of Chopra's relationship with the police chief, Sharma. Again, that's not something for which I can be held responsible. Now, listen to me, *my friend*: I'm the man who procured valuable stuff for you. I'm the man who took those bodies to Greater Kailash for you. And yes, you got me started, but now you're simply getting in the way. Your ego is getting the better of you."

"I strongly suggest that we should let this activity be confined to what I do in my hospital," said Arora menacingly. "If we have more deaths we'll all be in trouble."

Ibrahim scoffed so loudly that the old gentleman reading the newspaper looked across at them. "Take a look at what's going on around you. Hasn't it occurred to you that we're already in trouble?" he laughed.

Chapter 88

SANTOSH OPENED THE door of his hospital room and peered out. There wasn't a soul in sight. The corridor lights had been dimmed to night mode. Santosh knew that he was on the tenth floor. Room 1016. It was the same floor on which the chief administrator's office was located.

He should have been discharged by 5 p.m. but he had complained of severe stomach cramps. The doctor on duty had been forced to extend his stay by a day. Santosh had then requested Nisha bring him a flashlight. His cell phone—which had an inbuilt flashlight option—had been shattered during his altercation with Ibrahim.

He walked barefooted toward the nurses' station that was next to the elevator bank. The corridor ended there and a right turn from that point would take him toward the administrative wing. He wondered how many nurses would be on duty at that time.

He reached the end of the corridor and stopped. He needed to know whether any of the night-duty nurses were looking out of the glass panel that separated the nurses' station from the corridor. He peeped from the corner of the panel. Two of them were inside, both with their backs to him. They seemed to be helping themselves to coffee from a machine.

Santosh quickly crossed the station and took a right turn toward the administrative wing. Another corridor. This one was entirely dark. Administrative staff had left for the day and no lighting was required. Santosh squinted his eyes to adjust to the darkness and felt his way along the corridor. He tried to recall how far along the chief administrator's office had been. As far as he could remember, it was about halfway down the corridor.

He tried one of the doors but it was locked. The second door opened with a gentle push but it opened into a storage closet. He was in luck with the third. He entered the room and shut the door behind him. Once he was sure there were no footsteps in the corridor, he felt for the light switch and turned it on.

The harsh overhead lighting hurt his eyes. He quickly turned it off. The office had a window that overlooked the hospital's entrance porch and it was possible that the security guards could become suspicious seeing a light in a supposedly closed area of the hospital. He switched on the flashlight instead and headed to MGT's office, which connected to the outer office where his secretary sat.

The inner office door was locked. Santosh walked back to the secretary's desk, opened a drawer, and took out two ordinary paper clips. Putting down the flashlight on the desk, he straightened out both the clips. He converted one into a pressure pin by bending it at ninety degrees. The other clip he converted into a rake by creating a zigzag pattern using the secretary's scissors.

Santosh bent down and inserted the rake into the key slot and pulled down in an effort to push some of the lock levers down. He then inserted the pressure pin and rotated it left then right. Two minutes later the door was open.

He picked up the flashlight and walked into the office, shutting the door behind him. The desk was untidy and several files and documents lay strewn across it. Santosh began looking through the papers on the desk. Most of it was mundane stuff. Uniform requisitions, staff attendance and overtime reports, equipment repair orders, and canteen instructions.

Santosh tried the desk drawer. It was locked. He used his paper clips to open the simple lock and shone the flashlight inside. A single register with several slips of paper clipped together sat inside. Santosh took it out and began looking through it.

What he found were names of patients and the date and time on which they had checked in. The register then outlined their ailments and the date of surgery. So far so good. After that came the details of organs that had been removed and whether the patient had survived or not.

There were plenty who hadn't. Eleven? Santosh counted. More than that. He had a feeling that if it were possible to match the names here with the bodies found at Greater Kailash then they would indeed correspond.

What's more, in all cases there was only one consulting doctor. Dr. Pankaj Arora. The register was being used by MGT to maintain a macabre record of surreptitious organ removals that were communicated to him through those ubiquitous slips.

It was evident that he was fully supporting the activities of Arora. But why? He was from a very affluent family and certainly didn't need the money. Wilson's disease! MGT had lost his only son due to nonavailability of a liver. It would have been easy for Arora to emotionally blackmail MGT into allowing the racket to go on, almost convincing him that his son could have been saved if such a service had been available back then.

Santosh examined the back of the drawer. There was a carton of cigarettes. It was in silver finish with an impressive crest at the front. It read "Treasurer." That was the cigarette brand Nisha had found at the Greater Kailash house, the one by Chancellor Tobacco. Santosh remembered that MGT had lived in England as a young man. No doubt that was when he had acquired the taste for those expensive cigarettes.

There was the sudden sound of a door opening. Someone was accessing the outer office. Santosh froze.

He cursed himself for having switched on the lights initially.

He quickly put the register back inside the drawer, closed it, switched off his flashlight, and crept under the desk, fervently praying it wasn't MGT himself.

He heard the door handle to the inner office turn and the door open. Footsteps headed toward the desk and a beam of light from a flashlight danced around the room. Santosh attempted to bundle himself tighter while restricting his breathing.

The beam danced around some more. The man in the inner office called out to a colleague in the outer office, "It's empty. I told you that you were imagining it. Let's go back to that card game I was winning." Santosh heard the door close.

He sat crumpled like a paper ball under the desk until he was satisfied there was no one there but him. Then he gingerly began to make his way into the dark outer office, the door of which had been closed by the guards on their way out.

He didn't see who was waiting for him. Didn't see the blow coming. Just pain as he hit the deck.

Chapter 89

SANTOSH FELL TO the floor, dazed by the severity of the blow. He tasted blood in his mouth. He quickly spat it out and forced himself to get up and face his attacker.

"Bastard," said the hoarse voice. It was unmistakable. MGT!

He charged at Santosh, but this time Santosh was prepared. He deftly sidestepped the charge and kicked MGT between his legs.

MGT grunted and doubled over. "Motherfucker," he gasped. "I should have had you killed the day you walked into my office."

"That would be easy enough for you given the machinery you seem to have established for taking lives," said Santosh warily, looking out for any moves by MGT.

"I saved lives," said MGT indignantly. "Hundreds of

them. But it's something that I cannot expect people like you to understand."

"Level with me," reasoned Santosh. "Expose the network and we'll call it quits...quits. I know about your son. I understand why you're doing this."

The mention of his son only drove MGT to greater fury. He leaped up and grabbed Santosh by the ears, attempting to headbutt him. Santosh preempted it by headbutting MGT first. MGT staggered back, dazed by the shock. He picked up the slim vase on his secretary's table, knocked it against the desk, and held the jagged neck like a weapon.

"Don't you dare ever mention my son!" he said, taking a few steps toward Santosh. "No one was there to help him and I had to watch him die. Now you want to prevent others from being saved." MGT lunged at Santosh with the broken vase.

Santosh parried the lunge and swung the flashlight that was in his left hand. It caught MGT's right hand and the vase fell to the floor with a crash. "Fuck!" yelled MGT, his voice cracking.

"Don't fight me, MGT," urged Santosh as he assumed a defensive posture once again. "Help me unravel the network instead."

"Fuck off," said MGT. "You didn't give a damn about me in college because I hung out with the druggies and drunks. So high and mighty, you were! And now you want me to help you?" His hands were desperately searching for something on his secretary's table.

"There is only one way...one way...that this will

end," said Santosh softly, holding the flashlight like a weapon.

"Yes, there is," said MGT as he found what he was looking for. A letter opener.

MGT charged at Santosh, thrusting the metal letter opener.

Santosh swung the flashlight in his hand to deflect the blow. The letter opener stabbed into his forearm. His flashlight fell to the ground.

He then grabbed the hand in which MGT was holding the letter opener and simultaneously kicked MGT on the left side of his torso. It caused MGT to turn ever so slightly, just enough for Santosh to twist his arm behind his back. Santosh applied pressure until MGT yelled in agony and the letter opener clattered noisily to the floor.

"I give up," said MGT in pain, and Santosh let go of his arm. It wasn't a good idea. MGT swung around and planted an uppercut on his chin.

Santosh crumpled to the ground as MGT ran out the door.

Chapter 90

SHARMA ADJUSTED HIS belt, feeling exceedingly pleased with himself. His interrogation of Thakkar had gone very well indeed; the head of ResQ had given up the goods without Sharma needing to resort to some of the more tried and tested methods to be found in the Red Fort.

He sucked his teeth distastefully. No doubt Thakkar imagined he was somehow immune from prosecution. Perhaps he thought Jaswal would put in a call and get him off the hook. It didn't really matter now. Sharma had the names he needed. All the information he required was his.

Installed in his office, he maneuvered himself behind his desk and dropped to his chair with a corpulent grunt. This was why he was the Police Commissioner, he reflected. Crisis management. That was what it was all about. Firefighting. Turning an awkward situation to your advantage.

He reached for the phone and dialed.

"Hello, Guha?" he said.

"Commissioner. What can I do for you?"

"Well, I have something for you. Some more information regarding our little band of medical buccaneers. But first, how are the preparations for your story going?"

Guha sighed. "Not especially well, truth be told."

"Oh, really? What's the holdup?"

"A group calling themselves the Coalition for Freedom of Speech have applied for an injunction. Somehow they got wind of our story and want to stop it."

Sharma gave a low, throaty chuckle. "Such are the daily hurdles faced by a pioneering broadcaster such as yourself, Guha."

"It's serious. If the judge agrees with this coalition then my producer won't allow me to show the story."

"And the hearing is imminent, is it?"

"Very."

"Well, I suppose this means you won't want to hear what else I have to tell you then," said Sharma airily.

"Will it strengthen my case with the judge?"

"That's for you to decide."

And Sharma gave Guha the final details, straight from Thakkar's guts and poured into the journalist's ear.

When he had finished he relaxed into his seat, allowing himself a smile. "And that's it," he concluded. "Let me know how you get on with the judge and give me advance warning when you plan to broadcast. I intend to time my sensational arrests accordingly. I trust DETV will be there to record the historic events?"

"First things first, Commissioner."

Chapter 91

SHORTLY AFTER HIS conversation with Guha, Sharma's phone rang again. This time it was Chopra, asking if he could pay him a visit, hinting that cigars and whisky would be on offer. And after a hard afternoon spent interrogating Thakkar and schmoozing Guha, that sounded a very attractive offer indeed.

Sharma informed Nanda he'd been summoned and took a car to the Lieutenant Governor's opulent residence. There he was greeted by a housekeeper and led to the familiar study, where Chopra stood, indicating for him to settle into the same leather armchair in which he had spent so many happy hours.

He sat down. But Chopra remained standing, the welcome not as warm as usual, the atmosphere markedly less convivial.

"I have good news," said Sharma, feeling uneasy but

trying to behave as though nothing was amiss. "I have put into place a plan that will soon make life decidedly uncomfortable for our friend Jaswal."

Chopra's hands went to his hips. Big man though he was, Sharma was sitting and he felt small as the Lieutenant Governor towered over him. His eyes were fierce. His lips pursed. And when he spoke he roared: "I don't give a fuck about Jaswal!"

"But—" spluttered Sharma.

"No, you moron!" boomed Chopra. "This has gone beyond trying to score political points! You think I wanted to become Lieutenant Governor in order to watch Delhi tearing itself apart with gossip, suspicion, and innuendo? What point is there in wresting power from Jaswal if it is to rule over the smoking rubble of a riot-torn city? This has gone too far, Sharma." He pointed an accusing finger. "*You* have let this go too far. We have bodies piling up. Some kind of sick freak skinning his victims, for God's sake! We've practically got marchers on the streets. The newspapers are demanding answers; DETV is on the phone night and day asking all kinds of questions to which I don't have the answers: who is behind the killings? Why are we not releasing details? Is our ruling body riddled with corruption and pedophiles? You've been fiddling while Rome burns, Sharma. And now I want you to put away the fiddle. And get something done. I want you to put a stop to this! Is that clear?"

"Yes," gulped Sharma. "Yes, sir, that's clear."

Chapter 92

SANTOSH HAD NOT waited to be discharged from the hospital. He was well recovered, although the encounter with MGT had left him slightly unnerved. He hadn't wanted to have a nurse bandage the gash on his forearm so he'd helped himself to antiseptic and bandages from the supply closet he had passed. He'd then gone back to his room, changed out of the hospital clothes, and walked out through the service entrance a little after midnight. He had spent the night on Neel's couch.

In the morning, Jack and Nisha had come over and the four of them had dropped in for breakfast at a cafe in Khan Market.

Santosh was exceptionally fidgety without his walking stick.

"You don't need it anymore," Jack told him.

But Santosh was convinced he did. "It is my only

constant companion," he said. "It saved my life at the Tower of Silence in Mumbai. Moreover, it helps me think."

"Well, at least you have a new phone now," said Nisha. She had picked up a replacement unit after getting the old SIM deactivated and a new SIM initialized.

"Thanks," mumbled Santosh.

"The little run-in you had with MGT," began Jack. "Could he be mentally disturbed? Killing people while saving others?"

"Unlikely," said Santosh. "I could have caught him had I not trusted him in that final instant. I guess there was a part of me that felt guilty for his situation... I felt guilty."

"Why?" asked Jack.

"We treated him rather shabbily in college," admitted Santosh. "He was an outlier. Almost an outcast. A—"

"I have tracked down the registration number of his car," interjected Neel. "Passed it on to Ash. He'll get the cops to find him."

"I'm convinced they're all in it together," said Santosh.

"Who?" asked Jack.

"Patel and Thakkar. One man's company gets lucrative contracts to modernize hospitals. The other one drives American patients to the newly modernized hospitals and makes a killing on the insurance," said Santosh. "I call it having one's cake and eating it too."

"But Kumar was supposedly the partner of Patel," said Nisha. "In fact, my friend at the *Indian Times* says that Patel had promised Kumar extra equity for his help in managing the regulatory environment and that this extra stock was to come out of Patel's own shareholding."

"That makes him the third partner of this unholy alliance," said Santosh. "Both these businessmen would have needed Delhi's Health Ministry on their side. Solution? Make the minister your partner . . . your partner."

"But these men would have needed a godfather, someone who had vast amounts of capital to deploy," said Jack. "I called up Denny—the CEO of the National Association of Insurance Commissioners—and asked him to find out about the key investors in ResQ. It turns out that the major equity of ResQ is held by the same entity that is the major equity owner of Surgiquip. It's a company in the Bahamas."

"They're affiliated?" said Santosh disbelievingly.

"Santosh," said Jack, "they're practically the same company."

Chapter 93

IQBAL IBRAHIM ADDED milk and sugar into his tea and stirred it. He stared at the man who sat across from him. He had introduced himself as Dr. Khan. Ibrahim was not sure about what was being offered but knew it could mean freedom from Arora.

"We are well aware that you are the engine that drives ResQ's profitability," said Khan. "We have had you under surveillance for weeks. We know how you operate. We believe that your abilities and resourcefulness are not being appreciated at the moment."

He was right. Ibrahim busted his ass procuring the right material only to be reprimanded by Arora repeatedly.

"What are you suggesting?" asked Ibrahim.

"Our business model is different to that of ResQ," said Khan, avoiding staring at Ibrahim's hooked nose.

"In fact we are not even competing with them. But we believe that our business will become far bigger than theirs in a few years."

"Please explain."

"Unlike ResQ, which sells insurance policies to American clients and charges them low premiums to have their medical issues attended in India," said Khan, "our company operates differently. For starters, we're not an insurance company. We're transplant specialists."

"Transplant specialists for American clients?" asked Ibrahim.

"No. Our key market is the Middle East. Our patients belong to countries such as Saudi Arabia, Kuwait, Jordan, and the United Arab Emirates. Our medical infrastructure is entirely centralized at a spanking-new facility that we have established in Gurgaon. Patients from all over the Arab world come here for their procedures."

"Why?"

"Most of these customers have no option but to travel abroad," said Khan. "For example, transplants in the United Arab Emirates were legalized in 1993 but the law failed to include a medical definition of death, thus making it impossible to use organs from dead patients. The result was that no transplant operations could actually take place. Organ transplant infrastructure is virtually nonexistent in those markets."

"Why should I consider it?" said Ibrahim, rearranging the skullcap on his head ever so slightly. "I'm making good money where I am. Inshallah, the money may also increase."

"These are rich Arabs and hence we are dealing with a much more lucrative segment of customers—those who will pay high prices for these procedures. This also means that we can pay you double what ResQ pays."

Ibrahim sipped his tea. In his mind, he was totting up the numbers and figuring out what double the rates would mean for him. And what it would mean to be finally free of that Nazi Arora.

"The ResQ network is a strong one," he said. "They may come after me once they know I am working against them."

"Not if you destroy them first," said Khan.

Chapter 94

JUDGES AT THE Delhi High Court usually heard matters between ten in the morning and four in the afternoon. Weekends were off. But the high-powered appellants in this particular case had forced the bench to conduct a special sitting outside of normal working hours, that too on a weekend.

The appellants were a group calling themselves the Coalition for Freedom of Speech. They were worried that information had been received by DETV. DETV had already started airing commercials on the channel indicating that a major disclosure was on the way.

"What do you want?" asked the irritated judge. He had been forced to forego his Saturday bridge game in order to hear this matter, hence the annoyance.

"This may be privileged information," argued the counsel representing the Coalition for Freedom of Speech. "We believe some of the information is fabricated and could grievously damage the reputations of parties involved. For all of the above reasons, we request an injunction preventing the news channel DETV from broadcasting any story based on this information."

The judge looked at the counsel representing the appellants. "You call yourselves the Coalition for Freedom of Speech and here you are making an application to muzzle free speech?" he asked sarcastically.

"Your honor, freedom of speech comes with responsibility," said their advocate. "If you give us an early hearing, we will convince you that it is not in the public interest to broadcast the story."

The judge turned his attention to the lawyer representing DETV. "Any reasons why I should not grant an injunction?" he asked.

"Your honor," began the counsel for DETV. "This application deserves to be treated with contempt. It is a barefaced attempt by vested interests to prevent the truth from emerging. If you do pass an order restraining DETV, you will be playing with freedom of expression and the liberty of the press."

The graying judge looked at his wristwatch. If he passed interim orders, he could still make it to his bridge game, albeit a little late. Delay was the best way to play this.

"I need time to consider the facts of this case," he

said. "I am temporarily restraining DETV from airing the contents until Monday, at which time I shall hear detailed arguments to decide the case in finality."

It also helped that the judge was a friend of the Chief Minister, Mohan Jaswal.

Chapter 95

GUHA SAT AT his desk surrounded by his team, the atmosphere despondent. They were still attempting to come to grips with the temporary restraining order.

"How could the judge pass such a stupid order?" asked Guha's research assistant, chewing the end of her pencil vigorously.

"He was possibly intimidated by the powerful people who had applied for the restraining order," said Guha, looking haggard. His customary blue jacket and red tie looked even more worn out than usual.

"Who?" asked Guha's producer.

"Patel's company Surgiquip," said Guha. "Thakkar's company ResQ…Those are obviously affected parties. I believe," he continued, taking off his wire-framed glasses momentarily, "that it's also possible Jaswal may have played a role by influencing the judge. After all, he is a close friend of Thakkar, and a negative disclosure about Thakkar would have serious political ramifications for Jaswal.

"In business and politics there are no permanent friends or enemies. There are only permanent interests. It is a common interest that would bring them on the same side.

"Maybe what they want is time. But time for what? What can they do to make our story weaker?"

Guha paused in thought. "I wonder..." he murmured.

"They could try smearing you," replied the research assistant. "A hatchet job to make you sound less credible."

"Or someone could actually use the hatchet," said the producer, instantly regretting his words.

"Kill me?" asked Guha.

"Several people have already died," said his producer. "You need to be careful."

The producer avoided mentioning the fact that many media companies—including DETV—received their funds from questionable foreign sources.

"Are you asking me to avoid airing the story?" asked Guha, the anger evident in his voice.

"I'm not suggesting that," said the producer smoothly. "I'm simply advising that you should slow down. It's never a good idea to get emotional about news stories."

Guha nodded. "I'll take your advice," he said as he wound up the meeting.

Guha's research assistant felt a tad sorry for him. Guha was always among the last to leave the studio. Perhaps if he had a wife or family, he wouldn't devote his entire attention to pursuing the truth relentlessly. Guha hadn't gotten over his wife. Her photograph steadfastly remained on his shelf.

When everyone else had left, Guha quietly spoke to his research assistant. "I have decided I shall not give anyone the luxury of time," he said.

"What do you mean? We're legally prohibited from going to air," she said.

"I plan to defy the court order," said Guha, the determination in his eyes all too evident.

"It would be contempt of court. DETV could get into trouble."

"What's the worst that can happen?" said Guha. "I get arrested? Fine. Public opinion will force the court to release me within the day." He got up from his desk excitedly. He was pumped up once again.

"But why the sudden urgency?" asked his assistant.

"Because DETV is trying to bury the story," said Guha, putting a fresh lozenge into his mouth. "The longer I wait, the higher the chances that the story will never be aired."

"How do we manage our producer?"

"He won't know what hit him," said Guha as he packed up. "Make preparations for a completely different subject so that everyone is caught off guard."

Chapter 96

IT WAS BECOMING a little too easy these days. Or maybe the Deliverer was simply a genius. It was probably the latter. The Deliverer knew everything.

Over the past week he had killed so many people. With each kill, he had felt a sense of elation. And why not? He had done the world a favor in each instance! The world owed him a debt of gratitude and a medal of honor for making the world a better place.

After completing his twelfth grade at the cantonment school, he had joined the army at the age of seventeen as a soldier. He had loved every minute of his experience, surrounded by people who were bound by the call of duty. A couple of years later the war had happened and he had ended up with a bullet to his lung.

Luckily the doctor at the hospital had succeeded in patching him up, even though the wound had left him plagued with chest infections that refused to go away. It also left him with a persistent cough.

The army had no longer been an option for the Deliverer. It was almost like starting his life all over again. The newspaper stint had been just what the doctor ordered.

The Deliverer had been lucky to have survived the bullet to his lung but it had disqualified him from active duty in the armed forces. He had realized that he would soon be unemployed.

One day, while the Deliverer had still been recuperating in hospital, someone had visited the patient occupying the bed next to his. The visitor had struck up a conversation with the Deliverer and he had been forced to put down his book. The visitor had been an impeccably groomed man. It had turned out that he was the editor of a major newspaper. He had graciously offered the Deliverer an opportunity to come work for him—to report from the front lines for the newspaper. The Deliverer had gratefully accepted the offer and had spent several years providing the newspaper with scoops that were unprecedented.

While on the reporting beat, the Deliverer had begun to realize that the country was a shambles. Crimes went unpunished because of notorious delays in the justice system. Innocents lay locked up for years even though there was no real evidence against them. The law and order administration was inefficient and some police officers were busy lining their own pockets. The apathy and inefficiency had made the Deliverer's blood boil.

Men like him were giving up their lives on the nation's borders while others sucked the country dry! It had riled him to see that the mainstream press was turning a blind eye to many such injustices.

He'd decided the only way to change the system was to occupy a position of power. He'd decided that he would need to contest elections soon.

Chapter 97

IN A MEETING room of Delhi's Oberoi Hotel assembled a group of people who could never have expected to assemble in amicable circumstances.

On one side of the table sat the Police Commissioner, Sharma, who wore a uniform that strained at its buttons, as well as a distinctly sour expression, and beside him his assistant Nanda, who wore no expression at all, as though he were simply an interested bystander, an impartial observer.

Across from them sat Jack Morgan, relaxed, stubbled, his polo shirt open at the neck and a dazzling grin never far from the surface; Santosh, whose own stubble gave him a weary, troubled look; beside him Neel; and on the end Nisha, who glared with unreserved distaste at Sharma.

The cop cleared his throat to address the Private

team. "Thank you for agreeing to meet me. The reason I wanted to—"

"Wait a minute," cut in Jack. "Wait just a goddamn minute. I told you we would agree to meet on one condition. Let's see that condition met first, shall we?"

Sharma picked up a hotel pen then placed it down again. His eyes dropped to the tabletop and his color rose as he cleared his throat and mumbled something.

"A little louder, please," said Jack. "Aim for audible and we'll take it from there."

"Okay," said Sharma, throwing back his shoulders, "let's get this over with, shall we? I would like to say sorry to you, Mrs. Gandhe," he nodded toward her, "for your treatment at the station the other day. It was inexcusable. I of course accept that you have nothing to do with the spate of killings, and I should never have insinuated as much. Please accept my apologies."

"Thank you," said Nisha tightly.

Sharma's eyes rose to meet hers. "How is she?" he asked, with a tenderness that took her by surprise. "How is your little girl?"

"Oh, she's...Well, she's bearing up. She still has night terrors. She still talks about the killer as the good man. She hopes that he's read her essay."

Sharma nodded, tucking his chin into his chest. "And what do you think? Do you still think he's a good man?"

Nisha's hackles rose. "Oh? We're starting that again?"

"I'm interested to know what you think, that's all," responded Sharma.

"Okay then," began Nisha. "Our theory here at Private is that——"

Now it was Santosh's turn to clear his throat, sitting upright in his chair. "Wait a minute, if you would. Perhaps we might first learn what is the purpose of this meeting? Up until now, Commissioner, you've made it very clear that you have no intention of cooperating with us. Why the sudden change of heart?"

Sharma shifted. "Not long ago somebody said to me that the fervor we're seeing on the streets is the kind in which revolutions are forged. I didn't agree with him then, but I'm beginning to agree with him now. Things have gone too far, they've gotten out of hand. We need to put a stop to it and I'm proposing that in order to do that we pool our resources. We are, after all, investigating the same thing."

"The same *two* things," Nisha reminded him. "We have a serial killer on the street *and* an organ-harvesting network."

"If you're suggesting that my own investigations into either of those things have been half-hearted then you're wrong," said Sharma, with a touch of wounded pride. "In fact, I've established the identities of all the major players in the organ-harvesting network. I believe I know the identity of the killer."

Eyebrows were raised on the other side of the table.

"In return for you sharing what information you have with me, I will give you that information," he continued. "And in return for giving my team access to what I'm told is your state-of-the-art investigative technology," he waved a hand at Jack, "I'm prepared to patch you into a surveillance feed I'm setting up at the homes of Thakkar and Dr. Arora."

"We accept," said Jack happily. "That seems like an excellent pooling of resources. You're right: too many people have died. We need to prevent any more casualties."

"Wait." Sharma held up a hand. "As part of the treaty, I would like your assurance that you won't use any of your investigative findings against the Lieutenant Governor."

"Oh yes?" said Jack. "And what about you? Do you have anything damaging on the Chief Minister?"

For the first time since the beginning of the meeting, Sharma smiled. "Oh yes. Something very damaging to the Chief Minister. It appears that Jaswal and Thakkar are old buddies from NYU. No doubt you've been sitting on that information too?"

Jack ignored the question. "Do you have any evidence that Jaswal is implicated in the transplant network?"

Sharma let them dangle for a moment, then his smile broadened. "No. As far as I know, he's clean. But then as far as I know, Chopra is clean too. They *run* Delhi, for God's sake. Why would they get their hands dirty with something as tawdry as this?"

"The answer, Mr. Sharma, is money," said Santosh. "The answer is always money. But I grant you, all evidence points to both men being innocent." He paused. "At least in this particular matter."

"That's what you're here for, is it? To make sure that

nothing potentially damaging emerges?" said Nisha, her voice dripping with contempt.

"It was Chopra who insisted we put a stop to this, young lady," snapped Sharma. "It's to him we should be thankful."

Nisha scoffed. "Thankful? What's clear is that the state government has allowed things to reach boiling point in an attempt to score political points. And don't call me young lady."

"And what have you been doing at Private, then?" retorted Sharma. "Twiddling your thumbs?"

"The political situation made it difficult for us to come to the police with our findings," said Santosh calmly. Did he imagine it, or did he feel Nisha's eyes burning accusingly into him?

"Very well, very well," said Sharma, hands spread. "Then let this be the dawn of a new era between us."

"Good," said Jack. He looked left and right at his colleagues, drawing a line under the dispute. "You said earlier you know who the killer is. How about starting our new dawn by sharing that particular piece of information with us?"

"It's a man named Ibrahim," said Sharma. "He's been working with Dr. Arora at the Memorial Hospital, but he's gone rogue. He's been negotiating with someone else to shift his business to them instead of Thakkar's mob, ResQ. Most likely he's trying to destroy the entire ResQ network—Kumar, Patel, Thakkar. With all the key players gone, he'd have a free hand to expand with a rival corporation."

Nisha was shaking her head. "What about Roy's murder?" she said.

Sharma shrugged. "Roy was Health Secretary. We'll have to ask Ibrahim why he deserved to die when we catch him."

Still shaking her head, Nisha looked across at her colleagues. "No, no, this is wrong."

"Well, let me hear your better ideas, then," frowned Sharma.

"Wait. If you think it's Ibrahim, then why come to us?" said Santosh. "Why not just bring him in?"

"Because I want to be sure. Because I'm betting you can help find him. Because your associate Mrs. Gandhe here has seen the killer, remember?"

"And because you want to tie up any political loose ends," said Nisha.

Sharma rolled his eyes. "To our mutual benefit."

Jack signaled *cool it* and then turned to Sharma. "You've got surveillance on Thakkar and Dr. Arora?"

"Logic tells us they'll be the next victims," said Sharma. "In the meantime, if we could locate Ibrahim, that would be helpful as well. Unless you really have been sitting around scratching your asses, I'm guessing you've got to Ibrahim and I'm guessing you have something on him."

Santosh nodded. "We have cell phone numbers."

"Then we can trace him," said Neel, the first words he'd spoken since the meeting began. He looked at Santosh. "We can trace him more quickly than the police. We have the StingRay."

Chapter 98

"SURE, LET'S TRACE Ibrahim's numbers," said Santosh. "It's the easiest and most effective way to reach him. Neel, you think we can do it?"

Neel nodded. "We'll head to his usual area in the StingRay."

An hour later, Neel, Nisha, Jack, and Santosh were in the StingRay van. Nisha took the wheel because Neel needed to operate the equipment at the back of the van. Jack got into the passenger seat next to Nisha, his Colt .45 tucked away under his jacket.

Private had invested substantially in StingRay technology because all other wiretapping and tracking systems needed the cooperation of telephone companies. The telecom operators would usually only respond to law enforcement requests or court orders. This left agencies like Private out in the cold.

Neel had outfitted a van with international mobile subscriber identity (IMSI) catchers—also called Sting-Rays. A StingRay was essentially a portable "fake" cellular base station that could be driven to the area of interest. Once activated, the StingRay unit sent out a strong signal to cell phones within its range, thus causing such phones to attempt a handshake with the StingRay as though it were a real base station of the cellular company. Instead of latching on, the StingRay device would simply record the identity of each cellular phone that registered with it and then shut itself down.

The van made its way through the congested Delhi roads crossing Kalka Das Marg and Sri Aurobindo Marg. Nisha unashamedly blasted the horn to get auto rickshaws to move out of her way. She continued along Prithviraj Road, Tilak Marg, and Bahadur Shah Zafar Road to Urdu Bazar Road. She swerved the van toward an empty parking slot by the side of the road and asked, "Now what?"

"Now we activate the StingRay," said Neel, opening up his laptop. The screen immediately presented a map of the locality and little dots began to light up. Neel punched in the two cell phone numbers that ostensibly belonged to Ibrahim and waited for the next fifteen minutes, allowing the StingRay unit to make friends with various cell phones in the locality.

"Got him," said Neel, looking at the Delhi map on his computer screen. "He's heading toward the hospital."

"Arora," said Santosh. "He's going after Arora."

They looked at each other, all four members of the Private team.

"Come on," sighed Jack. "Let's go save the heartless butcher."

Chapter 99

THE OFFICE LIGHTS were turned off except for the desk lamp. Seated in the visitors' chair was Ibrahim with his hands tucked into the side pockets of his calfskin jacket, his head protected by his customary skullcap. Dr. Pankaj Arora sat on his usual executive chair, sipping hot water and honey. It was cold in Delhi and the hospital's heating system seemed to be on the blink.

"It has become clear to me that you will never allow me to receive a fair market value for my efforts," said Ibrahim. "I'm now evaluating other options that, inshallah, may be more lucrative."

"Don't forget who got you started," said Arora brusquely, baring the gap between his teeth. "If I could get you started, I can also get a hundred others to do my bidding. No one is indispensable—including you." The threat was unmistakable. Arora wiped his glasses.

Ibrahim felt his anger welling up. Sure, Arora had gotten him started and given him a fresh lease of life with the business. But did that mean lifelong servility? No! Enough was enough. It was time for Ibrahim to be his own man. The offer from the Middle East was an exciting one and Ibrahim was going to take it. But before that there was unfinished business. The ResQ network had to be debilitated.

Arora picked up on the determination in Ibrahim's voice. He would need to try a different tack—one of gentle persuasion. He got up from his chair and walked around to sit on the edge of the desk, near Ibrahim. He gently placed his hand on Ibrahim's shoulder. "You are like my son," he said. "I'm the person who trained you and taught you everything there is to know. If you want to work for someone else, I shall not get in your way."

Ibrahim's hands stayed inside his calfskin jacket as though he were attempting to stay warm. Inside the right pocket was a syringe with the plunger extended all the way up. Inside the plastic tube was a full dose of etorphine. Ibrahim held the syringe gently, his thumb stationed on the plunger. He was careful not to put any pressure on it, though. He did not want any of the liquid getting wasted before the needle met its target.

Chapter 100

FROM OUTSIDE CAME a noise, and when Ibrahim moved to the window and used a finger to shift the blind, what he saw was a van screech noisily into the forecourt below. From it tumbled several figures, one of whom he recognized: Santosh Wagh, the guy from the detective agency—supposed to be dead—as well as a woman and two other men.

And in the distance he heard the wail of sirens.

Shit, he thought. He'd told Arora they were in trouble, and now they really were. He glanced across at the doctor, thinking of the syringe in his pocket and wondering if he should finish the job, salvage something, but then decided that discretion was the better part of valor. It was time for his grand exit.

"What's going on out there?" snapped Arora.

"Oh, nothing," said Ibrahim airily. "Just an ambulance arriving. With any luck the occupant will have some fresh organs for us."

"You've seen sense at last, have you? You'll stick to doing things through the usual channels?" said Arora with audible relief.

"That's right, old man," said Ibrahim. "You win. But for now I have business to attend to. I'll be in touch."

And with that he left, trying to look as casual as possible, even as he hurried out of the darkened office and into the corridor beyond, heading for the elevator.

They'd be in the reception area by now, he thought, probably making their way to the elevator. There were four of them. If they had any sense they'd send one guy up the stairs, a couple in the elevator, one keeping an eye on the reception area.

In other words, they'd have the exits covered.

Shit.

He stepped away from the elevator, looking wildly left and right. Emergency exit. There. He trotted toward it, steeling himself for an alarm as he pressed the bar.

It stayed silent. It wasn't alarmed. *Yes.* Now he found himself on a set of gray-painted back stairs. Not that he was an expert on evacuation protocol, but he'd bet that going down would lead him out into the parking lot.

Bye bye, suckers, he thought, closed the emergency exit door softly behind him, and descended.

Sure enough, at the bottom was a second door. This time an alarm did sound, but he didn't care, the wailing accompanying him as he trotted away from the open door and toward his van. There were times he'd wondered about the wisdom of driving such a conspicuous vehicle, but the advantage was you could quickly find it in a parking lot. He fumbled for the keys and, glancing back at the hospital, he saw security men carrying walkie-talkies arrive at the open emergency exit. Abruptly the alarm stopped.

"Ibrahim," came a voice, and he swung around to see a figure standing between the vehicles, blocking his way to the driver's door. Moonlight scuttled down the long curved blade of a scalpel.

Ibrahim stood and gaped. It took a second, but he recognized the newcomer. "It's you," he said, forehead furrowing beneath his skullcap. "What do you want with me?"

"I've come to collect your dues," said the man.

He stepped forward, his knife hand swept upward, and Ibrahim looked down to where his clothes and the stomach beneath had parted. His hands reached to collect his intestines as they spilled from his stomach cavity, and for a split second he thought he might simply push them back inside and everything would be all right. But instead they slithered from his grasp and slapped to the asphalt of the parking lot, and in the next instant Ibrahim followed them, keeling forward to land on top of his own heaped insides.

Chapter 101

JACK AND SANTOSH stepped out of the elevator on the fifth floor of the hospital to be confronted by Dr. Arora, who looked taken aback.

"Is there something I can do for you two gentlemen?" asked the doctor.

Jack and Santosh both looked up and down the deserted corridor, Jack's hand inching toward the Colt slung beneath his leather jacket. "You all right?" he asked the doctor.

"Yes, I'm perfectly well, thank you. Now, I ask you again: what are you doing here?"

"Where's Ibrahim?" said Santosh.

Arora stepped back, suddenly wary. "I'm quite sure I don't know who you mean."

"We're working on a theory that Ibrahim is behind the recent spate of serial murders," said Jack. "You wouldn't happen to know anything about that, would you?"

"No," smiled Arora, as though talking to a small child. "But you can be assured that if I did I would convey my suspicions to the police rather than to...well, you two gentlemen. And if you've quite finished, I think I should like to go home for the evening. Perhaps you would care to share the elevator?"

Silently the three men descended to the ground floor, where Dr. Arora bid them farewell then left for his car.

The Private team watched him go, frustrated that Ibrahim had evaded them and hardly able to believe that Arora was simply walking away, the butcher strolling to his Jaguar.

Jack spoke for them all when he said, "You know what, guys? I think I'd have preferred it if he'd been murdered."

A second later there came a commotion from outside. They ran toward the noise and there found the body of Ibrahim.

Chapter 102

DR. ARORA ARRIVED home, closing the door behind him and locking it. Those people at the hospital, were they something to do with that agency Ibrahim had told him about? And while on the subject, what had gotten into Ibrahim? Why had he been acting so strangely?

On second thought, it didn't matter. Nothing mattered now. Dr. Arora had made a decision. He was leaving Delhi. Let them wallow in their own filth. Let them sort it all out. He'd always said, half jokingly, that the advantage of being a single man with no kids was that you could always make a quick exit if you needed to.

Half joking. Always in the back of his mind was the fact that the same extracurricular activities that had paid for the large, well-appointed house in which he now stood, the Jaguar, five-star hotels, and high-class hookers, might also one day require him to disappear at a moment's notice. He'd seen *Heat*. That De Niro quote about how you needed to be able to leave in thirty seconds if you felt the heat around the corner? Dr. Arora had taken that to heart.

But he was going to make things slightly easier for himself. He was going to leave in thirty minutes. He shrugged himself out of his jacket as he passed through the large reception hall of his home, opened the double doors that led into the dining room.

He stopped.

Laid out on the dining-room table were three large jars and a plastic funnel. Inside one of the jars was a human heart. The second was full of blood. The third one was more difficult to distinguish in the low lights of the room, but it looked like . . .

It was. Preserved in some kind of liquid was a large lump of skin that was pressed up against the glass, floating like a gelatinous marine specimen.

The killer. He was here. Arora turned and tried to run but a figure stepped out from behind the door, a glittering hypodermic syringe in his hand. The attacker's arm swung in a blur. The next thing Arora saw was the floor as it rushed to meet him.

Chapter 103

ARORA AWOKE FROM the sedative—etorphine, if he wasn't very much mistaken—to find himself taped to one of his own dining chairs and seated in a privileged position at the head of the table.

And there they were, still laid out in front of him. The jars.

Oh God.

"Are you hungry?" came a voice from behind, and he twisted his head to see the intruder move from his rear to the edge of his peripheral vision. All he saw was a man in black.

"What are you going to do to me?" he said, and was pleased to find that he sounded strong and resolute. Who knew, perhaps he could talk his way out of this.

The man gave a soft chuckle. "What I'm going to do

is serve you dinner." A black-gloved hand indicated the three jars.

"Come on," said Arora. "You don't really believe you're going to be able to get me to eat that."

"I'll have help," said the attacker, and he placed something on the table next to the jars, a piece of metal apparatus that Dr. Arora recognized as a speculum.

"Look . . ." the doctor tried to say, but his mouth was dry. The words wouldn't come. He gathered himself. "Look, why are you doing this? Whatever your reasons, let's talk about them."

"You don't know why I'm doing it?"

His voice was familiar. He was making an effort to disguise it but, even so, Arora recognized it. Just a question of trying to place it. If he could work out the man's identity then maybe he could establish some kind of bond between them.

"No, I don't know why you're doing it," he said. "Why don't you tell me?"

A gloved fist slammed down on the table, and even that gesture seemed familiar to Dr. Arora. "*You should know!*" he spat. "You tell me. You tell me now."

Again the voice was so familiar. It was as though the intruder's identity was there, on the tip of Arora's tongue, dancing around in his memory but not quite staying still long enough for him to recall it.

"Okay, okay, keep your cool," panted Arora. "It's the transplants, isn't it? Are you from Ibrahim? Do you work for people who want a cut? That can be arranged. Just say the word."

"Venal to the last. You shouldn't judge others by your own standards. No, Dr. Arora, this has nothing to do with wanting a cut and everything to do with... Well, I suppose it's revenge."

Arora changed tack. "Well, I can see that you're well informed and you've been told that I'm heavily involved. But you do know that's not strictly speaking true, don't you? I'm very much on the sidelines. It's true, I perform operations, but the life-saving operations, not those... other ones."

"What other ones?"

"You know..."

"No. What other ones? The other ones that Rahul told me about before I scooped out his eyes, perhaps? The other ones who were found at the house in Greater Kailash?"

"Yes, those."

"You had nothing to do with those?"

"No."

The man in black paused, as though mulling things over, then, as if suddenly deciding, said, "Well, I'm afraid I don't believe you. Now, shall we begin?"

"No!" pleaded Dr. Arora. That note of strength in his voice was absent now. He strained at the tape that bound him to the chair, whipping his head back and forth as the attacker inserted the speculum between his lips. With his mouth clamped he wanted to swallow but found he couldn't and began gagging at once. He heard the ripping of tape and saw the intruder advance, the black balaclava closing in as tape was pulled across his forehead and his head was jerked back. Arora bucked and gurgled, pulling against his bindings, but to no avail, knowing that his ordeal had only just begun—knowing only that he wanted it over with as quickly as possible.

"This won't be swift, you do know that, don't you?" said the intruder, as though reading his mind.

And now the man in black lifted the jar containing the heart above Arora's head so that the doctor could see it. The screw lid jangled as gloved hands unfastened it. Next he reached into the glass with one of Arora's own forks, speared the organ, and removed it. Preserving fluid splattered Arora's face as the heart was taken out of view, presumably to the table, and he heard the unmistakable sound of a knife and fork at work.

"Perhaps I should have cooked it first," said the man in black. More fluid dripped to Arora's face as the fork reappeared, this time with a smaller morsel on the prongs.

"Patel's heart," explained the attacker matter-of-factly. "A bit of it, anyway. Who knew he even had one?"

Arora could only make a dry sound, trying unsuccessfully to pull away as the fork disappeared into his mouth and he felt the meat touch his tongue, a taste that was at once gamy and metallic, before it slid down his throat. He spluttered. His mouth filled with vomit. His chest heaved and he coughed, expelling just enough vomit—and possibly even a bit of the heart—to allow himself to breathe, and then again he coughed, trying to clear his airways but dragging bits of meat and vomit into his windpipe.

Another jar was opened. "This is Roy's skin," stated the man in black, and continued to feed him, spooning chunks of skin into his mouth and using the fork to shove them into his throat. Trying to breathe through his nose, Arora snorted like a horse, but he could feel that airway blocking too.

"Now, let's wash it down, shall we?" said the man in black, and in the next instant Arora felt the plastic of the funnel against his teeth, the nozzle nudging it way down his throat, setting off his gag reflex. The jar containing the blood was presented to him. "Kumar's blood." Arora watched as hands unscrewed the lid, tossed it aside, and then began to pour the contents of the jar into the funnel.

As he poured, the man in black spoke. "This is for Rita," he was saying. "This is for my beloved wife."

The funnel filled. Arora felt Kumar's blood run thickly down his throat, spill out of his mouth and over his chin, knowing he would soon drown in it. And then, as the darkness beckoned, and Dr. Arora came to the end of his wicked life, the man in black reached to remove his balaclava.

Chapter 104

A TEMPORARY OFFICE had been set up in a conference room at the Oberoi. There a police tech guy in a headset sat watching the surveillance feed from vans parked outside Arora's and Thakkar's houses. Opposite sat Commissioner Sharma and Nanda. All three men jumped slightly as the door to the meeting room slammed open and in burst Jack, Santosh, Nisha, and Neel.

"Well?" said Sharma, standing. "Did you pick him up?"

"You were wrong," said Nisha bitterly, "just as I said you were. The killer is not Ibrahim. Ibrahim was his latest victim."

Sharma seemed about to take it up with her, but Santosh was already moving in to calm the situation. "It simply means that Private's theory currently remains the most plausible," he said, looking quickly between Sharma and Nisha, "and it seems as though the killer is reaching the closing stages of his campaign. If we stay here for the time being, we're perfectly situated to—"

"Hey," said Neel from the other side of the room. He'd taken a seat beside the tech guy. "What's this?"

The investigators clustered around his monitor. There on the feed from Dr. Arora's residence they could see a figure leaving the grounds then crossing the street.

"Who's that?" asked Sharma.

The figure was careful to keep his back to the camera as he stepped into a BMW parked at the curb. Rear lights flared. A moment or so later the car drew away.

The tech guy looked nervous as all faces swung toward him. "We didn't see anyone going in," he said defensively, hands upraised.

"Get Red Team in there, *now*," demanded Sharma, and the tech guy relayed the order into his headset. Seconds later they watched as armed officers from the surveillance van appeared on screen and ran to the gates of the house, nimbly climbing the low wall and disappearing into the grounds.

Sharma was pacing, hand to his forehead. "Jesus! Jesus! Somebody went in there right under our very noses. Run that plate, Nanda. Tell me you got the plate, right?"

"I got the plate, boss," said Nanda. "Running it now."

"He must have got in through the back," said the tech guy. Into his headset he said, "Red Team, get a couple of guys around the back, see if there's access."

"You didn't check access?" exploded Sharma.

The tech guy quailed. "I don't know, sir, I don't know. That would be down to the team commander on the ground."

"*For fuck's sake!*" Sharma swept a coffee cup from the conference room table that dinged off the wall and left a brown splat on the wallpaper.

Jack looked disdainfully from the stain to Sharma. "That's on your bill," he said, finger pointed. "Now, will you calm the fuck down and act like a professional."

All stood waiting now, watching the screen intently, the camera trained on Dr. Arora's gate.

Santosh glanced at Nisha, who stood with her hands on the small of her back, also watching. "Was that him?" he asked.

"I think so," she nodded. "Same build. Same height."

The call came back. The tech guy directed it onto overhead speaker. "Go ahead, squad leader."

"Sir, Arora's dead. No sign of the killer, just the body all tied up and jars full of . . . *stuff*."

"Stuff?" barked Sharma.

"Sir," they heard, "it looks as though the killer fed him bits of skin and heart, then poured blood into him until he drowned."

Chapter 105

"WE KNOW THE killer found another way in," said Santosh suddenly. "He's determined. Sharma, deploy more men at the house of Thakkar—send men around the back. My guess is he'll be on his way there now."

"The idea was to mount covert surveillance," hissed Sharma, rounding on Santosh. "We want to catch him, not send him scurrying for cover."

"He knew we were there," reasoned Santosh. "He was looking out for a surveillance van. He evaded it easily."

"If he knew we were there, then why did he allow himself to be seen on the way out?" said Sharma. "Why draw attention to himself?"

Santosh put a hand to his forehead, thinking hard. "I don't know," he said, feeling suddenly useless, knowing that the eyes of the room were on him, the great detective, head of Private India, outfoxed by a killer moving around under his very nose.

Now came a fresh development. The screen showed DETV news vans arriving at Dr. Arora's house. Sharma's mouth worked up and down in rank confusion. His deputy Nanda crossed to a television, snatched at a controller, and turned it to DETV, where a reporter was already broadcasting from the gates of the house: "Information received moments ago suggests that the killer may have struck again..."

"What the fuck is going on?" said Jack, his gaze going from the television to the two monitors. "How in the hell did they find out so fast?"

On the second screen more news vans arrived outside the gates of Thakkar's home.

"Blue Team, you see what I'm seeing?" said the tech guy. "Because I'm seeing a bunch of news vans arriving at Thakkar's house. What the fuck are DETV doing there?"

The reply came over the speaker: "Beats me, sir."

Sharma had scuttled over to watch what was going on, hardly able to believe his eyes. He snatched at the headset, tearing it off the tech guy's head. "Blue Team leader, get men outside—find out what the news people are doing there."

Nanda came off the phone. "They ran the plates, sir. The car was stolen an hour ago. It belongs to a woman in Noida."

Sharma cursed loudly then switched his attention back to the screen. "What are they doing?" he asked, indignant. "What are all these bloody news vans doing here?" Then, screaming into the mic, "Blue Team? Blue Team, are you reading me? Have you found out what all these news vans are doing?"

"It's a diversion."

Jack and Nisha both looked at Santosh, both familiar with the detective's sudden brainwaves, knowing one was on its way.

"The vans," said Santosh, pointing at the screen, finger waving from one screen to the other, "they're a smokescreen. It's a trick, a simple diversionary tactic to make us look one way, in one direction, and miss what's happening in the other direction." He turned to Sharma. "Get men at the rear of the property, at once. That's where he'll be."

"How, though?" said Nisha. "How could he organize all this?"

"Same reason he was able to recognize a surveillance van when he saw it. Same reason he was able to tip off his own news channel to attend the houses of Arora and Thakkar. Same reason he stole a car at Noida, the media hub of Delhi. Because the killer is Ajoy Guha."

Chapter 106

NOW SHARMA WAS bawling into the headset mic, "Blue Team, get men in the house, now! Report on the status of Thakkar. Do it at once, do you hear me? Do it at once!"

The investigators paced. Moments later the report came back.

"He's gone, sir. Thakkar has gone."

"What? You mean he's there and dead? Or he's gone, as in literally gone?" barked Sharma.

"The second one, sir. Literally gone. No longer there."

Sharma snatched off the headset and sent it the same way as the coffee cup. "We've lost him. We've lost them both," he said, suddenly ashen-faced. His eyes rose to meet Santosh's. "If it is him. Ajoy Guha. I was feeding him information. I was practically giving him a list of victims."

"I have a feeling there will be a great many recriminations on this one," said Santosh. Once again he was thinking. "He's got a show tonight. *Carrot and Stick* is on in just a few minutes."

"Is he likely to do the show now?" said Jack. "Won't he be busy scooping out Thakkar's vital organs?"

"No," said Santosh. "The other day, the judge handed down a gagging order on a story Guha wanted to run…" He looked inquiringly at Sharma, who nodded gravely.

"Yes," admitted the Commissioner. "It was the story about the organ transplants. Some coalition of Patel and Thakkar's companies was trying to stop him."

"He'll run it," said Santosh, certain of it. "He'll run the story and end it with the death of Thakkar."

"You seem awfully sure," said Sharma.

"He's a man on a mission," said Santosh, cursing himself for having been so blind. "He always has been."

Chapter 107

THE DELIVERER MADE his way to the studio, sucking on his lozenge. It was medication that he constantly needed to prevent upper respiratory tract infections. It had become a constant worry after he'd received a bullet to his lung during the Kargil War between Pakistan and India.

Guha recalled his early days as a newspaper reporter at the *Daily Express*. He had been one of their best reporters. He had imagined that his outstanding work would also make him popular among his colleagues. He'd almost imagined himself as universally loved and admired. That had been when he'd decided to contest elections for the Press Council of India.

It was a twenty-nine-member body ensuring press freedoms were maintained and that members of the fourth estate exercised responsibility and maintained ethical standards in their reporting. Guha had been convinced he would be able to force the mainstream press to report freely and fearlessly once he was on the council.

Of the twenty-nine members, thirteen represented working journalists, of whom six were to be editors of newspapers and the remaining seven were to be working journalists other than editors. These seven positions would usually be filled by nominations from newspapers around the country but the *Daily Express* was different and egalitarian. It allowed for internal elections that would decide who would be sent as the newspaper's representative to the council.

Guha had lost badly.

Dejected, he had been about to hand in his resignation at the *Daily Express* when his editor had called him into his office. "Even though you lost, I like your spunk," the editor had told him. "I had a chance to hear some of the talks that you gave to your colleagues. They were pretty good. Have you considered a career in television?"

The editor had proceeded to tell Guha that the *Daily Express* had decided to start a twenty-four-hour news channel called DETV. A consortium of investors had agreed to fund the project. The editor had felt that Guha would be ideally suited to anchor the primetime news show and spearhead the channel's investigations. Guha had jumped at the opportunity.

Life was suddenly being kind to him. During his stint contesting elections, he had met a young columnist who worked the entertainment desk. Her name was Rita and she'd had the most gorgeous dimples when she smiled. Guha had fallen head over heels in love with her and they had ended up getting married just three months later.

Guha had worshiped the ground Rita walked on. Never had a day gone by without him sending her notes, flowers, and little presents to tell her how much he loved her. They had taken weekend trips to romantic hotels and on one such trip Rita had collapsed as she was getting into the car. An ambulance had rushed her to hospital, where a series of diagnostic tests had been performed. The doctor had informed Guha that Rita had a condition known as cardiomyopathy. It was a disease in which the heart muscle—the myocardium—progressively deteriorated, eventually leading to heart failure. While less severe versions of the condition could be handled with medication, pacemakers, defibrillators, or ablation, the severest forms would eventually result in death. The only alternative was a heart transplant.

Guha's life had been turned upside down yet again. While Rita had remained in a hospital bed, Guha had begun to meet cardiologists and heart specialists to find ways to save the life of the woman he loved. He had eventually settled on a brilliant surgeon from Kerala whose practice was from a private hospital in New Delhi. He had successfully carried out eleven heart transplants and was acknowledged as India's leading specialist in the procedure. He had painstakingly put out the word to various hospitals that he was in need of a heart that matched the age, weight, and size requirements of Rita.

Usually such requests took months for any response, but then there had been a miracle. A young man who was brain dead was being taken off life support at a hospital in Pune and the family had decided that the best tribute they could pay their son would be to allow his organs to live on inside others. The Pune surgeon had telephoned Rita's doctor to convey the good news. "We'll ensure that the organ reaches you within four hours of removal," he'd said.

The next day they had waited. And then waited some more. And then there had been a call from Pune. There had been a delay in transporting the organ to Pune Airport owing to traffic. They had diverted the organ to Mumbai instead in order to ensure that the ischemic time requirement was met and that the organ was put to use for another patient.

A week later Rita had died.

Guha had been a broken man but he had refused to cry. After all, he was the Deliverer. How could the Deliverer go soft? His whole life had been a series of terrible events. Guha had picked himself up and gone back to the studio and that had become his new battlefield. It was Rita's death that had made Guha into the aggressive and relentless television crusader that people now knew him as.

Several months after Rita had died, his Kerala-based doctor had met with him. He'd revealed to Guha that he was suspicious of what had transpired. Upon making inquiries, he had found that there had been no transport delay in Pune. He had been convinced that someone somewhere had been bribed in order to make the organ available to someone else.

"Who?" Guha had asked.

The doctor had shrugged. "Difficult to say. There are many unscrupulous people and dodgy organizations that are profiting from such activities. This is nothing short of a war."

It had been no longer sufficient to seek the truth by ruthlessly pursuing criminals and scammers in his studio. The entire nation depended on him to clean up the mess created by politicians and corrupt officials. The nation wanted justice. It was the Deliverer's job to deliver it.

Chapter 108

CARROT AND STICK began. And what the watching public saw was Ajoy Guha in his usual black leather seat. Sharp-eyed viewers might have noticed that there was a splotch of blood on the sleeve of his white shirt, and that he was a little more agitated and unkempt than usual, but otherwise it was the same Ajoy Guha in his usual place, legs crossed, cheek bulging slightly with a lozenge that he sucked, beadily regarding his viewers through his glasses.

"Good evening," he said. "Tonight I would like to talk to you about our wonderful city's health care."

He held up Maya's essay and read the title. " 'Health Care, Fair and Square?' by Maya Gandhe. This essay came into my possession a few days ago, when I was in the act of murdering the pedophile Amit Roy."

Here Guha paused, as though to leave room for the

audience reaction. However, there was never any audience for *Carrot and Stick*, and on this particular occasion there were no production staff present either. Moments before the show had gone live, with the producer and various researchers panicking that their host had not yet appeared, Ajoy Guha had turned up. He had been using one hand to push a bound, gagged, and beaten-looking Jai Thakkar into the studio. In the other hand he'd held a Glock 17.

In moments Guha had cleared the studio, using locks designed to prevent intruders disrupting the show to lock himself and Thakkar alone into the studio. A skeleton staff had remained behind in the control room. Guha had warned them that Thakkar would die if they failed to broadcast events as they unfolded. Threats or not, all involved knew full well that the broadcast would continue.

Among those locked out were the Private team, Sharma, and a small squad of armed response officers, all of them watching on monitors in a corridor outside the studio. Guha had set the camera to roll but couldn't change the angle or depth of vision, so what it failed to broadcast was that at Guha's feet lay Thakkar, his eyes nervously fixed on the Glock Guha held to his forehead, also out of sight.

At the mention of Maya, Nisha's hand flew to her mouth. "Oh God," she said, as Guha continued his monologue.

"From the pen of this young girl comes hope for the future. A simple desire that health care for Delhi, for

the whole of India, should be delivered in a more egalitarian fashion." He held up the essay, now somewhat
dog-eared. "This essay—I've posted it to my Twitter account and I urge you to read it—this essay is a vision of
the future penned by a little girl. Just a child. However,
the piece of film I'm about to show you is a terrifying
vision of the present—though soon, I hope to consign
it to the past—run by the so-called adults, our leaders
and representatives, our corporate heads and ministers,
the doctors who command our trust—all of them committed not to saving lives as they would have us believe,
but to lining their own pockets at our expense.

"This bit of film will shock you, I guarantee it. And
you may watch it and feel the familiar sense of injustice
and impotence. You will ask yourself if things will ever
change. Well, ladies and gentlemen, when the report is
over, we'll come back and I will show you change. I will
show you change in action."

He looked over the top of his glasses at the control
room, waggling the Glock threateningly. Those in the
control room did as they were asked, and as newsmen,
they did it gladly. They ran the story.

In the corridor outside, cops and the Private team
gathered around a flustered studio manager. "The idea is
that if you know the code you can lock the door from
the inside," she explained nervously, "and of course Ajoy
knows the code."

"There must be a way to override it," said Santosh.

"There is. It needs two of us to input a master code.
The head of security is on his way now."

"Is there another way into the studio?" asked Sharma.

"The code controls all doors," she explained. "Once the doors are overridden, you can come in through the control room, or from the other end, but you'd be coming at Ajoy from the front. This is the only door that brings you in from the side."

"What kind of screwy security system is this anyway?" frowned Sharma.

An elderly security man arriving fixed him with a stare. "We have all sorts of celebrities, dignitaries, and notables in and out of our studios, Mr. Sharma," he said. "We need to be able to guarantee their safety."

Sharma indicated through the porthole window. "Mr. Thakkar doesn't look particularly safe to me."

"We've never had a journalist produce a gun before, Mr. Sharma," said the security guard reasonably. "This is what you call an unprecedented situation." He nodded to the studio manager, keyed in three digits to a door panel, and then stepped aside to allow her to finish the code. There was a click and a light turned from red to green.

Now a silence fell across those in the corridor as Sharma issued whispered instructions to his armed response team. Officers brought assault rifles to bear and took up positions by the door.

Back in the studio, if Guha was aware that the door lock had been circumvented, he made no sign. The film had ended. The story was out there, and now he was telling the story of the Deliverer, telling of his beloved wife Rita and how he pledged to take up arms against the same corruption and degeneracy that had killed her.

"I am sorry, people of Delhi, that my actions as the Deliverer brought you a period of unrest and uncertainty. But I promise with my hand on my heart that my intentions were benign, that I intended to rid the city of those elements that would seek to suck it of its lifeblood in order to deliver it into a better future."

He stood, kicking his seat aside, reached down, grabbed Thakkar, and hauled him backward so that for the first time the CEO appeared on screen. "Meet Jai Thakkar of ResQ." He stooped to rip off the tape from Thakkar's mouth. "Mr. Thakkar, say hello to the people of Delhi. Tell them what you have done."

In the corridor the elderly security guard spoke to Sharma. "I hope you know what you're doing, Commissioner. You may not realize, but out there in the city everybody is watching what's going on in here. Other channels are covering this channel. Traffic is at a virtual standstill. Millions of people are going to see every move you make."

Sweat glistened on Sharma's forehead. "Then millions of people are going to see us take down one of the sickest serial killers the city has ever seen."

"You sure the people see it that way?" asked Santosh.

"I don't give a fuck what the people think right now, Wagh," snapped Sharma, and then addressed the armed response team leader. "Go in there, take him out before he kills a CEO on air. Do it. *Now!*"

The team leader nodded, twirled his finger in the

air. Everybody else pressed themselves to the walls as the armed response team readied themselves and one of the men knelt, the barrel of his assault rifle pointing to the ceiling as with his other hand he reached to the handle and eased the door open a sliver.

Inside, Guha saw the door begin to open, the armed officers about to launch their incursion. At his feet, Thakkar was mewling, crying, and pleading, admitting all his many sins, spilling the beans to an audience of millions.

"But if the police come in here now, then I end it with a bullet to his head," said Guha loudly, directing his comments more to the doorway than to his audience. The armed officers froze. Something seemed to occur to Guha. "The person I would like to see is Maya Gandhe. Bring her here to me. Bring her so that she can appear to the people as a symbol of hope for the future."

In the corridor, the elderly security guard shot Sharma a look that said *I told you so* and the Commissioner cursed, knowing that Guha was giving him no choice. He couldn't play games with Thakkar's life. At least, not live on television. "Can we get her?" he said dreamily, as though he was far away. "Can we get the Gandhe girl?"

Nisha burst forward. "*I beg your pardon!*" she snapped. "Maya is coming nowhere near here!" Her face was right up to Sharma's. "What the *hell* do you think you're playing at?"

Sharma looked at her and his eyes were unfocused. He gave a tiny shake of his head and came back to himself. "I'm sorry. You're quite right. I don't know what I was thinking."

"Tell your men to stand down—I'm going in," said Nisha.

"No, Nisha, you can't," said Santosh.

Jack shook his head.

"He knows me." Nisha drew her gun, herding armed response officers out of the way like a harassed teacher, and then made her way to the door. "We have history."

And with that she slipped through the door and into the studio.

Chapter 109

SHE CAME INTO the studio, weapon raised, two-handed, taking short steps inside. There stood Guha. At his feet lay Thakkar, terrified and wracked by snotty sobs, his bound hands held almost as if in prayer. Guha stood with one foot on top of him, stooping slightly to hold the Glock to his head. When he looked up to see Nisha, the studio lights reflected off his glasses so that his eyes seemed to shine white.

"I'm sure I remember giving instructions that if the next person to walk through that door wasn't Maya Gandhe then I shoot Thakkar," he said. "Yes, I'm certain I can recollect giving those exact instructions. And yet, and yet, I am greeted by the sight of her mother." He addressed the camera. "Ladies and gentlemen, you probably can't see her, but I have been joined by Nisha Gandhe, the mother of Maya, our guide to a better future."

"How'd you know my name?" Nisha's voice sounded flat and muffled in the empty studio.

"Why, it's in the essay…You *have* read the essay, haven't you?" he said.

A guilty shockwave passed through Nisha as she stood with her gun trained on Guha. The truth was, she hadn't read it. She'd fallen asleep reading it and had never gotten around to finishing it. She hadn't been there to see Maya pick up her prize. Hadn't been there for Maya at all.

"How is she?" asked Guha. "How is Maya, the little girl I saved from the pedophile Amit Roy? How is that little girl?"

"She's very well, thank you. Now drop the gun and step away from Thakkar."

The light flashed on his glasses again. His Glock pressed harder into Thakkar, who whimpered in return. "Are you my assassin?" Guha taunted. "Have they sent you to kill me?"

"Nobody needs to die," said Nisha. She took a step forward.

"Oh, you know very well that's not true." His body language warned her to stay back. "I think we both know that Mr. Thakkar here needs to die. The last of the old guard, the final bloodsucker to extinguish before we can begin again."

"And you know very well I can't let you do that," replied Nisha evenly.

"You won't shoot. To stop me you'd have to kill me and you don't want to kill me."

"I don't want to kill you but I will if I have to."

He chuckled. "You had your chance to kill me the other night, and you didn't."

"I didn't have a clean shot. You were a shrinking target."

"Oh, and there was also the small matter of your little girl urging you not to shoot. Because she knows, doesn't she? Little Maya knows that the Deliverer is a force for good in this world, and that it's the likes of Roy, Thakkar, Kumar, and Patel who deserve to die. Essays are a start. They're a good start, but in order to effect true change—real, profound change—we need to show those who exploit us that we are not prepared to take it any more. And to do that we have to take up arms. The Deliverer has done more to root out corruption in Delhi in weeks than Ajoy Guha managed in years. You can't deny that."

"Perhaps," said Nisha. "And you're right, Maya thinks you're a good man."

"She does?" Guha seemed genuinely touched. "She really does?"

"Yes, she does. But what if she were to see you kill a man in cold blood on television. Would she still think so then?"

"She would understand in time that I did what had to be done."

"The fact remains that I can't let you do it, Guha."

The tension in the room rose. Nisha controlled her breathing, feeling her heart rate settle. Her hands were steady, her head inclined as she stared down the sight of her .38. Thakkar's whimpering increased in response to the increased pressure of the Glock pushed at his head, and Guha locked eyes with Nisha, a smile playing at his lips. He turned his head to address the camera. "We've reached that point in the show, ladies and gentlemen, where we have to say good-bye to one of our guests."

With no warning, Guha's Glock swung upward to point at Nisha.

She squeezed the trigger.

The two shots rang out simultaneously, like every other noise strangely deadened by the sound stage of the studio. Nisha felt a blow, staggered backward from the force of something that punched into her left shoulder, and knew right away she'd been shot. She looked down to see the hole in her jacket, warm blood already beginning to flow down her upper arm. She was struck by a dizzy feeling, knowing the pain would hit her any second now.

And then it did—with a rush of white-hot agony that sent her to her knees on the studio carpet. Her gun arm went limp and the .38 hung uselessly from her fingertips, but at least Guha was also wounded, his shirt bloodied and tattered along one side. Stooping, he bared his teeth in pain as he placed the Glock back to Thakkar's head.

"Don't," she called to him weakly, still unable to raise the .38, her vision clouding.

Guha's shoulders rose and fell. He shuddered and then pulled the trigger. Thakkar's head disintegrated, bits of blood, brains, and skull splattering Guha's face. Grinning. Triumphant. Behind Nisha the door opened and the armed response team burst into the studio.

All she heard as she lost consciousness was the sound of cops shouting. All she saw was Guha grinning.

Chapter 110

THE MAN CHECKED into the motel off the Delhi–Jaipur highway at around five in the evening. He paid cash in advance for one night and headed to his room without any luggage. The reception clerk did not bother about him. He was used to seeing all manner of strange people. Any type of business was welcome.

The man locked his room door, stood on the bed, and reached up to unscrew the fire alarm. He pulled out the batteries and screwed back the lid. He then sat on the bed for the next hour, chain smoking. In his head were images of his son in a hospital bed. Then images of his son's funeral pyre.

If someone had cared, my son would still be alive.

He stubbed out the last cigarette and stood up once more on the bed. He pulled off the belt from his trousers and looped it into the ceiling fan. He tugged at it to check the strength of the fan. Satisfied that it could take his weight, he placed his head into the noose that he had fashioned. He then bent his legs, allowing his entire body weight to shift to the belt.

MGT's body was discovered around six hours later after the police identified his car in the parking lot of the motel.

EPILOGUE

Chapter 111

IT WAS THREE months later, and everything about the case against Ajoy Guha had been expedited. The trial was fast-tracked, his plea had been guilty, and he had made no appeal against the sentence of death, asking only that it be carried out as soon as possible.

Shortly before the execution, Jack flew into Delhi. The day before, he summoned Santosh, Nisha, and Neel to the Oberoi. There they assembled in reception and were greeted by Jack.

"Santosh, you got your cane back," he said.

"Retrieved from Ibrahim's van."

"I'm pleased to see it," he said. "Neel, I trust things are going well with Ash? And how's the new car?"

Neel's smile said it all, and Jack turned to Nisha. "The last time I saw you, your arm was in a sling. Good to see you're better. How's Maya?"

Nisha had been smiling at the mention of Neel and the car she'd crashed, but at the thought of Maya her eyes clouded and she spent a moment or so composing herself. "I'm spending a lot more time with her," she replied. "Turns out we have a bit of catching up to do, and I have a lot of being-a-proper-mother to do. We go on holiday to Shimla in a couple of days, but she's still having nightmares, Jack. Not just about her ordeal."

Next, the four of them made their way from reception to the conference room. There they were greeted by a surprise. Waiting for them were the Chief Minister, Jaswal, Delhi's Lieutenant Governor, Chopra, and the Commissioner, Sharma.

The Private team took their seats. They eyed each other warily, unsure of the purpose of the meeting and looking to Jack as he moved to the head of the table, took off his leather jacket, draped it over a chair, and then rested his hands on the back of the chair.

He paused and then addressed the meeting. "Okay, I'll make this brief. I don't suppose there are many in this room who can claim to have covered themselves in glory over the Deliverer murder case, and I'm not asking for a postmortem; I'm not asking for each man to confess his sins. But what I will do is start by saying that I'm just as culpable as anybody else here, and I owe you an apology. To you in particular, Santosh, I'd like to say sorry for ignoring your advice and dragging Private into a politically motivated case when you warned me otherwise."

Santosh gave a short, grateful nod that Jack waved

away. Meanwhile Jaswal was about to speak up, but Jack held out a hand, politely silencing him. "Mr. Jaswal, I intend to reimburse you all of the fees you've paid, and please accept my apologies for having led you to believe that Private's allegiances lay with you in your turf war with Mr. Chopra here. We are an independent detective agency. My mistake was to believe—wrongly, as it turned out—that making high-level contacts in Delhi was the best way to establish my business here. What I should have done was concentrate on Private's core business, which is . . ." his head dropped for a moment, "trying to help people. Trying to do a bit of good in this cold world of ours.

"But, like I say, we've all made mistakes. Not just me. And what I want to propose now is that we don't compound those mistakes by making another one. I'm here to ask you, Mr. Chopra, and you, Mr. Jaswal, for leniency for Ajoy Guha."

Puzzled glances were exchanged. Chopra was about to speak up, but Jack cut him off and continued, "A little girl of my acquaintance is crying because she believes the state is killing the man who saved her life. I think we all know the little girl in question. Maya Gandhe, daughter of our very own Nisha, the girl who won the hearts and minds of Delhi thanks to her starring role in recent events. She's already held in such affection—she's become such a symbol of hope for the people—that I'm betting she could change things just by speaking out. Not that she knows that." He paused in order to let the implication sink in. "*Yet.*"

Chopra and Jaswal looked at one another, both aware they were being played. Jack went on, "Now, we in this room know more than most that there's nothing intrinsically *good* about Ajoy Guha. He did some terrible, wicked things. And yet..." Jack shrugged, spreading his hands. "He seems to have inspired people. Certainly he has Maya. And let's face it, he certainly wants to die, probably because he knows that dead he becomes a martyr, a much more potent symbol than if he lives, gets old, and dies in some prison somewhere. I ask you: are we in the business of giving a man like Guha what he wants? Is that a wise course of action, do you think?"

Jack swallowed and went for broke. Addressing Jaswal and Chopra he said, "What do you say, gentlemen? The execution is tomorrow. How about we find a way to cancel it?"

Chapter 112

PREPARATIONS FOR THE hanging began at 3:30 a.m. Not long after that, the crowds gathered in the courtyard. By daybreak, as Delhi awoke to a day of reckoning, the chanting had begun.

Guha was permitted a hot shower and a fresh set of clothes. The medical officer gave him a quick physical to certify that he was in sound health to face the calibrated drop to death.

There was a clicking of boots on the concrete floor as the warden and four deputies arrived at the cell. The guards stationed themselves front, back, left, and right of the prisoner. On an order from the warden they began walking toward the gallows, where Guha was handed over to the executioner. The Chief Judicial Magistrate read the verdict that had sentenced him to death.

The executioner was a police constable who had conducted eight previous hangings. He tied Guha's hands behind his back and bound his legs. He positioned him at the center of the platform's trapdoor, and then fastened the noose around his neck, adjusting it to ensure the knot was slightly to one side. He began reciting a short prayer to mitigate the guilt of killing another human being.

And now the hour was upon them. In the courtyard, and in the streets, it was as though the whole city held its breath. After all, Guha's case had been the most high-profile one ever seen in the country's legal system. Across the country people had held demonstrations demanding leniency for Guha. On social media, the hashtag #SaveAjoyGuha had been trending continuously, and to the followers of #TeamGuha he was a hero.

"*Ajoy Guha Amar Rahe!*" they chanted: "May Ajoy Guha forever remain immortal."

The man himself was determined to die. He wanted to die so that the Deliverer might live. That was his gift to the people.

The hangman tightened his grip on the lever that would release the trapdoor under Guha's feet.

Then along the corridor came a prison guard, huffing and puffing, carrying a letter. The Chief Judicial Magistrate indicated to halt the proceedings.

"I have a letter here signed by the President," said the guard breathlessly. "The execution is to be delayed indefinitely."

But Ajoy Guha wanted to die, and his eyes went to

the lever, knowing he could knock it with his feet, finish the job himself—and that he needed to act now.

For the first time he heard the chants from outside. "*Ajoy Guha Amar Rahe!*" they were chanting, and he realized they were calling for him, not the Deliverer, they were calling for Ajoy Guha. Abused, bullied, neglected, sidelined. Ajoy Guha. The people wanted him at last.

He smiled.

And moments later, as the news spread, the cheering began.

ABOUT THE AUTHORS

James Patterson received the Literarian Award for Outstanding Service to the American Literary Community at the 2015 National Book Awards. He holds the Guinness World Record for the most #1 *New York Times* bestsellers, and his books have sold more than 350 million copies worldwide. A tireless champion of the power of books and reading, Patterson created a new children's book imprint, JIMMY Patterson, whose mission is simple: "We want every kid who finishes a JIMMY Book to say, 'PLEASE GIVE ME ANOTHER BOOK.'" He has donated more than one million books to students and soldiers and funds over four hundred Teacher Education Scholarships at twenty-four colleges and universities. He has also donated millions to independent bookstores and school libraries. Patterson invests proceeds from the sales of JIMMY Patterson Books in pro-reading initiatives.

*   *   *

Ashwin Sanghi is counted among India's highest-selling English fiction authors. He has written four bestselling novels—*The Rozabal Line, Chanakya's Chant, The Krishna Key* and *The Sialkot Saga*—and co-authored the #1 bestseller *Private India* with James Patterson. Ashwin lives in India with his wife and son.

BOOKS BY
JAMES PATTERSON

FEATURING ALEX CROSS

The People vs. Alex Cross • *Cross the Line* • *Cross Justice* • *Hope to Die* • *Cross My Heart* • *Alex Cross, Run* • *Merry Christmas, Alex Cross* • *Kill Alex Cross* • *Cross Fire* • *I, Alex Cross* • *Alex Cross's* Trial (with Richard DiLallo) • *Cross Country* • *Double Cross* • *Cross* (also published as *Alex Cross*) • *Mary, Mary* • *London Bridges* • *The Big Bad Wolf* • *Four Blind Mice* • *Violets Are Blue* • *Roses Are Red* • *Pop Goes the Weasel* • *Cat & Mouse* • *Jack & Jill* • *Kiss the Girls* • *Along Came a Spider*

THE WOMEN'S MURDER CLUB

16th Seduction (with Maxine Paetro) • *15th Affair* (with Maxine Paetro) • *14th Deadly Sin* (with Maxine Paetro) • *Unlucky 13* (with Maxine Paetro) • *12th of Never* (with Maxine Paetro) • *11th Hour* (with Maxine Paetro) • *10th Anniversary* (with Maxine Paetro) • *The 9th Judgment* (with Maxine Paetro) • *The 8th Confession* (with Maxine Paetro) • *7th Heaven* (with Maxine Paetro) • *The 6th Target* (with Maxine Paetro)

• *The 5th Horseman* (with Maxine Paetro) • *4th of July* (with Maxine Paetro) • *3rd Degree* (with Andrew Gross) • *2nd Chance* (with Andrew Gross) • *1st to Die*

FEATURING MICHAEL BENNETT

Haunted (with James O. Born) • *Bullseye* (with Michael Ledwidge) • *Alert* (with Michael Ledwidge) • *Burn* (with Michael Ledwidge) • *Gone* (with Michael Ledwidge) • *I, Michael Bennett* (with Michael Ledwidge) • *Tick Tock* (with Michael Ledwidge) • *Worst Case* (with Michael Ledwidge) • *Run for Your Life* (with Michael Ledwidge) • *Step on a Crack* (with Michael Ledwidge)

THE PRIVATE NOVELS

Count to Ten (with Ashwin Sanghi) • *Missing* (with Kathryn Fox) • *The Games* (with Mark Sullivan) • *Private Paris* (with Mark Sullivan) • *Private Vegas* (with Maxine Paetro) • *Private India: City on Fire* (with Ashwin Sanghi) • *Private Down Under* (with Michael White) • *Private L.A.* (with Mark Sullivan) • *Private Berlin* (with Mark Sullivan) • *Private London* (with Mark Pearson) • *Private Games* (with Mark Sullivan) • *Private: #1 Suspect* (with Maxine Paetro) • *Private* (with Maxine Paetro)

NYPD RED NOVELS

NYPD Red 4 (with Marshall Karp) • *NYPD Red 3* (with Marshall Karp) • *NYPD Red 2* (with Marshall Karp) • *NYPD Red* (with Marshall Karp)

SUMMER NOVELS

Second Honeymoon (with Howard Roughan) • *Now You See Her* (with Michael Ledwidge) • *Swimsuit* (with Maxine Paetro) • *Sail* (with Howard Roughan) • *Beach Road* (with Peter de Jonge) • *Lifeguard* (with Andrew Gross) • *Honeymoon* (with Howard Roughan) • *The Beach House* (with Peter de Jonge)

STAND-ALONE BOOKS

The Family Lawyer (with Robert Rotstein, Christopher Charles, Rachel Howzell Hall) • *The Store* (with Richard DiLallo) • *The Moores Are Missing* (with Loren D. Estleman, Sam Hawken, Ed Chatterton) • *Triple Threat* (with Max DiLallo, Andrew Bourrelle) • *Murder Games* (with Howard Roughan) • *Penguins of America* (with Jack Patterson with Florence Yue) • *Two from the Heart* (with Frank Constantini, Emily Raymond, Brian Sitts) • *The Black Book* (with David Ellis) • *Humans, Bow Down* (with Emily Raymond) • *Never Never* (with Candice Fox) • *Woman of God*

(with Maxine Paetro) • *Filthy Rich* (with John
Connolly and Timothy Malloy) • *The Murder House*
(with David Ellis) • *Truth or Die* (with Howard
Roughan) • *Miracle at Augusta* (with Peter de Jonge)
• *Invisible* (with David Ellis) • *First Love* (with Emily
Raymond) • *Mistress* (with David Ellis) • *Zoo* (with
Michael Ledwidge) • *Guilty Wives* (with David Ellis)
• *The Christmas Wedding* (with Richard DiLallo) • *Kill
Me If You Can* (with Marshall Karp) • *Toys* (with Neil
McMahon) • *Don't Blink* (with Howard Roughan) •
The Postcard Killers (with Liza Marklund) • *The
Murder of King Tut* (with Martin Dugard) • *Against
Medical Advice* (with Hal Friedman) • *Sundays at
Tiffany's* (with Gabrielle Charbonnet) • *You've Been
Warned* (with Howard Roughan) • *The Quickie* (with
Michael Ledwidge) • *Judge & Jury* (with Andrew
Gross) • *Sam's Letters to Jennifer* • *The Lake House* •
The Jester (with Andrew Gross) • *Suzanne's Diary for
Nicholas* • *Cradle and All* • *When the Wind Blows* •
Miracle on the 17th Green (with Peter de Jonge) • *Hide
& Seek* • *The Midnight Club* • *Black Friday* (originally
published as *Black Market*) • *See How They Run* •
Season of the Machete • *The Thomas Berryman Number*

BOOK**SHOTS**

The Exile (with Alison Joseph) • *The Medical
Examiner* (with Maxine Paetro) • *Black Dress Affair*

(with Susan DiLallo) • *The Killer's Wife* (with Max DiLallo) • *Scott Free* (with Rob Hart) • *The Dolls* (with Kecia Bal) • *Detective Cross* • *Nooners* (with Tim Arnold) • *Stealing Gulfstreams* (with Max DiLallo) • *Diary of a Succubus* (with Derek Nikitas) • *Night Sniper* (with Christopher Charles) • *Juror #3* (with Nancy Allen) • *The Shut-In* (with Duane Swierczynski) • *French Twist* (with Richard DiLallo) • *Malicious* (with James O. Born) • *Hidden* (with James O. Born) • *The House Husband* (with Duane Swierczynski) • *The Christmas Mystery* (with Richard DiLallo) • *Black & Blue* (with Candice Fox) • *Come and Get Us* (with Shan Serafin) • *Private: The Royals* (with Rees Jones) • *Taking the Titanic* (with Scott Slaven) • *Killer Chef* (with Jeffrey J. Keyes) • *French Kiss* (with Richard DiLallo) • *$10,000,000 Marriage Proposal* (with Hilary Liftin) • *Hunted* (with Andrew Holmes) • *113 Minutes* (with Max DiLallo) • *Chase* (with Michael Ledwidge) • *Let's Play Make-Believe* (with James O. Born) • *The Trial* (with Maxine Paetro) • *Little Black Dress* (with Emily Raymond) • *Cross Kill* • *Zoo II* (with Max DiLallo)

BOOK**SH**TS *Flames*

FOR READERS OF ALL AGES

MAXIMUM RIDE

DANIEL X

Daniel X: Lights Out (with Chris Grabenstein) • *Daniel X: Armageddon* (with Chris Grabenstein) • *Daniel X: Game Over* (with Ned Rust) • *Daniel X: Demons and Druids* (with Adam Sadler) • *Daniel X: Watch the Skies* (with Ned Rust) • *The Dangerous Days of Daniel X* (with Michael Ledwidge)

WITCH & WIZARD

Witch & Wizard: The Lost (with Emily Raymond) • *Witch & Wizard: The Kiss* (with Jill Dembowski) • *Witch & Wizard: The Fire* (with Jill Dembowski) • *Witch & Wizard: The Gift* (with Ned Rust) • *Witch & Wizard* (with Gabrielle Charbonnet)

CONFESSIONS

Confessions: The Murder of an Angel (with Maxine Paetro) • *Confessions: The Paris Mysteries* (with Maxine Paetro) • *Confessions: The Private School Murders* (with Maxine Paetro) • *Confessions of a Murder Suspect* (with Maxine Paetro)

MIDDLE SCHOOL

Middle School: Escape to Australia (with Martin Chatterton, illustrated by Daniel Griffo) • *Middle School: Dog's Best Friend* (with Chris Tebbetts, illustrated by Jomike Tejido) • *Middle School: Just My Rotten Luck* (with Chris Tebbetts, illustrated by Laura

Park) • *Middle School: Save Rafe!* (with Chris Tebbetts, illustrated by Laura Park) • *Middle School: Ultimate Showdown* (with Julia Bergen, illustrated by Alec Longstreth) • *Middle School: How I Survived Bullies, Broccoli, and Snake Hill* (with Chris Tebbetts, illustrated by Laura Park) • *Middle School: My Brother Is a Big, Fat Liar* (with Lisa Papademetriou, illustrated by Neil Swaab) • *Middle School: Get Me Out of Here!* (with Chris Tebbetts, illustrated by Laura Park) • *Middle School, The Worst Years of My Life* (with Chris Tebbetts, illustrated by Laura Park)

I FUNNY

I Funny: School of Laughs (with Chris Grabenstein, illustrated by Jomike Tejido) • *I Funny TV* (with Chris Grabenstein, illustrated by Laura Park) • *I Totally Funniest: A Middle School Story* (with Chris Grabenstein, illustrated by Laura Park) • *I Even Funnier: A Middle School Story* (with Chris Grabenstein, illustrated by Laura Park) • *I Funny: A Middle School Story* (with Chris Grabenstein, illustrated by Laura Park)

TREASURE HUNTERS

Treasure Hunters: Peril at the Top of the World (with Chris Grabenstein, illustrated by Juliana Neufeld) • *Treasure Hunters: Secret of the Forbidden City* (with Chris Grabenstein, illustrated by Juliana Neufeld) •

Treasure Hunters: Danger Down the Nile (with Chris Grabenstein, illustrated by Juliana Neufeld) • *Treasure Hunters* (with Chris Grabenstein, illustrated by Juliana Neufeld)

OTHER BOOKS FOR READERS OF ALL AGES

Jacky Ha-Ha:My Life is a Joke (with Chris Grabenstein, illustrated by Kerascoët) • *Give Thank You a Try* (with Bill O'Reilly) • *Expelled* (with Emily Raymond) • *The Candies Save Christmas* (illustrated by Andy Elkerton) • *Big Words for Little Geniuses* (with Susan Patterson, illustrated by Hsinping Pan) • *Laugh Out Loud* (with Chris Grabenstein) • *Pottymouth and Stoopid* (with Chris Grabenstein) • *Crazy House* (with Gabrielle Charbonnet) • *House of Robots: Robot Revolution* (with Chris Grabenstein, illustrated by Juliana Neufeld) • *Word of Mouse* (with Chris Grabenstein, illustrated by Joe Sutphin) • *Give Please a Chance* (with Bill O'Reilly) • *Jacky Ha-Ha* (with Chris Grabenstein, illustrated by Kerascoët) • *House of Robots: Robots Go Wild!* (with Chris Grabenstein, illustrated by Juliana Neufeld) • *Public School Superhero* (with Chris Tebbetts, illustrated by Cory Thomas) • *House of Robots* (with Chris Grabenstein, illustrated by Juliana Neufeld) • *Homeroom Diaries* (with Lisa Papademetriou, illustrated by Keino) • *Med Head* (with Hal Friedman) • *santaKid* (illustrated by Michael Garland)

For previews and information about the author, visit JamesPatterson.com or find him on Facebook or at your app store.

JAMES
PATTERSON
RECOMMENDS

INTRODUCING THE MOST SUCCESSFUL
AND SEXIEST PRIVATE INVESTIGATION
FIRM IN THE WORLD

#1 *NEW YORK TIMES* BESTSELLER

JAMES PATTERSON

PRIVATE

NEW YORK · LOS ANGELES · LONDON · PARIS

& MAXINE PAETRO

PRIVATE

I've always been a curious person. It's one of the many reasons why I'm a writer. Something I always asked myself was: "What happens if a 'one percenter' gets into trouble?" The answer: Jack Morgan and PRIVATE. On Jack Morgan's agenda in his debut outing is investigating a multimillion-dollar NFL gambling scandal and solving a series of schoolgirl slayings. Then, the unthinkable—his former lover turned best friend's wife is murdered. One thing you should know about Jack is that beneath his Lamborghini-driving, red-carpet-event-attending surface, he's a very smart guy. And he takes no prisoners. Just wait till you get to the end of PRIVATE. You'll see what I mean.

JACK MORGAN
IS WANTED
FOR MURDER

THE WORLD'S #1 BESTSELLING WRITER

JAMES PATTERSON

PRIVATE

#1 SUSPECT

& MAXINE PAETRO

PRIVATE: # 1 SUSPECT

Over the years, I've learned that reputation is everything when it comes to business. While Private's Jack Morgan has a reputation for being effective and discreet, he's also known for being quite the lady killer. But when an ex-lover shows up dead in his bed and all evidence points to him, Jack realizes someone wants to kill more than just his good name. To make things worse, another event threatens Private's stability, and Jack suddenly finds himself with his back against the wall. Characters will do the most shocking things when they have no other options, especially characters like Jack who are used to being in control. I won't tell you what happens, but I will say it'll blow your mind.

THE WORLD'S #1 BESTSELLING WRITER

JAMES PATTERSON

Was Hollywood's most
famous couple kidnapped?
Or murdered?

PRIVATE
L.A.

MARK SULLIVAN

PRIVATE L.A.

If you've ever wondered what celebrity power couples do behind closed doors, you can stop all of your conjecturing—the answers are all in PRIVATE L.A. America's most popular celebrity couple has made an exit...from their lives. No one knows where they went or why, and it's up to Jack and his Private team to breach the walls of security and hordes of paparazzi to find the power couple. But when has anything good ever come from a pile of secrets buried under miles of genius PR? Jack's about to find that out, up close and personal, and he's in for the shock of his life. Because in the city of big dreams, nothing is what it seems. Especially if I'm involved.

PRIVATE UNCOVERS A
SHOCKING PAST AND A
LETHAL CONSPIRACY—
IN MODERN-DAY BERLIN
THE WORLD'S #1 BESTSELLING WRITER
JAMES PATTERSON
PRIVATE
BERLIN
MARK SULLIVAN

PRIVATE BERLIN

Every now and then, I find myself wanting a big change in scenery. Don't get me wrong. Jack Morgan and the Private team are great fun, but sometimes a little taste of the foreign makes life a bit more exciting. And by "exciting," I really mean dangerous. At Private's German headquarters, Chris Schneider—superstar agent—has gone rogue. He's the keeper of quite a few pieces of sensitive information, but one in particular could have earth-shattering consequences. Hang on tight and don't blink. This one is a rollercoaster of tension that'll leave you reeling.

BOOK**SHOTS**

THERE'S A REVOLUTION IN READING—IT'S CALLED BOOKSHOTS.

BookShots are a whole new kind of book—100% story-driven, no fluff, always under $5, and written and co-written by James Patterson himself.

At 150 pages or fewer, BookShots can be read in a night, on a commute, even on your cell phone during breaks at work.

FOR SPECIAL OFFERS AND THE FULL LIST OF BOOKSHOT TITLES, PLEASE GO TO: WWW.BOOKSHOTS.COM

35674058325797